*He's as dangerous as he is irresistible . . .*

The heir to his family's fortune, Aidan Wollstonecraft is ready to put his prodigal ways in the past and prove himself worthy of his illustrious name. Going undercover in a factory to expose the wretched working conditions, Aidan believes his noble act will lead him to a better future. Until he's reunited with the sweet beauty who saw him through his darkest days. Cristyn Bevan stirs him like no other woman before. Makes him yearn to claim her, despite the damning curse that dooms any Wollstonecraft wife to an all-too-early death . . .

To fall for Aidan would be her undoing. Yet, something about the blue-blooded scoundrel draws Cristyn to him like a moth to a deadly flame. Is it a desire to heal him that keeps the lovely nurse close? Or her secret hope that somehow, some way, Aidan can let go of his dark past and see the light—and the love—waiting for him?

# Books by Karyn Gerrard

The Hornsby Brothers
*The Vicar's Frozen Heart*
*Bold Seduction*

The Ravenswood Chronicles
*Beloved Beast*
*Beloved Monster*

The Men Of Wollstonecraft Hall
*Marriage With A Proper Stranger*
*Scandal With A Sinful Scot*
*Love With A Notorious Rake*

**Published by Kensington Publishing Corporation**

# Love With A Notorious Rake

*The Men Of Wollstonecraft Hall*

## Karyn Gerrard

**LYRICAL PRESS**
Kensington Publishing Corp.
www.kensingtonbooks.com

Lyrical Press books are published by
Kensington Publishing Corp. 119 West 40th Street New York, NY 10018

Copyright © 2018 by Karyn Gerrard

All Kensington titles, imprints, and distributed lines are available at special quantity discounts for bulk purchases for sales promotion, premiums, fundraising, and educational or institutional use.

To the extent that the image or images on the cover of this book depict a person or persons, such person or persons are merely models, and are not intended to portray any character or characters featured in the book.

Special book excerpts or customized printings can also be created to fit specific needs. For details, write or phone the office of the Kensington Special Sales Manager:
Kensington Publishing Corp.
119 West 40th Street
New York, NY 10018
Attn. Special Sales Department. Phone: 1-800-221-2647.

Kensington and the K logo Reg. U.S. Pat. & TM Off.
LYRICAL PRESS Reg. U.S. Pat. & TM Off.
Lyrical Press and the L logo are trademarks of Kensington Publishing Corp.

First Electronic Edition: December 2018
eISBN-13: 978-1-5161-0548-9
eISBN-10: 1-5161-0548-6

First Print Edition: December 2018
ISBN-13: 978-1-5161-0551-9
ISBN-10: 1-5161-0551-6

Printed in the United States of America

*A big thank you to my agent, Elaine Spencer, who exceeded every expectation I had. To Kensington Publishing/Lyrical Press and everyone involved at whatever step of the writing/publishing process, I thank you. To my family, love and hugs, especially to my husband.*

# Author's Foreword

Elizabeth Gaskell's *North and South*, and the 2004 BBC miniseries based on the book, was a definite inspiration for this story. The more I researched about factory working conditions in the early-to-mid Victorian era, the more I was appalled.

Many worked fourteen-hour days in incredibly unsafe conditions with few or no breaks or rest periods. The Factory Act of 1847 at least limited the workday to ten hours and reduced the number of hours women and children under age eighteen could work, but it would take to the end of the century and into the 20th before real reforms took hold.

Although this fictional story is not about such reforms, it is still the backbone of it.

# Prologue

How fortunate that Cristyn could study under her father, Dr. Gethin Bevan, at his private sanatorium. Women could not attend medical school—which was a vile injustice in Cristyn's mind—so she soaked up everything her father taught her. There was no formal instruction or recognition for nurses, and the positions were often taken by volunteers, for the pay was low. Although much of Cristyn's work consisted of cleaning and serving meals, there was more involved as her father's sanatorium treated those suffering from addictions—specifically opium.

Cristyn moved about the clinic's kitchen, preparing a tray for a patient. She toyed with the idea of a more solid fare, but decided to stay with the broth for the time being. This particular patient had her concerned.

The people—more specifically, men—often arrived with multiple injuries and their health in a precarious state. This meant she was able to utilize her skills to treat wounds and diseases of the mind, which her father vehemently believed—though the medical community did not—was the cause of addiction.

She had managed to remain compassionate toward her patients, but professionally distant.

Until Aidan Black.

Mr. Black had arrived five days ago in dramatic fashion. He was in a ghastly condition: barely conscious, malnourished, dehydrated, in the firm grip of an opium addiction, and quite out of his mind. He had been accompanied by his Uncle Garrett and another man, Edwin Seward, from London.

Mr. Black's first few nights were harrowing as he experienced the various stages of withdrawal. Cristyn stayed with him every step of the way, cleaning up his vomit and wiping his brow. Try as she might to remain detached, she had been immediately struck by the vulnerability and loneliness that radiated from him. Never had any of the male patients she'd treated affected her this way. It was entirely inappropriate.

Sighing, she ladled the beef broth into a bowl, then placed it on a tray along with a spoon. How could this attraction be happening? Yes, beneath the illness and addiction was a comely man, but it was more than his looks. He touched her heart, burrowed his way in deep. As much as she tried to stay professional and emotionally disconnected outwardly, inside she could not.

Pushing the thoughts from her mind, she carried the tray down the hall, then entered Mr. Black's room. The curtains were closed to keep out the winter sun. He lay on the bed wearing nothing but his drawers, since he alternated between perspiring and vomiting and had already ruined two nightshirts. Lord above, she should not be staring at him. He was finely made, though far too thin—his ribs were clearly visible. His shoulder blades were barely hidden by thinly stretched skin. How surprising to find that some delineation of lean muscle remained, considering his shocking physical state.

These wayward and inapt thoughts were not worthy of her. *Focus on the patient's needs.* Not that she was in a profession acknowledged by men in the medical field, or society as a whole—another entirely unmerited inequality.

Mr. Black's breathing was ragged, wheezing with every exhale, for he had a chest infection and a low-grade fever to accompany the symptoms of opium egression. Not to mention the flea and rat bites on his hands, arms, and chest, which she had treated the first night; he was covered in gauze dressings.

"Mr. Black," she called out.

His shallow breathing ceased momentarily, and his glassy eyes tried to focus on her. "No. Leave me be!" he exclaimed in a raspy voice, trailing off with a slight groan, as if the act of speaking was a great effort. With a sweep of his arm, he knocked the tepid broth from her hand, sending it careening across the room, but not before it splashed across her apron and part of her face.

Mr. Black leapt from the bed, but couldn't stand on his shaking legs and promptly slid to the floor. Cristyn rushed to his side, then fell to her knees, gathering him into her embrace. He was trembling, and she couldn't tell if it were tears running down his cheeks or beads of perspiration, or perhaps both. "Hush now, it's all right," she soothed.

"Let me die," he whispered. "My angel of mercy—end it."

His stark, pleading words caused her heart to contract with sympathy. "No, Aidan, you will *not* die. I won't allow it." As she said the words, she gently caressed his forehead, moving his matted hair aside. She had called him by his first name, which was far too familiar; another constraint between a nurse and a patient that should not be ignored. Cristyn didn't care.

He curled into her embrace, grasped her arm, and rested his head against her chest. "Lost... I'm...lost."

"I've found you, and I will never let you go."

Aidan began to sob, his shoulders quaking with each mournful lament. The somber sound arrowed straight to her soul. It was utterly improper for her to allow her unfettered emotions to enter this situation—emotions she had never experienced toward any man. The truth? She was attracted to Aidan, and Cristyn would own her feelings and not be ashamed of them, though she would keep them to herself. It was not as if she'd become besotted with every young man who had come through the sanatorium's doors.

Cristyn held Aidan close, speaking soothing words of comfort. "All will be well, *cariad*. On this, I vow."

She was falling for her patient, and had no idea what to do about it.

# Chapter 1

*From the papers of the Earl of Carnstone, 1704:*

Hear ye future men of Wollstonecraft Hall. Misery awaits! For ye shall never find love. We are cursed. If ye marry, she will die. There is only one way for the curse to be broken, affirmed by Morag the Scottish sorceress: only a love bond accepted by all the men of the family alive during a lunar year will break the curse. I pray that somewhere in time, the cycle of grief ends.

*Standon, Hertfordshire*
*Late May 1845*

As Aidan Wollstonecraft came to learn, there were consequences for being a notorious rake. There was an exacting penalty for allowing yourself to sink to the lowest depths, wallowing in vice and sin, abandoning all restraints, moderation, and good sense. And he'd had plenty of time to reflect on it. What else could he think about all these hours alone, staring out the window, watching winter turn to spring?

Since early January he'd been at the Standon Sanatorium under the name Aidan Black—no one knew his real identity, except for Dr. Bevan. Aidan had arrived barely conscious, a complete wreck, suffering the ill effects of an opium addiction, accompanied by his uncle, and, he was informed later, Edwin Seward, a private investigator. They had found him in St. Giles, living in absolute squalor in a den of thieves and prostitutes. It was as low as a man could possibly descend.

In the ensuing months, he slowly recovered, thanks to Dr. Bevan's empathic treatment and Cristyn's compassionate care. Once he gained control of his emotions he hid them away, protecting them from exposure, though it had become increasingly difficult in Cristyn's presence. His angel of mercy was a true beauty, inside and out, and he would be wise to keep clear.

As he took his seat in Dr. Bevan's office, Aidan knew he would have to depart soon. And do what? Go where? An unknown future yawned before him. *Damned unsettling.* But he'd vowed to be honest in his dealings with the good doctor and remain as unemotional as possible.

Bevan opened the folder before him. "You've gained close to ten pounds since January. Excellent."

Aidan was still far thinner than he had been. Food continued to hold little interest, but perhaps he would feel differently when he returned home, to more sophisticated meals than those served here. If he saw another bowl of stew, he would have what one American acquaintance called a "conniption fit."

When Aidan did not reply, the doctor continued. "Yesterday afternoon, we were discussing the reasons for your descent into addiction and the accompanying lifestyle. Have you any further insight as to why?"

"I was bored, needed stimulation and excitement. Complete disregard for convention. Contempt for responsibility."

Dr. Bevan scribbled notes as Aidan spoke. "At what point did it turn into contempt for yourself and complete disregard for your own preservation?" he asked.

*Ah.* There stood the crux of his downfall. "Perhaps since I'm cursed, I decided to indulge in all manner of sin and vice."

"Cursed? Truly? How fascinating. Tell me about it," the doctor asked, pen poised.

Aidan crossed his legs. "It has been in the family for centuries. It's said that women, either born or married into the family, do not live long. My mother died of a heart infection when I was four—or was I three years of age? I have no memory of it. My grandfather was widowed three times. His own infant daughter did not survive. There is a cemetery on the corner of our property with rows of tombstones of women who dared to love Wollstonecraft men. I admit, when my grandfather first told me of this at the susceptible age of thirteen, it made an impact."

"In what way?"

"I decided that when old enough, I would partake of pleasure. No curse would touch my life, as I planned to indulge and forego any serious attachments to anyone. Of course, at thirteen, I was not aware of exactly what pleasures were to be had. But I would cause no pain or suffering to anyone but myself."

Aidan frowned as Dr. Bevan continued to take notes, dipping his pen in the inkwell every so often. Speaking of the family curse would no doubt have the good doctor come to the conclusion that he was completely daft—or he would think that Aidan was making rationalizations for his reckless behavior. In truth, the curse *had* played a significant part.

He believed in it more than he'd let on to the rest of his family, perhaps almost as much as his uncle. But Garrett had recently tossed aside his solemn oath to never fall in love, which made Aidan wonder if any decisions he'd made in his own life were sound, past or present?

"Can the curse be broken?" the doctor asked.

"I heard that only true love will break the curse; however, my father and grandfather proved that caveat to be untrue." He stared at the doctor. "You are acting quite blasé about this."

"It's not important that I believe it, only that we explore the reasons why you do. Continue, please."

"Eventually, the 'serious attachments' grew to include my family. I became increasingly distant. The complete disregard? The steep decline? I cannot pinpoint the exact moment. Perhaps it occurred when I stopped returning home for the laborious monthly family meetings."

"Why call them 'laborious?'"

Aidan snorted derisively. "You know my family name. My grandfather is the Earl of Carnstone; my father is Viscount Tensbridge: progressive heroes of the British Parliament. My perfect schoolmaster brother is a paragon of decency. My uncle... Well, Garrett is a little of all of us mixed together. How could I possibly live up to their exacting high standards? Their lives are consumed by good works. Helping the poor. How tedious, and, for me, meaningless. For I care not."

Bevan arched an eyebrow. "Are you not the heir apparent?"

"I am the heir, though I loathe being referred to as 'lord.' What does that matter?"

"One day you will be in the British Parliament. These good works will become your responsibility."

Aidan snorted in response.

"You've told me more than once that you are proud of your family and their accomplishments," Bevan said.

"They are not *my* accomplishments," Aidan replied, flicking a speck of dust from his shirtsleeve.

"Then perhaps you should select something to focus your attention on instead of indulging in your own gratification." Aidan rolled his eyes, but Bevan held up a hand. "Before you give me a snide response, hear me out. To keep temptation at bay, you *must* have an objective, to aspire to something greater than your own ego. Make one of the Wollstonecraft causes yours alone. Not superficially, but truly immerse yourself in it."

Grudgingly, Aidan admitted there was merit in what the doctor said. After all, he was determined to recover. "I will seriously consider it."

"Excellent. I believe you will be ready to return home in two weeks. At the end of the first week of June, I imagine."

Trepidation moved through Aidan as swift as a flash flood. "I thought I would remain here until early autumn."

Bevan folded his hands on top of the folder. "You've already stayed far longer than any other patient."

"My wealthy family is not paying you enough?" Aidan snapped irritably.

The doctor ignored his outburst and shuffled the papers in the folder. "I wish to discuss the reason Mr. Colm Delaney made an appearance at my clinic to threaten you three months past. We will address this incident today, Aidan. You've delayed this discussion for far too long."

*Damn it all.* "I am not convinced he came to threaten me. It appears that I inspire passion in certain men as well as women." Another egotistical statement, but it held a kernel of truth. Delaney claimed he'd come to discuss what happened between them at that blasted, depraved party, but never had a chance to elaborate. Aidan had tried his damnedest to push what little he could remember of his last month of debauchery from the forefront of his mind.

"You always deflect from examining your emotions with sarcastic, self-centered comments. Be honest, Aidan, and tell me what occurred."

"I sincerely do not remember much of the final month of my decline. I had attended a wild party in Mayfair. It was decided, since I was the prettiest of my filthy crew of thieves and whores—which isn't saying much—that I would be sold to the highest bidder. We needed the money for opium. And gin." Aidan paused, and frowned. "I was handed over to some aged peer, who Garrett later informed me was the Marquess of Sutherhorne. He, in turn, gifted me to his man, this Delaney character. I don't remember much. Blocking it out? Perhaps. For a while, I thought it a recurring nightmare, but..." Aidan's voice trailed off. Thinking on it made his insides lurch.

"When Delaney showed up here, you realized the nightmare was real," Bevan interjected.

"Yes. Why he wanted to talk to me hardly matters. He whispered in my ear like a lover might. Offered to care for me, nurse me back to health. Hardly a threat, but I suppose it is how you look at it. I told him our brief encounter meant nothing. And it didn't. He was a means to an end." *Jesus, talking of this is damned embarrassing.* "I have no idea if this man, who is seemingly obsessed with me, will seek me out again. I can only hope he does not. I don't prefer men—far from it. But I do hold with my family's progressive view that what people do behind closed doors is no one's business, which makes me wonder why you insist on discussing this topic. It is rather salacious."

"It is that. It's not for me to approve or disapprove. I want to ensure you will no longer be haunted by this episode. You referred to it as a nightmare. Will it impede your libido in any way? Is it disturbing enough for self-loathing to overtake your life to such an extent that you will seek out oblivion again with an opium pipe? Or bottles of cheap gin?"

*Impede my libido? No, Doctor, seeing as I lust after your daughter.* But he did not dare divulge such information. "No. My first stop before I head to Wollstonecraft Hall will be the Crimson Club in London."

"Is that wise? Indiscriminant sex is what led you down this destructive path." Aidan frowned at the doctor's judgmental tone—or maybe he'd imagined it. "Besides, isn't the gossip about this Mayfair incident making its way about London?"

"It has been close to four months; I am certain the old hens of society have moved on to other scandalous tattle. Besides, I won't be in the city long." *Only long enough for a quick rut.*

"Do you still crave opium?" Bevan asked.

"I could deceive you and say, 'Why, no, Doctor, you have cured me of all my vices,' but it would be false. I do crave it, though not as fervently as I once did."

"Thank you for your honesty. The cravings will lessen with time. They have for most others."

Aidan crossed his arms, giving the doctor a dubious look. "But not for all of your patients."

A sad expression covered Bevan's features. "Not all. There are no guarantees in life, and certainly not with addiction. The onus for a full recovery will lie with you—hence the reason I suggested you focus your energy elsewhere. Decide on a few of your family's causes, and we will discuss which one will suit you. Speaking of your family, you're keeping up with the correspondences?"

When he'd met with Garrett briefly in February, his uncle had dropped off numerous letters from his grandfather, father, and twin brother. It had taken him close to five weeks to even break the seals on the envelopes; it took another two before he responded.

Riordan had married, and his wife, Sabrina, was expecting a child. He would be building a progressive school in Kent as soon as he could arrange it. Garrett had married Abigail Wharton in Scotland last month, and they had a fourteen-year-old daughter from their brief, intense love affair at age eighteen. Aidan's father was courting a neighbor, Alberta Eaton, and his grandfather was involved with Sabrina's ex-lady's maid, Mary Tuttle. From what he could ascertain from the letters, the association was serious. Life had carried on without him. It was rather sobering to discover the world did not revolve around him.

"Yes. I'm answering their letters."

"It's imperative at this stage of your recuperation that you allow your family to reenter your life. No more avoidance. If your uncle is any indication, you have a strong support structure in place. Use it. Accept your mistakes, learn from them. Wear them like badges of honor."

"Oh, come now, Doctor." Aidan tsked. "Honor?"

"Yes, honor. You have accepted your faults, agreed to treatment, and chosen the path to recovery. It takes fortitude, inner strength, character. Never doubt you have all these—along with honor. Hold your head high, continue to convalesce, and you shall not falter again. I stake my reputation on it."

A ball of emotion lodged in Aidan's throat. He was genuinely touched by the words. "Thank you."

"Take a walk, as it is a lovely spring day. We're having a special treat for dinner tonight: a crown roast of pork with all the fixings. Join Cristyn and me at seven. I expect you to eat it all."

Aidan stood, then bowed. "I shall. See you at seven."

He left the office and sauntered down the hall. It was the first time he'd been invited to the doctor's home; he must be nearly recovered if he was granted entry. The invitation filled him with elation at the prospect of seeing Cristyn outside the clinic walls, but also trepidation in the fact that he was about to be released. When was the last time he attended any type of proper social event? Could he even remember his manners?

Dr. Bevan and his daughter lived in a small cottage behind the sanatorium. Aidan passed the rooms of other patients, some of whom he had met—two were still in seclusion, and no doubt going through each stage of withdrawal and recovery he had.

Last night he'd heard the agonized cries of a recent inmate in addiction hell. God, had he acted the same when coming off the poison? He could not recall, but what little he remembered chilled his black soul.

He entered his room and stopped short at the sight of Cristyn. She was her father's most trusted, loyal assistant and nurse. Her presence always caused his heart to skip a beat. It made him fully aware he was a man, and she a woman. Cristyn's beauty never failed to capture his interest. She had a coal-black shade of hair similar to his, and violet-blue eyes he could happily become lost in. This glorious young lady was far too stunning to be toiling away in a country clinic for addicted reprobates.

Cristyn was making his bed, going about her chores efficiently and cheerfully. Early in his stay, there were times when she had annoyed him with her sunny smile and optimism; then he'd learned to bask in it, savor it. But nothing had prepared him for her touch. Even the lightest brush of her fingers seized his breath. He was shameless, being attracted to her while in such a pathetic state.

Could he be drawn to her because she was the only attractive woman around for months? Perhaps, for surely it could not be more. Despite his poor health, the rake still lurked under the surface. Yet during his horrible first few weeks here, Cristyn had stood at the vanguard, coaxing him to eat and attending to his every need. She'd spoken to him in soft, reassuring tones, all the while acting compassionate and kind and encouraging him to embrace his recovery. *My angel. My savior.*

One particularly vivid memory recalled him as a crumpled heap of tears and self-pity. Cristyn had held him, speaking soothing words of support. She had called him *cariad* more than once. Aidan found out later it meant "love" in the Welsh tongue. A term of endearment? Did she refer to all her male patients as *cariad* in her sensual, musical voice? What made him worthy of her special attention?

Beyond such questions, his blatant display of emotion and weakness embarrassed him the more his condition improved. In increments, he slowly tucked away such vulnerabilities and allowed the old Aidan to emerge, at least in her presence. The cool, detached, I-couldn't-care-less rake. It was a solid shield to hide behind. *You damned coward.*

Cristyn turned to face him, gifting him with one of her open and friendly smiles. No matter how standoffish he acted, she still treated him with kindness.

"I could have made the bed," he said. "Keeping my room neat and tidy is part of the treatment here at the clinic, is it not?"

"I don't mind helping out. Done with your daily dialogue?"

"Yes. I was ordered by your father to take a walk. I've come to fetch my coat. He also informed me that I am to be paroled from this desolate prison in two weeks."

Her smile faltered. Would she be sorry to see him depart? Strangely, that thought pleased him. "You will be glad to see the back of me, I am quite sure."

Cristyn met his gaze. "No. Not at all."

The look that she gave him was heated, and his swift reaction took him by surprise. He must be nearly well if a wave of lustful hunger was tearing through him. He was tempted to pull her into his arms and kiss her. Instead, he gazed at her through half-lidded eyes and said, "Why not join me on my walk?"

"I have my duties to see to."

"Surely you are able to spare fifteen minutes? I may need your arm to keep me steady."

"You're recovered enough to walk under your own steam."

"Perhaps, or maybe I wish to be alone with you." What was he doing? One sultry expression from the beautiful nurse and his shield had crumbled into dust.

Color spread across Cristyn's lustrous cheeks. "Do not tease me," she replied softly.

The honesty in her lovely eyes made his heart stutter. Damn it all, she *did* have feelings for him. While the knowledge gave him a jolt of satisfaction, it also filled him with dread. What he'd denied the past several months was crystalline clear: they were fiercely attracted to one another. For weeks, months even, this inappropriate interest had hovered about the edges of every encounter and conversation. Stopping at the Crimson Club took on a fresh urgency—it would banish his inappropriate desire for this young woman.

He couldn't be with her. Nor could he pursue this passion, even though he was drawn toward her like a thirsty man to cool, refreshing water. What harm could a simple stroll about the grounds do? Surely he could maintain control of his impulses. And more than anything, he wanted someone to talk to. Yes, he was lonely. "Come and walk with me."

Cristyn untied her apron and laid it on his bed. "I'll fetch my shawl."

As she scurried away, Aidan slowly ran his fingertips across the heavy cotton apron, still warm from her body. He glanced about, then picked it up, rubbed the material against his cheek, and inhaled the fragrance of crisp cotton, laundry soap, and the faint scent of violets. It was an appropriate flower, considering the shade of her eyes. His senses came alive, and he closed his eyes as if the apron itself was her gentle embrace. Again his reaction proved he was close to being fully recovered. Another reason to stay well clear of her.

At the sound of light footfalls, he placed the apron on the bed the way he'd found it, giving it a last touch with his fingertips. Discomfited by his actions, he turned to face the window, schooling his features into complete indifference. Difficult to achieve, considering his insides were aflame.

"I'm ready."

Strange emotions were whirling about him. Some he recognized, like lust and desire. Others were more elusive, probably because he'd never experienced them before. It was best to put all of this out of his mind. Aidan slipped on his coat, then turned to face her. "Shall we set off?"

Once outside, they sauntered along the lane side by side. Politeness stated he should offer his arm, but touching her would light him like a firecracker.

"This is rather familiar," Aidan said. "We often took walks together as I was recuperating. Granted, you were pushing me in a wheeled chair on many of the excursions."

"Yes, and many of the conversations were one-sided." Cristyn's eyes twinkled with amusement.

"Well, I was barely able to feed myself, let alone form coherent sentences." But he remembered it all, every word she had ever said to him. Every smile he'd been gifted with.

"I'm pleased with the progress you've made. I'm proud of you, Aidan."

He cleared his throat but didn't respond, for he believed he was not worthy of any praise. Embarrassment covered him, and regret for all he had done.

"Have you heard from your family recently? Is your uncle much recovered?" she asked.

Cristyn had never allowed his petulant silences to dissuade her from discourse. Though he'd mentioned snippets from the many letters from his family, he hadn't told her everything. Garrett had been shot; he had shown up in Standon in February with a sling on his arm, but it was much later when Aidan found out the particulars. The drama his family had endured the past ten months was staggering, and he had only added to their woes.

"Yes, completely. No lasting effects."

"I am glad."

They walked on in companionable silence, heading toward a cluster of oak trees.

"I would like to think we've become friends," she said, her voice soft.
*Friends?* "Hardly appropriate, considering the circumstances."

"I thought as much at the beginning, but I've since amended my thoughts on the matter. Over the course of the past several months, once you began to recover, we've had many interesting discussions. I believe we have much in common."

*Oh, God.* Aidan did not like where this was leading. It was better to remain silent than to acknowledge that she was correct.

"Aidan, will you write to me?"

He stopped and stared at her incredulously. She could *not* be serious. "Do you ask all your former patients to correspond with you?"

She gazed up at him. "No. You're the first."

"Why, for God's sake? What is to be gained?"

Cristyn turned her gaze to the blue sky above. "I cannot explain it. I wish for us to stay in touch."

"It's not wise," Aidan replied, his voice devoid of emotion. He started forward, but Cristyn laid her hand on his arm, halting him. Her touch seared his skin through the layers of clothes.

"Because you're recovering from an addiction? That is not an impediment."

Aidan shook off her hand. "Well, it should be." He continued forward.

"We are not even to be friends, then?"

"I make it habit not to be friends with the fairer sex. It leads to complications. Like infatuations—with me. Messy things." He winced inwardly at the pompous statement, but even though he was attracted to her, and had been from the first, he was not ready to enter into any sort of relationship, innocent or not. Perhaps he never would be.

"Your ego knows no bounds, Mr. Black," she scoffed. "I thought we shared...something. It appears I was gravely mistaken."

Aidan gripped her arm, pulling her behind a large oak tree. The hurt he had heard in her last few words tugged at his heart. He stood close, and he was aroused. If only she knew the maelstrom of confusing emotions blazing through him. A soft moan left her throat as his body adjoined hers. They were almost touching—not quite, but close enough to savor the heat. Nuzzling her neck, he briefly leaned against her and rolled his hips to allow her to feel his arousal. His cock was hard, to the point of sweet, agonizing pain.

Her fingers tunneled through his hair, making him release an animal growl from deep in his chest. How he yearned to kiss her and taste the sweetness within. He inched closer to her mouth. Her lips parted, as if anticipating.

Aidan froze. He was losing all control and could not allow it. He swiftly stepped away from her. "I apologize. How inappropriate of me to take such liberties. You have my assurance it will not happen again."

Cristyn exhaled and smoothed her skirt. "Apology accepted. I should not have allowed it. However, I will not deny I quite enjoyed it."

God spare him from plainspoken women. "Are you always this frank?"

"I was raised to be honest on all fronts, and to be forthright in my dealings, especially with men. Then there are no misunderstandings," she replied matter-of-factly.

His angel was bold. He damned well liked it. Imagine all that fearlessness in his bed. *Cease this at once.*

"Forget I said that," she muttered. "Forget anything happened at all."

"Allow me to be equally forthright."Aidan lifted her chin with two fingers and made her look at him. "When I leave here, we will not see each other again. It is for the best, for I am not a man to pin any hopes or dreams on. There will be no correspondence, no hope of more. I am not a nice man, Cristyn. I would use you and toss you aside, as I have with many other women. You are too fine of a person to be subjected to the likes of me."

Her eyes glistened. "Isn't that for me to judge?"

"Not in this case. I would taint you with my wretched, completely miserable past." He caressed her blushing cheeks with the tips of his fingers. "I must end this before it begins. You will thank me."

"A pretty speech. And condescending. I know you're from a wealthy family, though that is all I know about you. A daughter of a poor country doctor would not be suitable. *We* are not suitable." She pushed his hand away. "Shall we continue on our walk?"

He was genuinely surprised at her response. Class difference never entered his mind, but perhaps it was better that she believed such, for it would be easier for her to forget him. All that remained was the difficult task of forgetting *her*.

They strolled along the lane, and the awkwardness between them crackled with life. He had acted a haughty fool. But then, hadn't he always? For Cristyn spoke the truth: there was…*something*. Beyond lust or desire. At this stage of his turbulent life, he had no right to enter into a relationship with a kind, honorable woman who was no doubt a virgin.

Aidan had always avoided virgins in the past. There was too much drama, tears, recriminations—or so he had witnessed with other men of his acquaintance. Also, there was the chance of being trapped into marriage. At a young age, he'd sworn a vow to keep his assignations to widows and other women of experience. Pleasure with no emotional attachments.

Already there were too many complicated emotions swirling between him and Cristyn.

Glancing at her, he grudgingly admired how candid she was regarding her feelings. No tears at all. "Your father invited me for dinner tonight. I can send my regrets, if you prefer."

"There is no need." she huffed. "It will be a farewell dinner." She gave him a brief, brittle smile, then marched ahead of him.

*Well. Goodbye it is.* As he'd said, it was for the best. *Crisis barely averted.* He was proud of the restraint he'd showed, but why did he feel dejected about it all? It was complete torture not taking her in his arms and kissing her soundly. Is this what the rest of his life would be like, denying his pleasures until the end of days? God, what a horrible prospect. Aidan was frustrated beyond words, but also gratified that he'd ended this before it even started.

# Chapter 2

Cristyn hurried toward the sanatorium, not daring to turn around, for she could feel Aidan's stare boring through her. He often spoke in that conceited, who-cares tone of his, but there were occasions she'd caught him gazing at her with heated interest. Then he would quickly show his apathetic mask. But in her heart, she knew Aidan was attracted to her as much as she was to him. What had just happened between them more than proved it.

Granted, his devilishly handsome looks were a factor in her interest. Who wouldn't be drawn in by his wavy black hair and sky-blue eyes? His tall, lean form? His near-perfect face, which held a masculine beauty that took her breath away? But it was more than the outer shell. Perhaps it was the loneliness radiating in those cerulean eyes, or the etched lines of weariness bracketing his sensual mouth. The fact that he'd been brought low, but found the inner strength to accept his flaws and embrace his recuperation. Cristyn had witnessed his vulnerability, had seen him at his worst. He felt things deeply, though he was adept at hiding it. Aidan had touched her.

Oh, she'd betrayed her own rules about staying professional in her dealings with patients. Cristyn had crossed a line, and it troubled her. What an utter and complete fool she'd made of herself. She had done well up until now, keeping her feelings for Aidan under wraps.

Heavens, when he had stood close to her, leaning her against the tree, her entire body came alive, her insides thrumming with anticipation. She wanted his hands to roam and explore, for feeling his warm breath against her cheek and him briefly nuzzling her neck was not near enough. And the almost-kiss. For all her talk of being bold, why hadn't she moved a fraction of an inch and met his perfectly shaped lips?

Thanks to her nursing and study of anatomy, she was well aware what the hardness pressed against her thigh portended. It had thrilled her, and because of it she had not suppressed her moans of desire. The passion between them had sparked and flamed, there was no doubt of it.

Yet he'd stepped away. "I am not a man to pin any hopes or dreams on." How those words had broken her heart. "I would use you and toss you aside, as I have with many other women." Despite their many conversations, Aidan had never spoken to her of his past. Considering the condition in which he'd arrived, she could only make assumptions. To hear he was a heartless seducer should have given her further pause—yet Cristyn remained firm in her belief that underneath was a man worthy of her compassion. Yes, he had touched her heart.

As she headed for the entrance, she glanced up and saw her father standing at the window, with arms crossed and his mouth pulled into a straight line of annoyance. *Oh, no.* What had he witnessed? Hadn't they been hidden well enough behind the tree?

Crossing the threshold, she pulled her shawl from her shoulders. "Hello, Dad. I will look in on Mr. Holmes."

"Cris, could I speak to you in my office?" he asked, his voice grave.

*Blast it!* "Yes, of course."

Her father motioned for her to take a seat. "Your mother, rest her soul, wanted you to take a different path. Attend a finishing school, perhaps find a suitable match with a young man of solid middle class standing and adequate wealth. She made me promise to steer you toward that exact course. Alas, when you showed interest in medical studies, I abandoned my pledge." He frowned. "I allowed my ego and my desire to have you follow in my footsteps to cloud my judgment. You are bold, fearless, intelligent, and confident. If you were a man, you would be a prime candidate to attend Oxford or Cambridge and study medicine." He exhaled, shaking his head.

"But you're not a man, and you're not allowed to enter medicine. I should have remembered that salient fact. I should have protected you. What opportunity have you had to meet young men except here at the clinic?"

Cristyn did not like the direction of this conversation. Her father's tone was a combination of apprehension and annoyance. She remained quiet.

"I watched you and Aidan Black. The discussion appeared emotional, at least on your end. I lost sight of you behind the huge oak, but I can well surmise what happened." Her father rested his hands on the desk and frowned once again. "There have been more than a few handsome young men here the past five years. Why him?"

*Why him, indeed.* Flushing with mortification, Cristyn was not sure how to proceed. She and her father were close, as it had only been the two of them since her mother passed seven years ago. But speaking of her inappropriate infatuation for Aidan Black caused the flush to spread right to the tips of her toes. "I'm not certain I am able to explain why," she offered in a hushed voice.

"Try."

"He touches my heart," she replied quietly.

"He's not for you."

Cristyn frowned at her father's stern tone. Two men had told her this today, and it rankled. As if she did not know her own mind. Or heart. When told in the past she could not do or have something, it had made her all the more determined to achieve her objective. "You believe I'm not good enough for him—"

"On the contrary, my dear. *He* is not good enough for *you*."

She cocked an eyebrow. "In what way? The fact that he's recovering from an addiction? I thought you did not hold with such prejudices."

"I don't, but without breaking doctor-patient confidentiality, I can state his desolate past would give *you* pause. I do not wish to see you hurt."

"I know nothing of his scandalous past; he's never spoken of it to me. And you have instructed me not to ask questions of the patients, to ensure their privacy. But I can well speculate, considering the bruises and marks of abuse on his body when he first arrived. Has this to do with that brute of man showing up here this past February? Delaney, wasn't it? He threatened Aidan, did he not?"

"Again, I cannot reveal anything."

How infuriating. She'd briefly witnessed the confrontation after Aidan's Uncle Garrett had burst into the room. Delaney stood behind Aidan, holding him tight, brandishing a knife. It had been frightening to observe. But then Delaney had yelled at Cristyn and her father to leave, and she didn't witness what happened next, nor hear anything of the conversation. "You think he will slide into his old lifestyle, don't you?" What did he know about Aidan to make him believe that? How horrid was this "desolate past?"

"Cristyn, not all discharged patients meet with complete success in their recovery. Will Aidan Black? I can only hope. But due to his wealth and selfish ways, he will be exposed to more temptation than most. He could slide into his old habits."

"You don't like him," she accused.

"It's not my job to like or dislike my patients." He paused, took her hand, and squeezed it, his expression concerned. "I don't want that kind of life for you, never knowing if he will wander off the path of sober living. The uncertainty of it. I've revealed too much. It hardly matters, as he will be leaving shortly."

Cristyn was rather shocked by her father's blunt opinion. "Well, regarding his selfishness, he does come from a privileged background, correct?"

Her father gave a brisk nod in reply.

"Surely this is not the essence of the man. I believe Aidan feels things deeply, but keeps his emotions hidden. I believe he *is* on the right path, and merely needs—"

"A caring and compassionate woman to bring him out of his shell? To guide his way?" He released her hand and sat back in his chair. "Along with the reasons I've already stated, he's not of your class; he's far above us in station. It would not work."

Frustrated, Cristyn frowned. "I don't agree. But as you say, it hardly matters. Aidan has already informed me that once he departs, we will not see each other again."

Blast her father for looking relieved. "It's for the best."

She stood. Simmering anger caused her to clench her fists. She knew she should leave before saying something she would regret. "I will go and attend to Mr. Holmes."

"I am sorry you're upset. As difficult as it is, you cannot allow emotions to enter into caring for a patient. Empathy of course, but nothing else." He blew out an exasperated breath. "I'm proud of you, Cristyn. Never forget that. You have accomplished much these past years. I love you, and I don't want to see you hurt in any way." He gave her an affectionate smile.

Biting her lower lip, she nodded, too overwhelmed to reply. As she exited her father's office, her heart contracted in pain, as if it had suffered a permanent fissure.

What did she want from Aidan Black? For him to admit they had formed a bond. That the bond went beyond intense physical attraction. That it was passionate, if the brief burst of desire at the oak tree was any indication. She wanted him to accept they had much in common, were already good friends, had shared a certain…intimacy with regard to his recuperation.

Far above us in station? How far above? Should she confront Aidan and demand that he own up to his feelings and reveal his past? He had purposely avoided any topic concerning his life. She knew nothing, other than he was rich and resided somewhere in Kent.

No. She had some pride. Tonight at dinner she would act the polite hostess. And when he departed, she would think on him no more.

\* \* \* \*

Mrs. Williams brought in plates of food and laid them in front of Cristyn, her father, and Aidan. The woman had been hired recently, and besides doing the cooking and cleaning in their small cottage, she did the same at the sanatorium.

"The meal looks wonderful, Mrs. Williams, as always." Her father smiled.

The widow flushed, smoothing her apron. "Thank you, Doctor. If you need anything else, call out." She departed. The room was rife with undercurrents—not only between Cristyn and Aidan, but the housekeeper and her father as well. Was something developing there? Cristyn wouldn't mind; he'd been alone for years. Everyone deserved a degree of happiness.

Cristyn glanced at Aidan, who was staring at his food with disinterest. Though he may not have believed it, he deserved happiness as well. What she would give to see the sadness gone from his beautiful azure eyes. It had been her experience at the clinic that, on the whole, most people did not succumb to addiction unless there was underlying melancholy—she had seen it in him.

He wore a crisp white shirt, matching neckcloth, and a gray and black waistcoat, looking entirely too handsome for his own good. *And for my own good.*

Picking up his utensils, Aidan cut into the meat, making small, bite-sized pieces. He appeared to be in no particular hurry to consume his meal. "I wish to thank you both for your humane and empathetic treatment during my incarceration."

Her father chuckled. "How amusing, though it's true your sentence is nearing its end. You can be proud of your achievements."

Aidan scoffed. "I was not a brave soldier, injured on the field of battle, drowning in such pain and agony that opium was the only choice for relief."

"You were drowning in pain and agony of another sort," her father replied between bites.

Aidan's brows knotted, perhaps in displeasure at the honest assessment. Cristyn was fascinated at his reaction as his mouth twisted into a cynical frown. "Do not make excuses for me, Doctor. I willingly chose the course I traveled. Excess and thrills. Sin and adventure. No other reasons."

"I beg to differ," Cristyn interjected. "The soul can be wounded as deeply as any part of the body. I've witnessed this firsthand with many patients. Especially with you."

Aidan finally looked at her, for he hadn't given her anything more than a cursory glance since he arrived for dinner. His glaring eyes held a seething anger. "You presume to know me?"

She met his annoyed gaze, not intimidated by him in the least. "Yes, I do. Better, perhaps, than you know yourself."

"You do not know me at all," Aidan replied, his voice tight.

"Cristyn," her father said sternly. "Enough."

Suitably admonished, she looked down at her plate of food. Obviously still hurt and angry from their afternoon walk, she was allowing her emotions to run amuck, causing her to act inappropriately. The room was quiet for several minutes; the only sound was utensils clattering against stoneware plates. She picked up her fork and poked at the carrots, her appetite all but gone. Blast it! She must gain control, but inside she was in turmoil.

"I've been thinking, Doctor, and believe it best I depart before the end of this week," Aidan declared.

Cristyn's turmoil escalated at his statement. He couldn't wait to get away from her. It stung, and her heart ached at his coolly spoken words.

"Won't it take time to send word to your family to dispatch the carriage?" her father asked.

"I've decided to find a serviceable horse. I have funds. But it will mean leaving my trunk here until I can send someone to fetch it."

"Of course. But we should discuss this further, in a private session."

*Away from her.* Frustrated at both men and their secret conversations, Cristyn blurted, "And where is your home in Kent, exactly, Mr. Black?" She was going to get answers to a few of her questions before he departed. To the devil with proprieties and rules.

Aidan shrugged. "What does it matter?"

"Is it a government secret?" she demanded.

"No. My family home is not far from Sevenoaks. Do you know it?"

"Hardly, but I can find it on a map, I'm sure." Cristyn popped a few buttered carrots in her mouth and chewed, watching Aidan closely. "And what does your family *do,* Mr. Black? Do you have an occupation?"

"You mean besides dissipation and indulgence? Alas, I am a wastrel. A disappointment to my family and, it turns out, to myself," Aidan replied with annoyance.

"Cris," her father began, but this time, she ignored him.

"As for my family," Aidan continued, also ignoring her father, "we breed horses. It is a lucrative enterprise. Perhaps you wish to know how lucrative?" he sneered.

"And what if I do?" Cristyn snapped. The conversation was quickly veering into an argument, emotions heightened on both sides. You could carve the tension with a knife. Dismissing it, she plundered forward. "But then, you are far above us, and no doubt find such conversation about money crass and tedious. I'm sure you find most subjects tedious, as well as those below you in social ranking, whatever that ranking is."

Her father sucked air through his teeth, shocked at her rude words.

Aidan's mouth quirked, but his eyes narrowed in irritation. "Well, I am certainly finding *you* tedious at the moment."

"Cristyn, Aidan, perhaps we should—"

"It is entirely mutual. Not used to a woman speaking her mind, I'll be bound. By all means, return home to your horse stables and find a biddable young lady who will simper and acquiesce to your many whims." She slammed her knife and fork on the table and pushed away her half-eaten meal, which sat like a lump in her stomach, churning and grinding and causing a wave of nausea to pass through her. "Someday, you will be sorry that you denied what's between us."

"Cristyn!" her father cried.

"No, Dad, I will *not* stay quiet. The first time that I've given my heart…" The words died in her throat. What had she done? Her father was mortified. Aidan was clearly incensed, but heat shimmered in his half-lidded eyes. It was all too much. Cristyn stood, damned if she would apologize. The sentiments she had expressed were honest and true. "If you will excuse me. I've had enough." Enough of the meal. Enough of feeling lost in inestimable emotions she could not name. Enough of Aidan.

She marched from the room, then broke into a dash until her bedroom, where she slammed the door hard enough that the pictures on the wall rattled. With a slide of the lock, her hands flew to her flushed cheeks. She had made a fool of herself.

Never again.

\* \* \* \*

Aidan watched her flounce from the room. Hell, she was magnificent. Never had a woman spoken to him in such a way. Leave it to him to imagine all that powerful fervor unleashed in his bed. His angel was a passionate creature. God, to have Cristyn writhe in his arms while he plunged in and out of her, bringing her to an earth-shattering climax. He was sorely tempted to follow her and kiss her senseless.

"I must apologize—" Bevan began.

"No, Doctor. Do not. Cristyn spoke her mind. Although I found it irksome, I admire her for it."

"I should go after her, see if she's all right." The doctor stated, worry knotting his heavy brows. "But I know Cristyn; she would rather be alone. At least for now."

Aidan took another forkful of food. "This will pass. In time." How pompous he sounded. *To hell with it.* "Perhaps it is habit, but I cannot bring myself to lie to you. The attraction is mutual, and the undercurrent in this room more than proves my point. There. I said it. Inappropriate as you or I may believe it to be, there is something rather profound between your daughter and me. I will admit it to you as my physician, not as her father." He paused, watching the doctor for any sort of reaction. He gave none. "I thought you would be angry at my confession. You are acting far calmer than I expected."

"Oh, believe me, inside I'm livid. But I will not exacerbate this situation by reacting in a violent way—though it's quite tempting."

*Thank Christ.* Aidan was not much in the mood for fisticuffs. Besides, he was not recovered enough for fighting. The fifty-year-old doctor could take him easily. "I believe we can both agree that I'm in no position to do anything about this mutual attraction at present."

"And the future?" Bevan asked as he continued eating.

"My future is a blank page. Completely uncertain. Another reason to stay away from your daughter."

Bevan sipped his water. "There is an uncertainty to everyone's future."

"Mine more than most. I've wandered about this world with no purpose for long enough."

"I'm gratified to hear it."

"Since you've mentioned me immersing myself in one of my family's causes, I've thought of nothing else. I believe I have found one."

"And what would that be?" Bevan asked.

"My father's main cause, and, to a lesser extent, my grandfather's, is revising the Factory Act. I will focus my attention there. In what capacity, I haven't yet worked out."

"Are the earl and viscount part of the Radicals faction?"

"In sentiment, as they certainly wish to pull the Whigs toward a more liberal platform. The Radicals are not a party, more of a philosophy."

The doctor reached for the wine decanter and refilled his glass. Aidan's mouth twisted into a wry smile at the fact that Bevan did not offer him any. "I read in the paper last week that Prime Minster Peel is siding with the Whigs to repeal the Corn Laws."

*Fascinating.* Aidan had stayed away from newspapers since his confinement. Except for scraps of news in letters from his family, he had no idea what was going on in the world. "His party will not appreciate that. It could spell his end as prime minister."

"I agree. But regarding the Factory Act, it is a worthy cause. It's abhorrent how workers are treated—and how little they're paid. I commend your choice." Dr. Bevan laid his utensils aside. "On the topic of Cristyn, I am not sure how to say this except to speak as her father—as someone who loves her dearly. You're heir to the earl."

"The men in my family are blessed with good health and longevity; it will be many years before I'm earl—or able to use the courtesy title of viscount."

"Nevertheless, I'm sure your family will wish you to align yourself with an equally powerful family," the doctor interjected.

"The Wollstonecrafts do not place much stock in aristocratic alliances, yet two of my grandfather's three marriages were exactly that: products of his Regency and Georgian generational upbringing. He has since moved past such snobbish views. According to recent letters, he's fallen for an ex-lady's maid."

"I do not want to see Cristyn hurt," Bevan said softly. "Though it appears she is already. If I had known she harbored deep feelings for you, I would have ensured that she was not your prime caregiver. I only noticed it during the past week. I must have been blind, or you both hid it well in my presence." Bevan wiped his mouth with his napkin and tossed it on his plate. "You must have known that the attraction was mutual. Shame on you for not disclosing it," he reprimanded.

Staring at the man who had assisted him out of a pit of darkness and despair, ignominy covered Aidan once again. He deserved the rebuke. "Touché, Dr. Bevan. You are correct. However, I will reveal this: if it wasn't for Cristyn's compassionate care, I'm not positive I would have come out of this, although my complete recuperation remains an open question. Because of the admiration that I hold for you both, I will exit the stage and not have any further contact with her, or you, ever again." His tone was arrogant, as it often was when he hid deeper emotions.

Apparently he hadn't fooled the doctor, who cocked a dubious eyebrow at him. "As I said, you're adept at hiding how you truly feel. I don't wish for us to part on such an acrimonious point of contention. I will say it once more: I'm proud of your achievements. With regards to your departure, I cannot physically restrain you, but it is my recommendation you wait for your family's carriage and a suitable escort home. Perhaps your uncle can act as traveling companion."

"Why? Do you think I will go directly to St. Giles and seek out the pipe again?" he snapped.

"Why tempt fate? Regardless, I mailed a letter to your family this morning, informing them of your imminent release. You may arrive home before the letter does. But it is my responsibility as your doctor to inform your next of kin. Stay clear of temptations. As for alcohol, if you must imbibe, stick to wine, and in moderation. I wish you nothing but the best."

That was as decided a dismissal as he'd ever had. Wiping his mouth on the napkin, Aidan stood. "Then I shall take my leave, not only for tonight, but as soon as I'm able to make arrangements. Good night, Doctor." Aidan exited the room, peeved at both Bevan and his bold and beautiful daughter, and at himself for not keeping his emotions under tight rein. His departure from the clinic should not have been so fraught with emotion. Damn. Hell. *Fuck.*

He had thoroughly messed things up again. As he strode toward his room, he was all the more determined to embrace his chosen cause. Not only could it be the making of him, but it would assist in healing his hurt. Because, damn it all, his heart—and perhaps also his soul—ached. He cared for Cristyn more than he was letting on to anyone, including himself—and therein lay complete destruction.

# Chapter 3

It had taken Aidan two days to arrange the purchase of a serviceable horse, a gray-dappled gelding who looked similar to Riordan's Grayson. The horse was a fine specimen, and Garrett would no doubt deem him a welcome addition to the Wollstonecraft stables. Aidan named him Nebula, Latin for "fog," a reminder of where he had lived the past several months: in a vice-addled fog of his own making.

He'd packed a small valise, and left the rest of his belongings in the trunk Garrett had sent along months ago. Arrangements were made for someone to collect it at a later date. There was nothing of value in it, just a few books and various pieces of clothing.

It was a good thing his uncle had also sent one hundred pounds with the trunk, enough to purchase the horse and pay for his travels. After his quick stop in London, Aidan would ride to Carrbury to see his fraternal twin before traveling to Wollstonecraft Hall.

The brothers had been inseparable as small children. They'd even shared the same bedroom, though there were empty rooms aplenty. Aidan had been sent away to school first due to his constant misbehavior, but he had always come home for holidays.

Close to ten months had passed without Aidan seeing or talking to Riordan. Damn, he missed his brother, and he had suffered from their separation. Even though Aidan had eventually grown to resent Riordan's basic decency, he loved his brother fiercely. Being around Riordan had made him all too aware of his own shortcomings, but it was time he placed such destructive thoughts behind him.

Now came the goodbyes with Cristyn and Dr. Bevan. Aidan never liked farewells, whether they were temporary or not. Such emotional encounters often indicated change, which he disliked.

There was no mistaking his churning guts, for he would be going out into the world, with all its temptations and drama. The past several months here in Standon, despite feeling as if he were incarcerated, had actually brought much-needed peace and quiet to his tumultuous life. Cristyn was a huge part of his newfound tranquility.

The doctor and his daughter stepped outside as Aidan tied his small valise to the saddle. Dr. Bevan stepped forward and held out his hand. "All the best, Aidan."

He took the hand and shook it. "Thank you for all that you've done."

He turned toward Cristyn, and she quickly clasped her hands behind her back. It stung that she did not want him to touch her, not even to shake or bend over her hand. *Fine.* He gave her a curt bow. "My thanks, Miss Bevan. Goodbye."

"Goodbye," she whispered. Then, in a low voice he hardly could make out, she added, "Aidan."

*Damn.* This leave-taking was affecting him more than he'd thought it would. A lump had settled in his throat to go along with his plummeting insides. For a fleeting moment, he considered taking Cristyn up on her offer to correspond, but after their argument at dinner, and the fact that he was not ready to have any type of relationship complicate his already difficult life, he allowed the temptation to pass. With his booted foot firm in the stirrup, he mounted Nebula and gathered up the reins. Aidan touched his forelock, turned, and headed down the lane.

This part of his life was over. Now came the thorny part: the actual living. Finding purpose and meaning. Granted, stopping at a brothel was not exactly a feasible beginning, but damn it all, he wasn't a monk. Although his heart ached, and he longed to gaze at Cristyn once more, Aidan did not look back.

He arrived at the Crimson Club by early evening and quickly selected a solidly built, buxom woman with golden hair who went by the name of Bridget. He promptly buried himself inside her to forget the past several months. But each time he'd closed his eyes, he saw his angel's beautiful face and warm smile.

The sex with Bridget was fast, raw, wild, and completely meaningless.

He lay on his stomach, the blankets and sheets in a tangle on the floor. His body was covered in a thin sheen of perspiration, and as soon as he caught his breath he was having another go. Never had he been haunted like this, even to the extent that he thought of Cristyn during sex with another woman. It was disturbing.

"My, you were vigorous in your attentions." Bridget giggled.

"I'm not done yet," he murmured. He wasn't stopping until his body gave out, or the daydreams of his gorgeous, violet-eyed angel dissipated.

"I don't doubt it. Tell me, Lord Wollstonecraft, are the stories they're saying about you true?"

Aidan had hoped that in four months the gossip would have died down— apparently not. "What particular gossip? I cannot keep it all straight," he answered indifferently. "And cease with the 'lord' business. Address me as Aidan." He'd never cared for the designation, even requested the servants at the hall not refer to him as such.

"As you wish...Aidan." Bridget trailed her bare foot along the back of his leg to his arse, then with curled toes kneaded it. "The gossip? Why, the fact that you indulge in orgies with both sexes. You naughty lad." Bridget giggled, and Aidan was sorry he had not selected someone else. "And that there was an auction, and you were the grand prize, gifted to a rather wild-looking man." The sound of a drawer being opened filled his hearing. "Well, I have a prize for *you*, for bringing me much enjoyment. Look here, young lordling."

Aidan turned his head to stare at her. She dangled a small round bag in front of him. His blood froze in his veins, for he recognized the clothed ball. *Opium*. His heartbeat thundered in his ears, loud enough that he hardly caught what she said next.

"I've heard you will do anything for this. Even sell yourself. How about I sell this to you? I always keep some on hand for special guests. For a price, of course. My lord tiger." Bridget giggled again. "You'll be an earl someday, am I right?"

His insides roiled and cold perspiration broke out on his forehead. He was Lord Nothing, as far as he was concerned. His father held the only courtesy title, Viscount Tensbridge, connected with his grandfather, the earl. Someday, long into the future, Aidan would be a viscount, then the earl. It did not bear thinking about.

Aidan fought to keep his voice even and uninterested. "What has that to do with anything?" he mumbled, trying to tear his gaze away from the opium. His entire body tensed and his hands began to tremble, but he tucked them away. He would not show how close to the edge he teetered.

"You can afford my price, my lord." She shook the bag again, trying to entice him, but all it did was make his stomach turn. "I mean, Aidan." She giggled.

The heartbeat that thundered in his ears was now accompanied by a high-pitched whine. "Do not believe all the tittle-tattle you hear. I'm not interested. Besides, I am not here for conversation, or the procurement of opium."

Bridget shrugged, then popped the bag back into the drawer and slammed it shut.

Aidan exhaled in relief. His first test, and he had passed it—but barely. Slowly his body unclenched, and the sounds flooding his brain quieted.

She stood, unconcerned that she was naked. "Perhaps a drink, then?"

Not a drop of alcohol had passed his lips since January. Would a sip of scotch send him reeling? Push him off the wagon of sobriety? Not taking a drink would be suspicious, and cause for comment. "Red wine, if you please," he murmured. Surely wine would not unsettle him; Dr. Bevan said it was allowed. He need only sip at it.

"I've another proposition for you," Bridget continued as she strode toward the sideboard, her ample breasts bouncing with every step. "I'll be setting myself up as a courtesan. I want to give you first crack." She poured him a glass of wine and set it on the table next to the bed. After pouring another glass, she rejoined him, using her bare foot to slide along his backside as she nosily sipped. "I know you haven't been here in months, but I want two or three men as sponsors, and I'd like one of them to be you." Aidan stirred, and she laid her foot flat on his back to stop him from turning over. "You're one of the few men I actually enjoy in my bed."

"Do not be insulted, but I've been in your bed before?" Damned if he could remember. But then, he hardly recalled the faces of anyone he'd had dealings with since the beginning of his steep decline.

"Yes, you have. Multiple times last autumn."

No wonder he hadn't recalled any of it: he was in the grip of his vices by then. Much remained a blur.

"You made quite an impression on me. You were wild, and, when the need called for it, not caring exactly, but mindful of my needs. Rare to find in this business. And you're rich and well-connected. Handsome, tall, with dark hair and lovely blue eyes. A combination most women desire." Her toes caressed his arse again. "And insatiable. What more could a working girl ask for?"

Aidan grunted in response. It was good to know that despite his dissipation, he had still been able to satisfy a woman. But, God, would she ever stop talking?

"More importantly," Bridget droned on, "I know deep down you would not mistreat me. Hurt me." The last two words ended on a soft whisper.

Well, she was correct there. Aidan had never understood why men mistreated women. Growing up, he had been taught to treat women with the respect they deserved, that they were individuals who warranted equal footing with men, regardless of what society dictated. But having a courtesan on retainer? It had never appealed to him. He'd chosen Bridget today because she looked solidly built to take his fierce pounding. If he were to admit it, she looked the least like Cristyn of any of the available prossies. He batted her leg aside and rolled over, facing her. "I'm flattered. I'll think on it."

Her luscious mouth curved into a cynical smile. "That means no. I appreciate you being polite about it." She stretched her arms above her head, giving him a full view of her generous breasts, which stirred his arousal afresh. "There are other men in your family. Maybe I can entice one of them. Your father, for example."

Aidan arched an eyebrow. "You've been with Viscount Tensbridge?" He knew that through the years the men in his family had often visited the Crimson Club. It was clean, well-run, and had a respectable air about it—at least as respectable as a brothel could be.

"Not lately. Not for close to two years, but I recall he's as much of a tiger in bed as you are."

"Please. I don't want to hear of my father's attributes. Besides, his attention has been turned toward a woman. You may not see him here again." Aidan's gaze lingered on Bridget's lush, naked form. "In fact, I don't believe you will see any of them darken the door here in the future. I am the last man standing." Clasping his semi-hard cock, he gave it a couple of quick strokes until he was fully erect. "On your hands and knees," he demanded in a gruff voice.

"Oh." She licked her lips, giving him a hungry look. "Going full beast, are we?"

Aidan reached for a French letter and slipped it on his stiff prick. He was lucky he had not caught any poxes or diseases during his reckless sexual encounters, and he would make damn sure he wouldn't in the future. Beast? Indeed. He'd been referred to as one through the years for his prowess in bed.

"Full beast." He thrust into her and she moaned in response, arching her back as she took him deep.

*Forget.*

Starting slow, he built into fierce, rapid strokes.

*Oblivion.*

Aidan spent the night at the club, then, after a hearty breakfast, bid farewell, for he would not be returning for some time—if ever. It had disturbed him to hear the gossip was still being discussed, and the farther he was from London—and temptation—the better. The multiple sex sessions had taken the edge off his frustration, especially when Bridget brought in a silver-haired vixen called Madeen to join them. It was a wild night, to be sure. But it had done nothing to banish Cristyn from his mind. She was his first thought as soon as he'd awoken to find both women curled up next to him.

Yes, the sex had been hollow. And, surprisingly, it had left him feeling emptier than before—and more fatigued, which proved he was still recuperating.

Since he was tired, he stopped at an inn at the halfway point of his journey. He had taken his time, soaking up the sun and inhaling the fresh air. Once refreshed, it was onward to Carrbury and his reunion with his brother.

Carrbury was a small town in East Sussex, south of Wollstonecraft Hall. Aidan took a more westerly, circuitous route to avoid Kent altogether. It was a pleasant late spring day. Insects droned in the grass and in the bracken, mixing with birdsong high above. Aidan could not remember when he'd last appreciated nature. Perhaps he never had.

From reading Riordan's descriptive letters, he recalled that the school was nestled in a wooded area a mile north of town. It was going on five o'clock, and, according to Riordan, he usually stayed after dismissal to work. It would be prudent to meet his brother privately before venturing to Riordan's town house. He clicked his tongue and sank his heels gently into Nebula's flanks, and the gelding vaulted forward into a brisk canter. With luck, he would arrive at the schoolhouse before half past five.

At last, a large wooden structure came into view. Damn it all, he was nervous. Would Riordan be angry? Show his disdain, and be distant? No, that described himself more than his brother. Aidan did not know if he could handle seeing the disappointment on Riordan's face—or the face of anyone in the family. Especially their father.

Bracing himself for the emotional reunion, he slipped from Nebula, tethered the reins to the post, and gave the gelding a pat. The horse nickered gently in response. All was quiet; was Riordan even within? Aidan opened the door and crossed the threshold. Moving through the small alcove, he stepped into the schoolroom. There was his beloved brother, sitting at his desk at the front of the room, scribbling furiously.

"Riordan."

His brother looked up, his eyes widened in shock. He rose quickly from his chair, and it crashed to the floor. Before Aidan could form another thought, his brother ran toward him and gathered him in a fierce embrace. At first, Aidan stood stiffly, his emotions churning.

"Oh, God, Aidan. Aidan," Riordan said tenderly, his voice shaking.

Hearing the stark emotion in his brother's voice broke away any self-imposed restraints. He returned Riordan's embrace, clapping him on the back for good measure. "I've missed you, Brother."

At last they parted, but still gripped each other's upper arms. "Why didn't you send word? Have you been home?" Riordan asked.

Aidan shook his head. "No. I wanted—needed—to see you first."

Riordan leaned forward until their foreheads touched briefly, then, in unison, they clasped the nape of each other's necks. God, he *had* needed this. That connection only they shared: the link—despite time, distance, and circumstance—that would never break. Not ever. No matter what Aidan had done or said to damage it.

"Come, take a seat." Riordan grabbed a chair and dragged it toward the desk. "Tell me everything. You will be staying a couple of nights?"

"If you and your wife will have me."

"Sabrina will be thrilled." Riordan smiled as he sat at his desk. "As will Mary Tuttle. She is already part of the family."

"It is serious then, between her and Grandfather?"

Riordan chuckled. "He's been here for a visit every month since February, bringing gifts of flowers, chocolate, and books. I would not be surprised if there were a wedding before the autumn." Riordan winked. "He took her on a short trip to the seaside not two weeks past."

Aidan smiled. "The old dog. Good for him."

"You'll like Mary. She's warm, humorous, down-to-earth, and exactly what Grandfather needs."

"And what of our father? What romance is brewing there?"

"You know him; caution will win the day. He is taking things at a slower pace, but I believe it will end up in the same place as Grandfather's. Eventually."

Aidan scratched his chin. "I really am the last man standing. And we have a young cousin. What a revelation."

"Megan is a charmer; you'll meet her when you arrive at the hall. I've never seen Garrett so blasted happy. He and Abbie are a love story for the ages. I'm glad they found each other again."

"Much has happened...to all of us," Aidan murmured.

"Brother, I will not drill you about your absence. None of us will. But know I am here whenever you feel the need to talk. I don't like that we have drifted apart—"

"That is on me," Aidan interjected.

"Not all of it. I should have reached out. You will find that the rest of the family feels the same—about all of this," Riordan replied.

Aidan shook his head. "The state I was in? I would have refused all assistance. Probably would have sunk even lower, if that were possible. But I thank you for the concern, and in time, I will talk about it. As it stands, it's an open wound."

Riordan stood and gathered up his papers, shoving them into a leather satchel. "On that note, let us head home. Dinner waits."

When they stepped outside, Riordan pointed at Nebula and smiled. "A near twin for Grayson. Well met, Brother."

"Except Nebula's mane is white, not black. I couldn't resist when he was shown to me. I had to purchase him."

"I like the name."

Aidan untied the reins and began walking side by side with his brother, with Nebula following behind.

"The town house is a good size, completely furnished, with a small barn in the rear. Grayson is still boarded at Farmer Walsh's. With the carriage and two horses I recently purchased, I thought, for the rest of this school term, that Grayson was better served at the farm than crammed into a small shed. For a two-night stay, I'm sure that Nebula will be fine." Riordan gave him an appraising look. "You're too thin and pale. Not what I remember."

"Believe me when I tell you, I was in much worse shape than this. The recuperation is ongoing. My appetite has been slow in recovering, and, as you can imagine, I have been indoors for the most part. The ride was quite pleasant, fresh air, sun, all that blather. I obviously need more of it." Actually, the ride had fatigued him, but it was a good tired. "Although I did manage a quick stop at the Crimson Club."

Riordan laughed heartily. "Damn it all, you *are* recovering. I'm pleased to hear it."

Once they placed Nebula in the barn, giving him a quick rubdown and leaving him plenty of water and oats, they headed toward the house. Again, Aidan's insides twisted in apprehension. It made him wonder if he'd left the sanatorium sooner than he should have.

They entered through the rear, making their way to the front of the house. As they stepped into the parlor, two women stood and smiled. Riordan went to the younger of the two, kissing her on the cheek as his large hand splayed across the bump of her belly. She glowed, the love between them apparent. For a brief moment, Aidan was envious. The emotion was not a new one as far as Riordan was concerned, but it was high time he moved past such selfish indulgence.

"My darling, this is my brother, Aidan."

Sabrina stepped forward, holding out both hands. Aidan clasped them tight. "Dear, dear brother. How I have longed for this meeting." She stood on the tips of her toes and laid an affectionate kiss upon his cheek. Her words were lovingly and genuinely spoken.

Aidan was grateful for the happy reception. "As have I, Sabrina." His brother's wife was attractive, and warm kindness reflected in her eyes.

"And this is Mary Tuttle. Mary, my brother, Aidan." The older woman's eyes twinkled, and she looped her arms through his and his brother's. A handsome woman with threads of gray at her temples, she gave him a friendly smile.

"Sabrina, have you ever seen such a fine pair of bookends? Not a matched set, as such, but enough alike to warrant admiration."

Everyone laughed, and Aidan already felt at ease, the last of his apprehension slipping away.

He had been welcomed—pulled into his family's loving embrace.

Never had he felt so humbled. And grateful. Well, except for his care at the clinic—more specifically, from Cristyn. Aidan had managed not to think of her during his long journey, but experiencing this warm affection and acceptance had him thinking he'd made a grave error in saying goodbye to his bold and beautiful angel.

# Chapter 4

Dinner was an agreeable affair, and Aidan managed to eat three quarters of the food placed before him. When offered wine, he acquiesced, and sipped it slowly. Three quarters of the glass remained when the meal concluded.

"Mary made lovely ginger scones. Would you care for them now, or perhaps later this evening, with a cup of tea? Or do you prefer coffee? We have both." Sabrina smiled.

"I do prefer coffee, and will attempt a scone later this evening."

"Are you sure you've had enough to eat?" Mary asked, a worried look on her face. Her concern warmed him, which again made him think of Cristyn. God, would she haunt him forever? He gave his head a shake to banish the thoughts.

He agreed with Riordan; Mary was exactly what his grandfather needed. Hell, what the whole family needed: a caring and loving matriarch.

"Believe me, this is the most I've eaten in months. And I actually enjoyed it. I am still recovering, as it were." The first mention of his decline and fall in front of the ladies. Aidan waited for awkward looks and silence.

Instead, Mary squeezed his hand gently. "I cannot tell you how glad we are you're here. I've heard much about you, not only from Riordan, but also from your grandfather. You are loved, Aidan; never doubt it. I hope I'm not being too forward."

He laid his hand on top of Mary's. "Not at all. I've always wished for a grandmother. Looks as if I'm to have one, and I could not be more pleased."

Mary blushed. "You're a teasing imp, like your grandfather said."

Everyone laughed.

"Riordan, why not take your brother to your study? I believe after we see the dishes are cleared away, I will take a nap," Sabrina suggested.

Riordan brushed the back of his fingers along Sabrina's cheek, causing pink spots to color it. "Rest well."

The men headed toward the study, and as Aidan entered the room, he smiled at the books crammed into several bookcases. Riordan had always been a voracious reader, whereas Aidan read in fits and starts. He only rediscovered the joy of reading when Garrett had sent books along with his trunk.

The room was small in comparison to the various libraries and studies at Wollstonecraft Hall, but a fire blazed in the hearth, giving it a consoling, flickering glow.

"Not my books, though I'm pleased they are included with the residence. This house belongs to a magistrate who is away for a year, visiting his daughter and her family in Spain. I considered buying Sabrina's former home, Durning House, from her destitute baron father, but she said it held no warm memories and would rather it be sold. Did I mention in one of my letters that Baron Durning was sent to debtor's prison this past January?"

"Yes. Well deserved for the part he played in Sutherhorne's dastardly schemes."

"The baron will be released as soon as the royal verdict comes through on Sutherhorne. The Wollstonecrafts will pay his debt, in exchange for his testimony toward the prosecution of the marquess, and Durning's agreed to leave the country. What he will do and where is still up for discussion." Riordan chuckled as he observed Aidan checking his pocket watch. "You still have it."

His brother pulled out the identical one; they were given to them by their father when they had turned sixteen. It was inlayed with gold, with the Wollstonecraft family crest on the cover: a howling wolf standing on a large stone. Diamond chips decorated the face. Inside, the engraving read: *Brothers by blood, friends by choice. July 29th, 1818.* Their birth date.

"I had left it behind at the hall last September. Garrett sent it along with the trunk." Aidan ran the pad of his thumb along the etchings. "I would never sell this. At least I had the foresight to leave it," he murmured. Snapping it shut, he slipped it into his waistcoat pocket.

Riordan moved to the sideboard. "Drink? I have Mackinnon single malt. Or is it thoughtless of me to ask?"

Damn it, he was sorely tempted. His hand trembled slightly, for the scotch reminded him of his descent. Though still shaken at how close he'd come to succumbing to the temptation of opium at the brothel, he was proud he'd fought it. Perhaps he should avoid spirits of all sorts. "No, not thoughtless. But I'd better not. I will stick with wine."

"Would you like your glass from dinner? It's still full, or I can pour you a fresh one."

"The one from dinner is fine."

Riordan left to fetch it. A loud meow filled the air and Aidan glanced down. A white and orange cat was staring up at him with curious green eyes. "You must be the elusive Mittens. Too shy to show yourself until now." Aidan rubbed the cat's ears and received a rumbling purr for his efforts.

Riordan returned. "Now you've met the last member of the family."

"Good God, a young cousin, pets, a niece or nephew on the way, a sister-in-law, a new aunt, and a possible stepmother and step-grandmother on the horizon. What next?" Aidan mumbled. "Wollstonecraft Hall will be overrun. Not used to having women around. Or children."

Riordan laughed and handed him the glass of wine, then poured himself a tumbler of scotch. He settled into a chair opposite and met Aidan's gaze. "It certainly will be overrun when we return to the hall at the end of June. Then we will prepare for the birth."

"When is Sabrina due?" Aidan asked as he scratched Mittens under the chin.

"Mid-August. Maybe later; hard to ascertain."

"And what else is on the horizon?"

"I already have men of means in place to fund my progressive school. Thanks to my presentation on education reform before Prince Albert last month, it has garnered a good deal of interest."

"Especially among those who wish to impress the prince, no doubt." Mittens, apparently done with human interaction, headed to the fireplace and curled up in front of it. "Nevertheless, well done. I'm proud of you." And he was, as the prince did not give an audience to just anyone.

Riordan smiled. "Thank you. That means more than you know. As for those princely sycophants, I will take their money regardless. May I ask what your plans are? You know you're welcome here for as long as you like. Until the end of June, of course."

"I appreciate the offer." Aidan stared down into his wineglass. "My plans? Dr. Bevan suggested I immerse myself in one of the family's causes. To give my life purpose, I suppose, and to have me focus on something besides my self-seeking extravagances."

"I heartily recommend it. I never dreamed that I would find such contentment and satisfaction in teaching. It has changed my life. This was to be a temporary experiment, to try out my education reforms in a schoolroom setting. Now I see it as my life's calling."

Aidan sipped the wine. "It's not much of a covert action any longer."

Riordan chuckled. "No, though my students still call me Mr. Black, as it is less of a mouthful than Wollstonecraft."

Hearing of Riordan's strategy, a plan hastily formed in Aidan's mind. "I thought to choose factory reform. Considering your success as a clandestine operative, perhaps I could do the same. Continue to use the name Black, find work at one of the worst factories, mills, or mines, and observe and report. It would assist Father in his push for an improvement of the current Factory Act."

Riordan seemed to contemplate the announcement. "It would at that. He's still working closely with Lord Ashley and others on further amendments. Are you well enough for such a venture?"

"If nothing else, my wan and pale self would fit in with the working class. And I do not mean that in jest. I've always been appalled at how workers are treated, particularly the women and children who toil in cotton mills." Aidan paused. "The more I think on it, I believe this to be a sound plan. Surely Father can pull some strings and have me placed at a mill. I'm aware there are many that are not following the revisions of the Labor in Cotton Mills Act of eighteen thirty-one, or the Factory Act of eighteen forty-four. There are not enough factory inspectors, for one thing—only four for the entire country. And the fact that the workers do not report the owners, for fear of retaliation or losing their positions, makes it difficult to enforce the laws already on the books."

"Ah." Riordan smiled. "So you *did* listen at the family meetings."

"More than you know. Do you think Father will be amenable to my scheme?"

Riordan rubbed his whiskered chin. "If you lay it before him as you have with me. You're truly interested in pursuing this?"

"I've floundered about long enough. I'm weary of drifting through life with no purpose. How embarrassing to discover how low I sank." Aidan swirled his wine. "I am ashamed, Brother. Utterly humiliated by my thoughtless and reckless behavior." He met Riordan's gaze and said in a soft voice, "I wish to redeem myself, not only in the family's eyes, but, more importantly, in my own. I wish to banish this 'notorious rake' nom de plume once and for all. Hang society; I don't give a toss what they think about me. But I do care about what the people I love think."

"I will keep your confidence, and I'm gratified to hear you want to rejoin the living. Be part of the family. I admit life has taken a swift move forward for all of us."

"What has happened to the damned curse? To hear that Garrett—who believed in it more than any of us—has embraced love is hard to take in. And you, with Father and Grandfather following close behind."

Riordan took a long draw on his scotch. "As I said to Garrett, love means taking a chance. At the end of the day, I could not bring myself to turn away from Sabrina. She means more to me than the curse. Garrett inevitably reached the same conclusion. Perhaps you will too, someday."

Aidan snorted. "Not likely."

"And what of Miss Cristyn Bevan?"

Aidan's head snapped up and he glared at his brother. "Where in hell did you hear about her?"

"From Garrett, who heard it from Abbie. She observed the two of you exchanging yearning gazes—"

"Christ," Aidan huffed, annoyed. *Damned interfering woman.* "Nothing remains private in this family, does it?"

"Easy. Garrett told only me. Do you care for this young lady?"

Yes, fuck it all, he cared. "I've said my goodbyes. I'll never see her again."

"Indeed?"

"Regardless of any feelings, and I will admit this only to you, she played a great part in my recovery. I'm not sure I would have made it if not for her. To answer your question: I care. Let us leave it at that."

"Garrett says she's quite lovely. Why not see where the attraction will lead? It's mutual, is it not?"

Aidan set his wineglass on the table. "Yes. At least, I believe it is. Nevertheless, I've ended it before it began. She deserves better."

"Well, all I know is fate often takes a hand, whether we want it to or not. Garrett will tell you all about that."

Aidan scoffed, but deep inside, he had the distinct impression all was not over between him and Cristyn. Or perhaps it was wishful thinking. In any case, no matter how much he desired or admired her, or thought of her, he'd never act on it. There were too many scars, inside and out. He was too damaged, a complete and utter wreck, carting behind him a sordid past that would taint any woman who came in contact with it—or him.

The truth was he wouldn't subject his angel to someone like him.

\* \* \* \*

Three days had passed since Aidan departed, and he'd hardly left Cristyn's thoughts. She did not like that they had argued and sniped at one another. Thankfully, her father was sympathetic, and had not pressed her on details of her ill-fated infatuation. But she must talk to someone. Gathering her shawl, she decided during her afternoon off to head to the village proper, to her close friend Cynthia Doyle Tennant's residence. They had not seen each other much of late. Since Cynthia's marriage to the young vicar, Davidson Tennant, and Cristyn immersing herself in Aidan's treatment, the weeks had flown. It was past time to correct the oversight.

She knocked on the door and the vicar opened it. He gave her a welcoming smile, and all at once Cristyn was reminded why Cyn had married the young man. No, he wasn't handsome in the strictest sense. The vicar was of a medium height and build, and already his hairline was receding, but he possessed the most beautiful light brown eyes. They reflected a kindness and intelligence that never failed to impress her, and when he smiled, he took on a saintly beauty that fairly took her breath away—not to mention his soft, but slight, Scottish burr.

"Miss Bevan. It is very grand to see you. Do come in; Cyn will be thrilled."

"Please, call me Cristyn."

He stepped aside to allow her to enter. "Only if you call me Davidson."

She returned his smile. "Of course."

Davidson escorted her to the parlor, where the two women embraced. "I will order tea and leave you alone to catch up."

Once the vicar departed, Cyn took Cristyn's shawl and bade her to sit next to her on the settee. "Marriage agrees with you, Cyn. You're positively glowing," Cristyn marveled.

"Oh, it does agree with me," she replied breathlessly. "Davidson is all I ever hoped he would be." She smiled coyly. "Especially in the bedroom."

Cristyn giggled. Her dear friend always spoke her mind and never failed to make her laugh. "Oh, Cyn, how I have missed you these past weeks. Please forgive me for not returning all of your kind invitations. I became caught up in...in—"

"Aidan Black? Last you were here in March, you spoke of nothing or no one else." Cyn gave her a sympathetic look. Had she really gone on about Aidan? How pathetic. And here she sat in Cyn's parlor about to discuss him again.

Why deny her feelings? "I did, didn't I? I'm afraid the infatuation has grown by leaps and bounds since then. I have to talk to someone. Although Dad and I are close, there are things that one cannot discuss with a parent. Not in great detail."

The housekeeper entered, setting down a tray with a teapot, cups, and a plate of biscuits. "Thank you, Mrs. Bell. Would you please take a cup to the vicar?"

"Already have done, Mrs. Tennant." The housekeeper smiled. "If you need anything at all, call out." She exited the parlor, closing the door behind her.

Cyn poured tea into the cups and passed one to her. "Now we are completely alone. What has happened?"

"I'm not sure where to start. My emotions are a tangled muddle. Separating and identifying them has become difficult." Cristyn sighed wistfully. "Against all common sense, I believe I have fallen in love with him. Please, no looks of pity. I'm already feeling sorry for myself."

"No pity from me, I promise. But it is wonderful—to fall in love." Cyn gave her a smile of encouragement.

"I acted like an empty-headed ninny. Toward the end of his stay, I wore my heart on my sleeve. Blast it all! I threw it at him, and he kicked it away." She sipped her tea. "Perhaps I was mistaken about those heated looks he gave me. I caught him more than once before he hid behind his impenetrable shield."

Cyn passed her the plate of lemon biscuits and Cristyn took three. "Men are such contrary creatures. Many see such emotions as a weakness."

"I had already seen him at his most vulnerable. I think that is when my intense emotions began to take root, for he'd arrived in dreadful condition." Cristyn frowned. "Why would I fall in love with a thin, shivering man, covered in vomit and rat bites, going through opium withdrawal? It makes no sense."

"He touched you," Cyn whispered.

Cristyn nodded. "Yes. His vulnerability and sadness opened my heart in a way it had never opened before. I wanted nothing more than to hold him and protect him. Why him, and not another male patient? An intimate bond formed between us—surely I am not mistaken in that. Through sheer will, he recovered. I admire his courage, his strength, and, yes, as he grew stronger, I cannot deny that his dark, devilish looks also appealed."

"Perhaps his disreputable past appeals as well? I mean, I assume he has one, considering the opium. I've heard from various quarters that there is nothing like reforming a rake. Once tamed, he makes for spectacular husband material. Think of all that naughty sexual experience."

Cristyn laughed, and Cyn joined her. Oh, she needed that.

"Speaking of naughty, my cousin, Suzanne, wrote me about a particular piece of juicy gossip. Do you wish to hear it before we continue? It will make for a much-needed diversion, however temporary."

"Your cousin from London?" Cyn nodded. Cristyn had met Suzanne on many occasions through the years, when she'd come to visit Cyn during the summer months. They were all about the same age. "Oh, go on. I could use a good dose of salacious scandal." Anything to take her mind off her heartache, and Aidan, if only for a moment.

"Well, this concerns the heir to the Earl of Carnstone; she didn't say in her letter what the family name is or where they are from, and blast it if I know all the names of the peerage, but London had been chattering about this for the past several months. Apparently the heir attended one of those disgraceful parties aristocrats like to throw, with all manner of sin available for consumption." Cyn's eyes brightened as she relayed the sensational details. A vicar's wife talking about immoral aristocrats. Only Cynthia Doyle Tennant would dare to do it.

Cristyn smiled at her dear friend. Yes, she had missed these conversations. "In other words, you're speaking of an orgy."

"You shouldn't know of such things, and neither should I, but yes, exactly that." Cyn frowned. "I can't imagine it, all those tangled, sweaty bodies...."

Cristyn laughed once again, almost choking on her biscuit.

"Anyway, there was this auction," Cyn continued. "And the heir, a sinfully handsome young man, according to all reports, was the prize. He went for hundreds and hundreds of pounds. He was sold to an ancient, licentious lord. Can you imagine?"

Actually, Cristyn could imagine it. She'd heard many similar stories in the years she had assisted her father in treating addiction. People would descend to unknown depths for a variety of reasons, and bored peers were always looking for a thrill, especially if it were illegal. "That *is* juicy gossip."

"And it matters not to society, for I hear there are young ladies aplenty eager to make his acquaintance."

Cristyn shook her head. "There's no accounting for taste and discrimination."

"But it proves my point about how rakes as husbands are in high demand." Cyn reached for another biscuit. "And what the heir participated in is not only against the law, but against the rules of God. At least, that is what the church says. Davidson doesn't hold with such strict rules. He doesn't judge what people get up to privately."

"Good for Davidson."

"Now, back to the vulnerable, but devilishly handsome, Mr. Black. What will you do?"

A wave of sadness rolled through Cristyn. "He's gone, Cyn. Three days ago. We parted on awkward terms, arguing and the like. But not before he stood close enough to nuzzle my neck."

"Oh? Do tell." Cyn winked.

"Oh, his passionate touch was all that I hoped it would be. He was aroused; I felt it. Yet he stepped away, claiming that it would never happen again." Cristyn placed her empty cup on the tray. "He said, and I quote: 'I am not a man to pin any hopes or dreams on. There will be no correspondence, no hope of more. I am not a nice man, Cristyn. I would use you, and toss you aside, as I have with many other women. You are too fine of a person to be subjected to the likes of me.' Shouldn't I be the judge of that?"

Cyn whistled. "Goodness. Not only do you remember what he said word for word, but he has a low opinion of himself. What do you know of his past?"

"Next to nothing, except that his family is well off. They breed horses, live in Kent. That's it." Cristyn caught her dear friend's gaze. "Here's the astonishing thing: I don't have a low opinion of him. I can't explain it; perhaps I've been blinded. I will never see him again, and it blasted well hurts."

Cyn laid a comforting hand on hers and squeezed. "Oh, my dear. I don't know what to say to make it better. What will you do?"

"I've been thinking. Perhaps I need a change of venue. I thought I might travel to London and find a position at one of the hospitals."

Cyn's eyebrows shot up. "London? By yourself? Your father will never agree to it."

"I'm twenty-three, soon to be twenty-four. Besides, I have acquired a vast knowledge of medicine. I want to put what I've learned toward a more general practice. Set broken bones, treat wounds and the like, above and beyond what I have been able to do at my father's clinic."

"Surely he could find you a position in a smaller clinic nearer to home. Talk to him about it before you make a rash decision. London is overwhelming, and can be a dangerous place."

Cristyn had to admit: her friend made sense. Now that she had spoken of her plan aloud, it took on a fresh urgency. She did wish to ply her skills in a more varied setting, but more than anything she needed to escape. Everywhere she turned, she was reminded of Aidan. He haunted every nook and cranny of the sanatorium, and every part of her heart and soul.

The only way to banish him for good would be new surroundings. A new life. In time, her heart would heal—she could only hope.

# Chapter 5

On the road to Wollstonecraft Hall, trepidation moved through Aidan once again. Reuniting with the rest of his family brought on old anxieties and new concerns. Once all this reunion business concluded, he could commence with getting on with his life. In his head he could hear Dr. Bevan advising him to take a deliberate and straightforward path. But Aidan had never been the cautious type, or one to follow directions or commands. *Obviously.* He had always charged full-steam ahead without any regard to consequences—and look where he had wound up.

Visiting with Riordan had helped ease the way for the next step, which consisted of facing his father. All his life Aidan had been a disappointment; he'd seen it clearly on his father's face on numerous occasions. It started in childhood: misbehaving, tantrums, destruction of property (of which he was heartily ashamed; it was the reason he was sent to school before Riordan). Instead of trying to improve his behavior, he had purposely and stubbornly sought out more wickedness. Rather childish, when he reflected on it. It was well past time to grow up.

The trees took on a familiar look; he was close to the edge of the vast Wollstonecraft property. Aidan rode past the duck pond and was given quacking greetings from the feathered occupants. Every shrub and hedgerow was immaculately groomed. Wollstonecraft Hall and its grounds spoke of a more affluent age.

The hall itself was initially owned by a baronet in the medieval age, and once purchased by the seventeenth century Earl of Carnstone, renovations began immediately. He retained the use of the word "hall," even though the current residence did not resemble the original timbered structure, except at the front entrance. Eclectic in look with its Georgian and Gothic wings, the rambling residence had seen its share of heartache.

With regards to a more affluent age, how prudent that his father and grandfather had seen the change approaching decades ago, and took steps to ensure that their family had not become complacent when it came to the economic shift of the country. Many peers were nearing complete ruin because they hadn't kept up with the times or, more recently, had invested in dodgy railway schemes. His grandfather had invested the family's money in solid industrious ventures, and because of it, they were wealthier than ever.

Someday, long into the future, this would all be his. In the past, the prospect had terrified him. Bloody hell, he didn't ask to be born ten minutes before his fraternal twin. Riordan would have made a better heir; he was responsibility and sturdiness incarnate.

But fate had a sense of humor and laid the duty at his feet instead. Fingers crossed Riordan and Sabrina had a son, then there would be no need for Aidan to marry. His nephew could be the damned heir. How easy it would be to hand the responsibility off to someone else. His past self would have done it quick as a wink.

But Aidan wasn't that man anymore. *Surely not.* He hadn't come through opium hell only to slip into old habits. Besides, after all his father and grandfather had done to improve the family's circumstances, it would be reprehensible of him to allow it to founder.

Turning onto the tree-lined circular drive, he felt like a soldier coming home from battle. At least, how he imagined one would feel. No doubt soldiers felt strange, elated, to be sure, but also apprehensive, with everything holding a type of unfettered unfamiliarity. Not that he was any kind of hero. Far from it. Hero was something he would never be.

With a deep breath, he pulled up on Nebula's reins and halted before the front entrance. Slipping from the gelding, he patted his neck. Christ, his insides were churning. He grabbed the brass knocker, but before he could use it, the door opened. Martin, their venerable butler, opened the door. "My God, Master Aidan!" Martin quickly arranged his features into professional neutrality. "You were not expected, sir."

Aidan had instructed the staff long ago not to bother with the courtesy 'lord' designation when addressing him. He must have arrived before the letter from Dr. Bevan. "Are my father and grandfather within?"

Martin stepped aside to allow him to enter the front hall. "The viscount is visiting at the Eaton residence, but the earl is presently in his study."

"No need to announce me, I remember the way."

"It *is* good to see you, sir." Martin's deep voice had a soft, affectionate tone, something he didn't show often.

Aidan was genuinely touched. "And you, Martin. It is good to be…home."

As he made his way through the long hallways, nodding to a few footmen, it was as he'd surmised. All was familiar, but also strangely removed from reality. A door burst open and a dog bolted past him, with a young girl following close behind, her red hair flowing to her shoulders. They had nearly knocked him off his feet.

"Laddie! Come back here!"

The dog woofed playfully and disappeared around the corner, as did the girl. Out of the same room barreled a young man who knocked Aidan off balance. He hit the tiled floor hard, and his shoulder ached from the impact.

"Oh. Sorry, sir."

The man was huge, almost as tall as Garrett's six and a half feet, and their collision had Aidan gasping for breath. All at once he was pulled upright, causing another blast of pain to shoot through his shoulder.

"Laddie has Meg's new gloves," the golden-haired giant said.

"How exciting," Aidan replied drolly.

"Are you Aidan?"

"I am."

The young man thrust out his huge hand. "I'm Jonas Eaton."

The simpleton. *Easy. A little compassion would not go amiss.* He took the man's hand. Jonas was as breathtakingly handsome as Garrett had described. Good God, this young man would set London society on its ear. The young ladies would be completely agog, in spite of his limitations.

"Good to meet you."

Before he could speak further, the dog and the girl whirled around the corner and made a complete stop before them. The dog eyed him suspiciously, and a warning growl emitted from the beast, who opened his mouth far enough that the gloves dropped to the floor. The girl, Meg, picked them up, frowning at the saliva dripping from them.

Aidan held out his hand toward the collie. "We've met before, Laddie, remember?"

Laddie gave him a good sniff, and recognition dawned. Garrett had brought the Scotch collie—more of a half-grown puppy at the time—for a short visit in February when Garrett had been in Standon. Laddie's tail wagged and he gave Aidan a friendly woof. "There we are, friends again." He scratched the dog's ears for good measure.

"Meg, this is your cousin, Aidan," Jonas enthused.

Jesus, it was as if a feminine version of Garrett stood before him. Her hazel-green eyes blinked, then a shy smile broke out, making her prettiness all the more apparent. She had as many freckles as his uncle. Aidan reached for her hand and bent over it. "My distinct pleasure, Miss Hughes."

She laughed at his exaggerated bow and faux pompous tone. At least she realized that he wasn't being serious.

When he released her hand, she gave him an extravagant curtsey. "Lord Wollstonecraft."

He chuckled. Yes, he liked her already.

"Aidan!" Abigail stood in the doorway, a warm smile on her lovely face. He strode toward her. "Good to see you, Aunt Abigail."

"Oh, I'm your aunt. What a development. Please, call me Abbie." She took his hand and squeezed it affectionately. "We did not receive word of your visit."

"Apparently the mail is not as efficient as believed."

"I'll tell Garrett you're here," Jonas said. "He's in the barn. Then I'll fetch Tens."

"Thank you." Aidan assumed 'Tens' was his father, and his mouth quirked with amusement at the nickname.

"Your grandfather is in his private study. Go and see him, and I will order tea. Are you hungry?" Abbie asked.

*Food.* He would have to make an effort. "I wouldn't say no to beefsteak sandwiches."

"Consider it done. I'll send word when it's ready. Come, Megan."

Impulsively, Megan kissed his cheek. "I am happy you're here."

He was left alone in the hallway, as Laddie had followed the women. Damn it, all this flustering and emotion was spiking his anxieties. Dr. Bevan had stressed there may be residual disquiet from his decline into debauchery.

Taking a cleansing and calming breath, he headed to his grandfather's study. The door was ajar, so he stepped inside. There he sat, reading over documents. He looked up, and the astonishment was clear on his face. Overall his grandfather hadn't changed much—a few more lines etched into his handsome face, fewer threads of black running through his hair, for it had been close to ten months since they'd seen each other. "Grandfather."

He stood, and immediately strode toward Aidan, taking him into a warm embrace. "Welcome home, Grandson. Welcome home." His grandfather's voice shook, which caused Aidan's throat to grow tighter.

Garrett burst into the room. "Aidan!" His uncle grabbed his arm and pulled him into a crushing bear hug. "You're home at last."

*Yes. Home.* The word conjured up warm memories and a feeling of safety and comfort—things that had been lacking in his life of late. Damn it all, everyone seemed genuinely happy to see him. But would his father be as pleased? Could he blame him if he weren't?

\* \* \* \*

It wasn't often that Julian could find time alone with Alberta, but today he wished to take things beyond ardent kisses. Ever since she and her brother-in-law, Jonas, had taken possession of her late uncle's small manor house last September, his world had been turned upside down.

Julian had not seen Alberta during most of the spring due to parliament being in session, but he'd never stopped thinking of her. An omen, to be sure, proving that his feelings had already moved beyond friendly affection. While in London, he'd briefly considered taking a trip to the Crimson Club to banish his sexual frustrations, but found he hadn't wanted a casual encounter. Damn it, he wanted Alberta.

Frankly, he was tired of sipping tepid tea in her parlor. He gazed at her from over the rim of his cup. Fiona, the twins' mother and his beloved wife, had died more than twenty-five years past. No other woman had managed to capture his interest. *Except Alberta.* With her glorious crown of wheat-colored hair, pretty face, and lush figure, she certainly appealed to him physically, but it was more than that.

The thirty-nine-year-old widow spoke to his heart. She was a calming presence, generous and kind, vowing to her late husband that she would look after his younger brother, Jonas, and ensure that he was never sent to an asylum because of his intellectual and mental shortcomings.

Julian's caution seemed ridiculous in light of his intense feelings. He should be taking what sparked between them further. But, damn it all, he was frightened into inaction because he could not bear more heartache and loss. Fiona's death had scarred him. And what was etched on his heart and soul? The curse. Placing another woman he cared for deeply in possible danger made him hesitate.

With his youngest son, younger brother, and, it appeared, his father accepting love, it was well past time he showed the same conviction and courage. Enough vacillating. Perhaps there was still hope that the curse could be broken.

Julian placed his cup on the tray. "Alberta."

She looked up at him. "Hm?"

"Let's go to bed."

Alberta arched an eyebrow at him, her expression confused. "Pardon?"

"I've shocked you."

"Heavens, no. I've waited months for you to make the suggestion." She placed her cup on the tray, and Julian took note of her hand shaking slightly. "I was beginning to wonder if I would have to take the bold step and propose it. But then, I thought perhaps you may not wish to move forward on such a path." She paused, and huffed out a short breath. "I know of the curse. Abbie told me, as did my late uncle in his letters. Do you believe in it?"

"I do...to a certain degree. But there is a way to break it."

"Oh? By having sex in the middle of the afternoon?"

Julian stared blankly at her.

"I am teasing."

His mouth twisted into an amused grin. "Apologies. It's a touchy subject—the curse, not sex." She laughed lightly in response. "Riordan recently located ancient papers in the attic that stated all living Wollstonecraft men must form a love bond within a twelve-month period." He tugged on his earlobe, giving her a sheepish look. "Now that I speak it aloud, it sounds completely foolish. The truth is Fiona's death left me bereft. I hesitated—because of the curse, to an extent, but also because I did not want my heart engaged." He paused. Might as well lay it all out. "I was afraid to love."

"Love?" she whispered.

He stood and held out his hand. "Come, and let us make love."

"It has been a long time, Julian," Alberta murmured. "More than three years, since Reese passed." She slipped her hand in his, and her touch sent a bolt of desire through him, arousing him further.

He gently pulled her into his embrace. "It's been close to two years for me," he whispered hotly in her ear. Then he nibbled on the curve of her neck. When she moaned softly, he took her hand once again and led her upstairs. Julian hesitated. "Your room?"

Alberta smiled. "This way."

Once inside the room, he was taken by cozy yellow shades on the walls, carpets, and bedding. "I confess that one of the first rooms I had renovated was this one. The furniture, including the bed, are recent purchases," she said.

Julian glanced toward the four-post canopy bed with yellow sheers draped across the upper posts. "Beautiful, like you."

She blushed, making her even more attractive. God, how he wanted her. He shrugged out of his coat and tossed it onto the yellow rose divan. Unbuttoning his waistcoat, then his shirt, he tossed both next to his coat. Alberta's gaze remained on him, her eyes swimming with desire. "Should I keep going?" he asked, giving her a sensual smile.

"Please."

He stood before her naked and fully aroused. Alberta's gaze traveled the length of him.

"Oh, my, Julian," she gasped. "You are...quite stunning." Reaching for the buttons on her tea gown, she licked her bottom lip, causing his cock to jerk in response. "I do hope we will not be disturbed." She kicked her slippers aside.

Julian marched to the door, closed it, and turned the key. "Jonas is with Garrett this afternoon, working and training in the stables." He tossed the key on the bedside table, then leaned against the poster, crossing his arms. "Please, continue. Unless you need my assistance?"

"No, I've managed without a lady's maid for years." The copper-colored gown pooled at her feet. Next, the petticoats, then her front-lacing corset. She stood before him in a chemise and stockings, allowing him to look his fill. Curvy, lush. Her nipples were hard, pressing against the sheer material. Alberta pulled the garment over her head. Her breasts were full, glorious, and he ached to touch them. "Keep the stockings on?" he asked, his voice husky.

"As you wish."

In a few quick strides, he stood before her and gathered her into his arms. They were skin against skin, igniting the flame that sizzled between them. Julian captured her lips with his, kissing her fiercely. She ran her fingers through his hair, returning the kiss with equal fervor.

They tumbled to the bed, touching and kissing. Already this had moved beyond his few casual affairs. He removed the pins that held her coiffure in place, and her silken locks fell to her shoulders. As he nuzzled her neck, inhaling the rosewater scent of her hair, his hand trailed down her side and slid between her legs. *God. Wet.* Inserting two fingers, his thumb found that sensitive nub and he stroked her, faster, as she moaned and arched her back under his ministrations. With a piercing cry, she reached her peak. Damn it, he couldn't wait. Rising above her, he gripped his cock, moving it across her slick entrance.

"Yes, Julian," she urged, raising her hips to meet him.

He plunged into her, groaning as her inner muscles clutched him. They found a heart-pulsing rhythm, moving together. Alberta gasped, reaching another climax. Close to his own, he started to pull out.

She grasped his arse and held in him place. "No. Stay."

About to question her, his peak slammed him hard. He groaned long and loud, and it ended on an awed whisper of her name.

Alberta gently swiped aside the lock of hair that had fallen across his forehead, and Julian heard a door slam.

"Tens! Bert! Where are you?"

They stared at each other, still breathing hard. Alberta's eyes widened in shock. "Jonas!" she whispered harshly. "Quick, we must dress."

The heavy tread of boots hitting the stairs grew ever closer. Julian chuckled. "Too late, my sweet. We are caught, good and proper. How fortuitous I locked the door." He had no sooner spoken when the handle rattled.

"Bert, are you in there?" Jonas called out. "Tens?"

"I'll be out shortly!" Alberta buried her face in Julian's chest. "Oh, drat it all."

"Jonas, we will meet you presently in the parlor," Julian called out.

There was a long pause. "Oh. Right." The sound of his footfalls grew quieter as he descended the stairs.

"I believe he has deduced what we've been up to," Julian laughed. "Especially since Garrett and I gave him the frank talk a few months past."

"How mortifying," Alberta moaned.

Julian rolled his hips. He was still semi-erect, and could easily go again. Gratifying to discover he still possessed a modicum of stamina. He gently tilted her chin and met her gaze. "No need to be ashamed or embarrassed."

She smiled. "Truly, I'm not. Well, perhaps a little at Jonas guessing. This was wonderful, and it changes everything, doesn't it?"

He kissed her, his tongue plunging deep. Now fully erect, he moved in and out of her, increasing the pace as he laid her shapely leg on his hip. "Yes, everything."

Alberta moaned. "But Jonas—"

"Can wait."

Twenty minutes later, they strode arm and arm into the parlor. Jonas looked everywhere except at them, obviously flustered.

"What is it, Jonas? No need to be uncomfortable, lad."

He nodded, then smiled. "Aidan is home! I came to tell you."

Julian's breath caught. His oldest son. *God.*

Alberta clutched his hand. "Go to him. It will be all right, Julian. Speak from your heart. Mend the bridge between you."

"Thank you." Her words gave him the courage to do exactly what she'd suggested. *Mend the bridge. Speak from the heart.* After saying his goodbyes, he headed toward home at a brisk pace.

Julian entered the front hall and Martin stepped forward, taking his hat. "Master Aidan is in the earl's private study, along with Master Garrett."

"Thank you, Martin." He took the stairs two at a time, his heart pounding fiercely in his chest. Upon entering the parlor, he froze as Aidan turned to face him. He was thin; his cheekbones were prominent. Father and son stared at each other across the expanse of carpet. It might as well have been a ravine. Aidan's expression was guarded, his shoulders straight, as if bracing for a scolding. Julian recognized the stance from years of confrontations. Be damned if he would reproach his son. He crossed the space between them and pulled Aidan into an embrace, something he had not done for longer than he cared to remember. Aidan stood stiffly, not responding. Julian didn't allow it to deter him; he merely hugged his son tighter. "Aidan. I don't have the words, except to say I love you. I always have. I am glad you're home," Julian whispered.

With a strangled sound that to Julian resembled a choked sob, Aidan returned the hug.

His son was home. Safe. And in his arms.

All was right with the world.

# Chapter 6

Aidan hadn't expected such an affectionate welcome from his father. And when was the last time he'd said he loved him? When he was six? Eight? Ten? Certainly not after the age of ten. Aidan wasn't sure he could form words. Would he fall completely to pieces? Instead he gathered his inner courage, which had been stored away and safely protected these past several months, and said, "I love you, too."

They parted, and his father smiled. "Have you seen Riordan?"

"I journeyed there first."

"Ah. He is well?"

"Exceedingly happy, from all accounts. Oh." Aidan stepped away from his father, pulled an envelope out of the side pocket of his coat, and passed it to his grandfather. "From Mary Tuttle. I like her. She will be a welcome addition to the family. With Abbie and Megan already in residence, what is another woman about the place?" The men chuckled. "I was practically mowed down by my cousin and Garrett's collie. And I was knocked to the floor by Jonas Eaton." Aidan rubbed his shoulder at the memory. "Abbie is ordering tea, by the by, and will inform us when it is ready."

"In the meantime, please, sit," his grandfather said. "All together again, except for Riordan, but he is here in spirit, and will be here for good in about a month's time. I cannot be more pleased."

They sat on the opposite side of the large study, on the leather settee and wingchairs. Then silence descended, as if no one knew what to say next. Despite the affectionate welcome, awkwardness had settled in. It was time to say his piece while they were alone.

"I've lived in idleness and discontent, slipping slowly into the dark pit of debauchery." Aidan met the men's gazes. "I am not being flippant;

I'm speaking the truth, as hard as it may be for you to hear. I've made a complete muddle of my life. We all are quite aware of how low I descended—apparently, the rest of society is as well. I am not proud of my behavior. Allow me to apologize for it, and for any disrespect that I have shown." He paused, uncomfortable, but soldiered on. "I also regret any shame that has been reflected on the family."

His father cleared his throat. "You are forgiven, Aidan. You were long ago."

"Thank you. Now I have to learn how to forgive myself. There will be a time I'll be able to speak of it in more detail, but it is still too…raw, for lack of a better word. Have patience with me."

"Of course," Garrett said. "Take all the time you need. Just one question: What about Delaney?"

Aidan shrugged. "I want to put the incident out of my mind."

"I've asked Edwin Seward to trace his background and whereabouts, but the man has disappeared. All he's discovered is that he's originally from Ireland. Perhaps he has returned there," Garrett said. "I am awaiting the final report."

"Let's hope he's gone from England. I was going to wait to mention this, but I believe it best to put my plan in motion as soon as possible," Aidan stated.

"Shouldn't you rest before taking on any enterprise?" his grandfather asked, concern in his tone.

"I've had plenty of rest. I've discussed this with Riordan, and he agrees with my scheme. Dr. Bevan suggested I submerge myself in one of the family's causes." Aidan explained how factory reform held his interest, and how he wished to operate as Riordan had, observing as a covert operative, gathering information that could be used to push through much-needed amendments to the current act.

His father and grandfather exchanged glances. At least they hadn't discarded his suggestion outright.

"I'm particularly interested in cotton mills, since they exploit women and children more than any other industry," Aidan said.

"Dr. Bevan agreed to this strategy? Does he believe you well enough?" his father asked.

Aidan frowned. "I didn't discuss the particulars, but he would not have allowed me to leave if I wasn't ready to move on with my life."

"Aidan should do this, and he should be given our full support," Garrett said.

He gave his uncle a nod of thanks. His six-years-older uncle was more of a big brother, and Aidan was glad of his assistance. "Father, between you and Grandfather, you know of the worst mills in the country. Using your influence, you can have me placed at one. Think of the information I could gather—enough ammunition to push for improvements."

"In what capacity would you work at the mill? You hardly look and sound like a factory worker," his father interjected.

Aidan smiled. "I've thought of that. Surely there are middle management positions, such as a floor supervisor."

"That would not be easy to arrange," his grandfather said. "Such positions are coveted, and usually held by men who have been at the mill many years."

"I have great faith in your power, Grandfather, and in Father's. You could arrange something, even if it's temporary."

His father rubbed his forehead. "You cannot be plunked down in the middle of a cotton mill. You will have to be trained on the machines, learn the inner workings of the production of cotton. Study all of the laws—"

"Like the Labor in Cotton Mills Act of eighteen thirty-one? As I said to Riordan, I listened more at those family meetings than you know." Aidan leaned forward, resting his elbows on his knees. "I have to do this. I want—need—to do something worthwhile. It's not an immediate necessity that I be dropped into a mill; I *will* do the due diligence, be trained on the machines, study laws and procedures. It will have to be one of the worst mills in the country. Surely you know of one."

His father sighed, "There is more than one, unfortunately. Government grinds at an agonizingly slow pace. Even Riordan's presentation of education reform before the prince will not bring about swift change. Passing amendments to present acts, or crafting new ones, takes months, years. God, even decades."

"It's true," his grandfather interjected. "It is deuced frustrating. You could go to all this trouble and see no satisfactory result."

"Even bringing the mill owner to justice would be a victory, would it not?" Aidan asked. "Think of me as a de facto factory inspector, albeit a stealthy one."

"Sounds like a victory to me," Garrett stated. "Surely Da, you're able to find a mill owner who deserves to be prosecuted?"

"Yes, Garrett, there are a number. If you are determined to do this, Aidan, then allow your father and me to make inquiries. I know of a man who can train you on the inner workings of a cotton mill, but it may take a few weeks."

Aidan beamed. Hope bloomed inside him for the first time in—well, longer than he could recall.

Abbie knocked and entered. "Tea is served, gentlemen. And Aidan, when I informed Mrs. Barnes you were home, she and Mrs. Teague prepared a veritable feast."

The housekeeper and cook had been at the hall since before Aidan was born. Even when he misbehaved as a child—which, he reflected, was often—the ladies always had a biscuit and a ready hug when he had needed it most. He would visit them after dinner.

Later, once tea then dinner had concluded and he'd spoken to Mrs. Barnes and Mrs. Teague, Aidan entered his suite of rooms. He marveled at the cleanliness—not an item out of place, and in the exact condition he'd left it last year, as if waiting for his return. Aidan tore off the layers of clothes, tossing them to the divan. Naked, he sat on the floor facing the end of his bed. Hooking his feet under the iron rungs of the footboard and clasping his hands behind his head, he began his regimen of one hundred sit-ups. After this, he would do one hundred floor presses.

He'd been introduced to this routine a couple of years past, in his boxing phase. The trainer at the club stated the ancient Romans used to do a version of these particular exercises, which the trainer referred to as calisthenics. The physical exertion kept disquiet from his soul, and allowed him to focus on something other than haunting memories.

It also kept him focused on his goal. Recovery. Rebirth. Redemption. Not to mention it aided in building up his strength, muscle, and stamina, which had been sadly lacking. His brother was right; he was far too thin. He moved quicker, and sweat popped out on his forehead from the effort.

Banish the demons. Keep temptation at bay.

And, more importantly, try to forget Cristyn. She invaded his erotic dreams. He could not shake the memory of her. At times, he swore he caught the scent of violets. She haunted his every step. No woman had ever affected him to this extent—she was yet another addiction to overcome. Or perhaps she wasn't. Perhaps she was more. Best to put it out of his mind. Putting her out of his heart, however, would require greater effort.

\* \* \* \*

It was well into June before Cristyn decided to speak to her father about her plan to pursue nursing. She'd broached the subject once more with Cyn and Davidson, and they'd agreed that any place but London would be a better choice. Davidson had attended university there and painted a rather grim picture of dirty streets, foul air, rude people, and expensive lodgings.

With the city out of the question, perhaps a smaller town or village would suffice. It was what she was used to.

There was no time like the present to raise the topic. "Dad, since a recent medical graduate from Oxford will be here by the end of the month, I thought I might look for work elsewhere."

Her father dropped his fork in shock, and pieces of beef and vegetable smothered in gravy bounced across the tablecloth, leaving a greasy stain. "What?"

"The training program that Mr. Garrett Black, Aidan's wealthy uncle, is funding? Young doctors will be learning your methods of addiction treatment. You will have a young man arrive here with another in August. You no longer need me to act as your assistant. I would rather not be relegated to the position of head maid." Cristyn dabbed the corner of her mouth and laid the napkin on the table. "I have learned much from you, and I wish to put it into practice in front-line medical situations. At first, I thought London—"

Her father's eyes widened. "No, Cristyn."

She held up her hand. "I've already ruled it out. There is no formal training for nursing, and if I applied for a position at a hospital there, I would be treated no better than a servant. There is nothing wrong with being a maid, but that is not what you've trained me for. I know as much or more than any apothecary offering medical care to the lower classes. Perhaps more than a surgeon treating those who can afford to pay to have a broken bone set." Cristyn exhaled.

"Yes, you *are* highly knowledgeable."

"But it is not enough to have it recognized by anyone other than my father. Women are not welcome in the medical field, or even allowed to train and study formally at an accredited university. It's not fair."

"No, it isn't. But here at the sanatorium you will receive the respect that you deserve. Regardless of who comes here to train, I would never relegate you to a subservient position. You're my assistant, and that will *not* change. Not as long as I run this facility. And if these young men can't accept it, they can return from whence they came."

Her father's passionately spoken words of support touched her heart. "I do appreciate it, Dad. Truly. But as I said, I wish to put my skills to practical use."

"We treat the villagers for various maladies," her father replied.

"Yes, lancing a boil or pulling an infected tooth. I'm speaking of those in true need, those too poor to pay for medical care. Surely there must be a place my experience and learning can be put to good use. Besides London or any other large city."

"You're serious about this."

She nodded. "Yes. Completely."

"Is there more to it? Is it because of Aidan Black?"

Her father knew her well. "Perhaps a little."

He cocked a dubious eyebrow at her.

"All right, perhaps more than a little," she whispered softly.

Her father's eyes widened. "Dear God, you're in love with him."

"I don't want to be."

"Damn the man. I am sorry I ever allowed him to stay here," her father snapped irritably. "How dare he hurt you."

"I hadn't meant for it to happen. He did nothing to encourage my feelings. The blame can hardly be laid at his feet."

Her father patted her hand. "The heart is a tricky thing; it rarely listens to common sense. If you feel strongly about it, I won't stand in your way." He frowned, as if puzzling out the dilemma. "There is a possibility with a friend of mine from university. He attended with Elwyn and me. His name is Dr. Paris Middlemiss. He's around forty-eight years of age, and a confirmed bachelor."

Cristyn's mood brightened. "What else can you tell me about him?"

"He strongly believes in helping those less fortunate. Although he is the third son of a viscount and has credentials enough, he was able to set up a fashionable and lucrative practice in London, though he has walked away from that life. For the past four years he has been moving about Great Britain, staying a year in each place, tending the sick and using his own fortune to finance his good works."

Cristyn smiled. "He sounds wonderful."

"Paris is a good man."

"Why would he give up a profitable practice in London?" Cristyn asked.

"He mentioned a doomed love affair, but I'm not aware of the particulars. I suppose he is trying to take his mind off it by keeping busy. If I contact him, and he agrees to take you on, you must give me your word it will only be for a period of three months. I cannot spare you any longer than that. Besides, I would miss you terribly."

"Oh, Dad. I will miss you as well. But I need to do this. I must stand on my own two feet." Cristyn twirled the stem of her wineglass. "And forget how much of a fool I've made of myself over a man who didn't return my feelings. Perhaps there is something wrong with me."

"Blast it! I cannot and will not allow you to think you're not worthy of love." Her father slammed his napkin on the table. "I'm breaking a confidence, and it is not sitting well with me, but my dear, the attraction was mutual. Aidan confided in me that night at dinner."

Her eyes widened in shock. Then a slow, simmering fury crawled through her at the reminder. At the fact it had not been merely in her imaginings. "He said he was attracted to me, and still left?" Her voice shook with anger.

"I agreed with his reasons. As I said earlier, he's not for you. Aidan still has much to work through. He stated—rightly—he's in no position to enter into any sort of relationship, and I concurred."

Damn men and their high-handedness! Somehow, it hurt even worse to know Aidan was interested in her and departed anyway, as if what had existed between them wasn't worth exploring. Her eyes narrowed as she glared at her father. How dare they discuss her over dinner, making decisions about her life without allowing her any contribution. "You had no right to pass a verdict on my feelings. Neither of you did. How arrogant. My opinion hadn't mattered at all."

Her father took her hand. "I *am* sorry. But try to remember: I'm aware of aspects of his past that you are not. Know that I acted in your best interests."

Cristyn pulled her hand away. Perhaps it was best she would be leaving for three months. She was angry and hurt, and afraid of saying something she would regret. "In the future, allow me the courtesy of living my own life, on my terms, and if that means I take a misstep along the way, then I learn from it. You cannot run my life under the guise of protecting me. I won't be smothered or manipulated."

"Of course," he murmured. "Again, I offer sincere apologies. You're a grown woman, and I had no business interfering."

Too late. Aidan was gone and they would never see each other again. They were not even given a chance. Blast her father! And damn Aidan for leaving without even discussing it with her, for keeping his past and present such a secret. Damn him for capturing her heart. Cristyn admonished herself for giving her heart so readily. It was a mistake she would never make again. She folded her arms and frowned, stewing about the entire situation.

Her father cleared his throat, no doubt uncomfortable under her withering look. *Good.* "Well, I should tell you where Paris is living at the moment. You're still interested in your plan?"

"More than ever," she replied coolly.

"I deserve that. At any rate, Paris is living in a village called Earl Shilton in Leicestershire, north of here, in the East Midlands. I will contact him at once."

\* \* \* \*

During his first two weeks home, Aidan tried to follow the hall's daily regimen and strict meal and tea times, but it was difficult fitting into a *normal* life once again. Though the family embraced him warmly, there was a definite aura of discomfiture hovering over everything.

Perhaps he was mistaken in demanding no one mention his fall from grace, as it was patently obvious when people were trying to avoid the topic.

He spent many hours in the stables, assisting Garrett and Jonas. He also came to know Megan and Abbie better. Having females in the house was strange, but entirely welcome, along with an energetic Scotch collie that enjoyed running through the halls. Aidan's family had certainly changed. It was merely a matter of becoming used to the transition.

A meeting had been called in his grandfather's study. On the sideboard sat trays of sandwiches and fruit, along with coffee and tea. The men helped themselves, then took a seat at the table. Martin, after seeing everyone had sufficient food and drink, sat next to the earl, ready to take notes. His grandfather kept meticulous annotations on all their major family meetings. People may scoff at the men's gatherings, but it was a generations-old tradition that kept them close and involved in each other's lives—and focused on mutual objectives.

Aidan gobbled up two sandwich wedges and reached for another. Working outdoors had restored his appetite, and he wouldn't be surprised if he'd gained a pound or two in the past couple of weeks.

"We are here to discuss you, Aidan, for I have news on your cotton mill venture," his grandfather stated.

Abbie and Megan walked into the room.

Garrett smiled warmly at the sight of his wife and daughter. "Come, my loves. Take a seat. Martin, if you would be kind enough as to serve the ladies?"

Martin stood. "Right away, Master Garrett."

"This is a family meeting; all the members should be here," Garrett stated.

"Of course. A decided oversight on my part. My apologies, Abbie, Megan. Chalk it up to my age and forgetfulness, for you are more than welcome." His grandfather smiled.

"How exciting," Megan said. "I cannot wait to hear about Aidan's plan. And if there have been any developments on my suggestion for the private home for those with special needs."

"On that point," Julian stated, "it is still a work in progress. I do have several donors lined up. It's a matter of where we would like to locate it. Be assured, Megan, I will include you in the meetings when they occur."

"Thank you, Uncle." She beamed.

"And quickly," Garrett interjected. "I have received word from Dr. Bevan confirming that the first medical graduate from Oxford will arrive for training in Standon at the end of June, with another joining them at the end of August. Both young men will be staying in Abbie and Megan's former home."

At the mention of the Bevan name, Aidan's heart ached with regret. After time to reflect, he'd come to the conclusion that he had handled the situation with Cristyn as clumsily as one man could. She never left his thoughts, day or night. What could he do about it? How many mornings had he awoken to an aching erection because she'd haunted his dreams?

"Do you have all that, Martin?" his grandfather asked, pulling Aidan away from his thoughts.

The butler, seated once again, was scribbling frantically. "I do, my lord."

"Good. I believe I have found a mill to serve our purposes. It is in an area that is suffering grinding poverty. The queen has started an inquiry and sent a man to investigate. The main industries in the area are the making of boots and stockings, usually done in people's homes from rented stocking frames, and the cotton mill, which is the only factory in the vicinity." His grandfather took a sip of tea while he referred to his papers. "It is called Morris Mill, a medium-sized enterprise, owned and operated by Rupert McRae. While no formal complaints have been registered, there are a lot of whisperings of rampant abuse, including mistreatment of the workers, underpayment of wages, long hours, safety violations, and the like."

"How is he getting away with it?" Abbie asked.

"There are only four factory inspectors for the whole of England, for starters. We are working in parliament to increase that number tenfold, and for that provision to be included in the next revision of the Factory Act," his father replied.

"Many workers do not report these violations for fear of losing their employment," his grandfather interjected. "Not only is poverty rampant in the area, but so is crime involving poaching game—no doubt because of hunger. It is not safe to go out after dark, for robbery is rife as well." His grandfather caught his gaze. "After hearing all this, Aidan, do you still wish to insert yourself into this dire situation?"

"I do. While there, I can gather enough information to see this Mr. McRae is held accountable for his various violations."

"Excellent. His present overseer will be met with a dire family emergency, and will have to leave the country for two months. Your name, Aidan Black, will be put forward in his stead for temporary employment," his father said.

Aidan's eyebrows shot up. "How are you going to arrange this?"

His grandfather chuckled. "The wheels are already in motion. This overseer will do as bidden if he wishes to have employment the future. After all, he has a wife and five children; he does not want to be ruined, nor invoke the wrath of an earl and a viscount."

Aidan laughed. "You would never ruin the man."

"He doesn't know that," Garrett stated. "But beyond the particulars, this sounds as if it could turn into a dangerous circumstance."

"We will put provisions in place for Aidan's safety. You've been reading up on the various rules and laws regarding mills and factories the past two weeks?" his father asked.

Aidan nodded. "Yes, I have."

"Excellent. You will train on the spinning looms and carding equipment for a couple of weeks, as well as learn the inner workings of a cotton mill."

"Where is this place? You never said."

His grandfather referred to his papers. "I didn't? Well, let's see…here it is. It is located about one hundred and forty miles north and west of here, in Leicestershire. The name of the village is Earl Shilton."

# Chapter 7

Gazing out the window, Cristyn watched as the countryside passed by. She had never been on a train, and she had been excited to learn she would be traveling on one partway. The train would go as far as Hinckley, which was five miles from Earl Shilton. Cristyn was an independent woman, and how thrilling to be making the journey on her own.

Once Cristyn's father wrote to Dr. Middlemiss, all had fallen into place quickly. It was agreed that Cristyn would be billeted with a widow whose residence was located near his practice.

She and her father managed to mend the fracture between them before her departure—not that it was much of a crack. Cristyn had been more annoyed at his interference than truly angry. Though she had a quick temper, she believed life was difficult enough without holding grudges. Her father had pressed several pound notes in her hand before she left and made her promise to keep them well hidden, and to write if she needed further funds.

Steam expelled and the shrill whistle blew as they pulled up to the recently constructed train station. To think that one day all of Great Britain would be accessible by rail. Cristyn scanned the platform, trying to speculate which person was Paris Middlemiss. Standing in the rear of the crowd was a tall, slim man with sandy blond hair and spectacles. *This must be him.* Cristyn grabbed her small case and opened the door of the train car.

The bespectacled man stepped forward. "Miss Bevan?"

"Yes. You are Dr. Middlemiss?"

He smiled. *My, what delicate, attractive features.* He looked younger than forty-eight years. His eyes were the darkest brown; she could not make out the iris from the pupil. The color was a startling contrast against his fair hair. "I am. Please, call me Paris when we are alone. I am pleased to meet you." He took her case. "You have more luggage?"

"Yes, a small trunk. Ah, there it is." They strolled along the platform toward the baggage car, where the porters were unloading. "And I am pleased to meet you, Paris. Dad spoke highly of you."

Paris blushed. "Gethin always was a kind soul. We keep up a rigorous correspondence, and because of it, I'm fully aware of your training and medical skills. I must say, they will be put to good use in Earl Shilton." Paris motioned to a porter. "I will need assistance loading a trunk onto a wagon."

Cristyn's gaze slid to a rough-hewn wagon hitched to a black horse.

"Not fancy as such, but serves the purpose," Paris said good-naturedly.

"And the trunk, sir?" the porter asked.

Cristyn pointed to hers, not far from where they were standing. Once loaded, Paris assisted her up on the bench, then climbed on next to her. Taking the reins, he clicked his tongue, moving the gelding forward. "Enjoy the fresh air between here and the village," Paris said. "Because of the cotton mill and its use of coal as well as steam, the air is rather foul at certain hours of the day. The village is rife with lung ailments, not only from the coal haze, but from working in the cotton mill. Most of the workers suffer from varying degrees of byssinosis."

He paused, as if waiting for her to ask what byssinosis was. "It's also known as brown lung disease," she said, "caused by exposure to cotton dust in poor ventilation. Because of a narrowing of the airways, it can lead to respiratory failure and death." Cristyn gave him a satisfied smile that caused him to laugh.

"Brilliant. Well done." Then he sobered. "It is a blasted shame. I tried on numerous occasions to appeal to the owner to install a wheel, which is often used in cotton mills to dissipate a portion of the dust and fluff in the air, but he claimed that the expense would cut into his profits. Also, the mill has to be kept hot and humid, to prevent breakages in the threads, which in turn exacerbates the lung conditions." Paris sighed. "There will be work aplenty, and, I'm sad to say, not much in the way of payment. Because of the Truck Act, all goods and services must be paid in cash, which hits the poor hard. Some pay me with what they can spare, but mostly I offer my services gratis; it was the only way I could encourage the villagers to come for treatment. I will pay you a salary, never fear, as well as your room and board with Mrs. Ellen Trubshaw."

"Oh, Dad gave me several pounds, I would never expect—"

He patted her hand briefly. "You keep that money. I can well afford the expense. Besides, I am grateful for the assistance. Shall we say a weekly salary of four and ten?"

Four pounds a week? "My, that is much more than I expected. Thank you."

"You will be earning every shilling. There are near to twenty-three hundred souls living in and around Earl Shilton, and nearly all have one type of malady or another."

"I cannot wait to start. Inasmuch as I've enjoyed working at the sanatorium, I do wish to use all I have learned in a more general practice."

When they neared the village, the air turned hazy as Paris had predicted. The roads became rougher, with deep ruts carved into the earth, jostling her until her teeth rattled. Paris pointed to several homes. "Some of these are empty. Many villagers have sought temporary shelter at the Union Workhouse in Hinckley, known to the locals as the Bastille."

"Heavens, things are that dire?"

Paris nodded. "Unfortunately, yes." He turned the wagon down a narrow lane. "See there? That is my practice. I live in the few rooms above. Two doors beyond is Mrs. Trubshaw's house."

A group of people wearing tattered clothing was standing outside Paris's office. "I have patients," he stated.

"I can assist you right away."

"Tomorrow morning is soon enough to begin. I have breakfast with Mrs. Trubshaw, and often supper, and as a result, we will be in each other's pockets for the next three months."

Cristyn glanced at Paris. She wouldn't mind. Already she liked him. His face was kindly, his eyes reflecting genuine warmth. His soft voice was calming, perfect for a physician. She couldn't wait for this new chapter of her life to begin.

* * * *

After spending two and a half weeks in Manchester learning about cotton mill operations, Aidan returned to Wollstonecraft Hall for a brief respite before heading to Earl Shilton and his covert mission.

The hall had even more occupants, as Riordan, Sabrina, Mary Tuttle, and the orange and white tabby, Mittens, had recently arrived with the end of the school term in Carrbury. Riordan was given a larger portion of the wing, and Mary had her own small suite—not far, Aidan noticed with amusement, from his grandfather's rooms.

Surprisingly, after a wary introduction, Mittens and Laddie hit it off, and most afternoons the two could be found curled up before a fireplace in one of the three libraries. Also, a governess was hired for Megan, Miss Eliza Barton, and nurses were being interviewed for the upcoming birth of Riordan and Sabrina's child.

The hall was more alive than any time in Aidan's recent memory. He found all the activity caused a roll of disquiet to move through him, which had him wondering, once again, if he were fully recovered. After months of tranquil peace at the clinic, he'd forgotten life could be noisy and chaotic. Would he be tempted to relieve his anxiety the way he had done in the past? Would he be able to pull off this ruse at the cotton mill?

The men were attending a brief meeting in his grandfather's study; the ladies decided to forego this particular assembly in favor of other duties. It was the first time the men had all been together since last September. How much had changed.

"I've invited Bastian Faraday to visit us for the month of August," his grandfather stated.

Garrett beamed. "Brilliant. Aidan, it's too bad you will be away and not only miss the birth, but Bastian's visit. I believe the two of you would get along famously."

His uncle and the doctor had become good friends after Faraday was called in to treat Garrett's gunshot wound in February. Being his grandfather's exclusive physician gave Bastian a standing in society he might not otherwise have achieved, because his mother hailed from the West Indies. Though the prejudice existed, the Wollstonecrafts did not tolerate it at all.

"Not only is he a family friend, but he'll also be on hand to oversee Sabrina's care. How shrewd," Aidan teased.

His grandfather held up a fancy envelope. "Communication from Prince Albert." He turned the envelope around to show them. "The royal seal. Now that we are all here..." His grandfather broke the ornate wax seal and scanned the letter. "Well, news on the Marquess of Sutherhorne. He has been relocated to the British colony of Newfoundland in the North Atlantic, a rocky, rugged island six hundred miles off the east coast of Canada. He was settled on the west shore; it is sparsely populated, and he will have to learn to fish for his supper."

The men laughed, but soon sobered.

"Truly, is this just punishment for kidnapping Sabrina and shooting Garrett?" Riordan asked.

"It was the best we could hope for under the circumstances," his father replied.

"He will be living under reduced conditions, barely enough to survive. If he leaves the island or has money sent to him and the crown discovers it, the prince will put the Bill of Attainder into effect and Sutherhorne's heirs will lose the title, lands, and money. He won't chance it," his grandfather stated.

"Good riddance," Garrett snarled. "May we never discuss him again."

"I concur, Son. The case is closed." His grandfather placed the letter in the envelope and slipped it under the pile of papers. "On to Aidan. I've inquired as to train routes to Earl Shilton. Alas, it would take four different changes of trains, and layovers, with part of the journey by mail coach. It would take twice as long as if you traveled by our private carriage. Samuel Jenkins will accompany you. He is an ex-soldier and a trusted employee of our stables."

"I cannot arrive in an earl's coach," Aidan mused. "There may be questions."

"True. We thought to install Samuel in nearby Hinckley, close enough you can reach him if you need his assistance, but far enough not to reveal your true identity and purpose. Bring Nebula on the journey, and Samuel can leave you on the outskirts with the gelding. He will see to it your trunk is delivered to the Dog and Gun Inn. You will be staying there," his grandfather said.

Aidan nodded with approval. "That makes more sense."

"There is one thing," his father said. "Confide in no one. Your identity must remain secret. If this is to work, you must gain the trust of McRae. It will be a fine line to straddle in order to gather the damning information that we require, and there cannot be any doubt as to your masquerade. You may have to act the part of a superior, a cruel bastard, at least around McRae. Perhaps others." His father gave him a grave look. "No one can be told."

"If you wish," he replied. "No one." Realistically, it would depend on what situation he found at the mill. Best to decide for sure once he arrived.

"Messages and reports may be sent to Hinckley. Samuel will send them on to us," his grandfather stated.

"Five miles is quite a distance," Riordan interjected. "What if Aidan is in danger? What good is Samuel in Hinckley?"

"Not sure what danger I will find in a village full of poor souls barely eking out an existence," Aidan replied.

"Exactly that. Grandfather said thievery and other crimes are rife in the area. It could have potential for peril," Riordan stated.

"If I feel the situation, in whatever way, becomes a hazard, I will send for Samuel immediately. Besides, if this mill owner is as horrible as we hear, I may not need the full two months to collect the evidence. Trust me to handle this." Aidan glanced around the table.

While his family nodded, Aidan couldn't help but notice faint expressions of doubt from them. He frowned. "If you don't believe I am up for the task, speak, or forever hold your peace," he retorted.

"Son, I do not doubt your abilities, I only question your readiness for taking this on after what you've been through. Perhaps we can do this in the autumn, and you can take the rest of the summer to rest and recuperate," his father offered.

Aidan fought to control his temper. His family meant well, but they didn't understand. No one could, unless they had experienced it for themselves. "It's hard to describe what led to my slide into hopelessness. This sounds rather self-indulgent, considering I am rich, heir to an earl, and am attractive enough to have the world handed to me. Dr. Bevan claims I have a disease, not merely a bad habit. I do not use that as a justification, but as an explanation. I no longer wish to live that way. I want my life to have meaning. I want to care about something other than myself and my own pleasures." Aidan expelled a shaky breath. "There has to be hope for a better future, or why even try? I'm fighting for my life, to reclaim what I have lost: my dignity. Support me, by all means, but do not facilitate me too much. I must stand on my own two feet."

"Well spoken," Garrett murmured. "We will do as you ask. But the moment you feel unsafe, extract yourself from the situation with all haste. Since you brought up your state of affairs, and we're speaking of dangerous propositions, I've had a letter from Edwin. The final report."

Edwin Seward was an ex-Bow Street Runner who'd assisted Garrett in locating Aidan in London last January. He was also the one who suggested the Standon Sanatorium.

"As you know, I asked Edwin to find out anything he could about Colm Delaney, Sutherhorne's hired man," Garrett said.

At the mention of Delaney's name, Aidan's apprehension kicked up a notch.

His uncle continued, "The landlady at his flat stated he was quiet and paid his rent on time. He left many of his meager possessions behind when he vanished, instructing the landlady in a note to sell and keep the proceeds. Edwin found out where he engaged in his illegal boxing. Delaney had a reputation as being a brutal and merciless fighter; not many wished to face him."

Garrett took a sip of his tea and continued. "From what he could glean, Delaney is forty years of age, arriving from Ireland about twenty years past. No mention of family. No attachments of any kind, except he often frequented molly houses. There was not much more to discover there, as you imagine there is a code of secrecy in order to protect the men from arrest, as sodomy is a capital offense."

Aidan winced inwardly. God, how uncomfortable this was; it reminded him of how he had debased himself in order to procure drugs. "And your point in mentioning this man once again? And why even open an investigation in the first place?"

"To ensure he will stay well clear of this family. That he is not a threat. But since we do not know where he is, you must remain vigilant. Samuel knows what he looks like; he will keep an eye out, in and around Hinckley and beyond."

"I appreciate your thoroughness, Uncle. I will take your advice. But I believe we have seen the last of this man." At least, Aidan hoped. How he wanted that harrowing chapter of his life closed once and for all. He'd already acknowledged his mistakes, accepted assistance in recovery, and was determined to travel a different path. Dr. Bevan was correct: "Accept your mistakes, learn from them. Wear them like badges of honor."

Aidan had emerged from his traumatic experience a different man. Not better as such, but he thought he should give it a go. "I do not know who I am; perhaps I never have. But this fall from grace allowed one article of worth—for me to begin anew. To reshape myself into the man I always should have been."

"And what man is that?" his father asked softly.

"I wish to be a compassionate man who genuinely cares for the world and its inhabitants. A man of honor. A man with a heart. In other words, a Wollstonecraft. For I have been none of this, for more years than I care to count. I am selfish at the core; perhaps I always will be, to some extent. For I do this for me—to cleanse my soul. And it needs a rigorous scrubbing, I assure you. But I also do this for altruistic reasons. I wish to make a difference, as you all do in your various ways. Thank you for supporting me in this venture. I will make you proud."

A pretty speech, and heartfelt. Cristyn crept into his thoughts, for the truth of it was he wanted to be a man *she* could be proud of, regardless if they never saw each other again.

Now to follow up his words with actions.

# Chapter 8

Cristyn had been in Earl Shilton for over three weeks. How invigorating to be at the forefront of medical care for people who truly needed it. Using an antiseptic-soaked cloth, she cleaned the wound of the patient sitting before her. "There. Now I will stitch it for you."

"Aye, miss," the young woman murmured.

As she continued with her nursing duties, Cristyn's mind turned to her new circumstances. Mrs. Trubshaw was a strict landlady, but kind in her gruff way. Cristyn welcomed the early curfew, for she was exhausted by the time she returned to the rooming house for supper.

"It is not wise for young ladies to be out and about on the streets once the sun goes down; it is not proper. You could be robbed. It is best to be safely tucked away by eight o'clock," Mrs. Trubshaw had advised.

Cristyn concurred. Most nights Paris accompanied her, and stayed for a meal. She tried to observe any romantic undercurrents between the landlady and the doctor, for they were a like age, but Cristyn couldn't sense any. Not like the ones between her father and the housekeeper.

Or her and Aidan.

Yes, blast him! Though she'd kept occupied, Aidan still managed to drift into her thoughts when she least expected it. The open wound ached afresh in each instance. The hurt, the lingering, throbbing pain had never left her, and she silently cursed him for it.

Cristyn returned her attention to her patient, Tessie, who had a gash on the lower part of her arm. The injury was a result of her working at the cotton mill. As she set about stitching the cut, Tessie coughed and sniffled.

"I do thank you, Miss Bevan. Mam says I'm to give you a penny for your trouble."

Paris had instructed her early on to accept all payment, no matter how small, whether it was coin or a loaf of bread. It gave the village folk a sense of accomplishment that they had paid for the treatment.

"Thank you, Tessie. How goes work at the mill?" Cristyn found that if she kept the patients talking, they wouldn't focus on the needle and thread.

"Same as always. Though there be a new overlooker."

Cristyn glanced up at Tessie questioningly.

"An overlooker watches over us all, to make sure we be working hard. Reports to Master McRae."

"Ah," Cristyn murmured. "A supervisor."

"Aye, that be it. I heard tell he be only passing through like. Too bad, for he is an eyeful and more, he is. Young, handsome, tall. He has all the women in a flutter, even the old ones." Tessie cackled, but it ended in a cough. "He came three days past; not sure if he's as cruel as the master, or...I shouldn't be talking such. Could get me in a right fix."

"I would never repeat anything you tell me, Tessie. You have my word."

"Aye, I heard from others you be a good 'un."

Cristyn tied a small knot and snipped the thread with a pair of scissors. "I'll place a dressing over the cut. You must come twice a week to get it replaced until the stitches are ready to be removed."

Tessie frowned. "I can't afford no more healing, Miss Bevan."

"This is all the same treatment, Tessie, do not fret." Cristyn placed the sticky dressing over the wound. "There now, a good thing I'm capable at embroidery; when the stitches come out, the scar will be barely noticeable."

Tessie chuckled.

"You should rest for the remainder of the day."

Tessie ceased laughing. "Oh, no, miss. I must go back to work, or Master will have me replaced. I promised I'd return sharpish."

Cristyn sighed. It was the same old story. No matter how injured or ill, the workers at the mill did not dare be sick, or they would be out of a job.

"As you say, but you must keep the wound clean."

Tessie slipped the penny into Cristyn's hand, then departed. For the first time since eight o'clock this morning, the place was empty.

Paris came out of the back room that served as his office, wiping his hands on a cloth. "Speaking of the cotton mill, I managed to get Mr. McRae to agree to a meeting this afternoon. Why not accompany me?"

"Shouldn't I stay here in case a patient comes in?"

"No, we won't be long. I often draw a picture of where I will be in case of an emergency, since most people cannot read."

Cristyn smiled. "How clever."

"You should meet this McRae, and see what I am up against. I hope to persuade him to purchase the wheel for the bad air conditions within the mill. Also, I mean to examine the orphan children in his employ. He finally agreed to allow it when I said there would be no cost to him. You can assist me."

"He has orphans working for him?"

"Well, I am not quite sure if all of them are technically orphans, but most are no doubt pauper children dependent on poor law guardians. Mill owners often make contracts with these guardians to supply them with a cheap work force."

"That sounds barbaric, bordering on slave labor."

"All the more reason to look in on these unfortunate children. Are they being fed properly? Housed properly? Limited to twelve-hour workdays, as outlined by the Health and Morals of Apprentices Act? We will have to be subtle in our inquiries, or McRae will not allow us to see the children at all." Paris tossed the cloth aside. "I've met the man on a couple of occasions. I do not like him. Too arrogant by half, and the cruel gleam in his eye certainly gave me pause." Paris pointed to a cloth bag. "In there I have placed slices of apple and fresh bread. We will slip the children some food when we can."

"Is it as dismal as all that?" Cristyn exclaimed.

"Yes. These children were no doubt malnourished when they arrived at the mill. We had best head there directly, before the man changes his mind."

Donning their coats, they started out on the journey to the cotton mill at the edge of the village. Since it was the first week of July, they decided to walk. The sun was out, burning its way through the coal haze of the morning. The wretched poverty in this village always struck Cristyn afresh; the poor condition of the houses and roads were testament to that. The villagers' expressions of dreary hopelessness made the situation all the more tragic.

Paris did say an inquiry had been opened by the queen, and a Mr. Muggeridge had made several trips to the village the past year to investigate the lingering poverty. However, government ground at a snail's pace, and any improvements would be slow in coming. Those villagers who did not work at the mill often toiled in their homes morning to late night on stocking looms they had to pay rent on.

As they emerged from the pathway through a small area of woods, the L-shaped brick mill came into view. It had a water wheel, and was located next to a river.

"The mill uses water to power a steam engine, which in turn runs the spinning looms. Coal is also used. There are a little over one hundred people employed here; I am not sure if that figure includes the children," Paris stated.

As they walked through the stone archway, Cristyn could see a man standing in front of the second story window, watching them closely. His imperious stare had her guessing he was the owner, Mr. McRae. In the courtyard, men were unloading bales of cotton from wagons pulled by large dray horses. The bales were bundled onto handcarts and dispatched to various locations of the mill.

Before they reached the front entrance, a short man with a receding hairline and a nervous gaze hurried out to greet them. "Dr. Middlemiss? I'm Mr. McRae's personal secretary, Mr. Meeker. He bade me to escort you to the children. They are awaiting you in the storage warehouse."

"I thought to examine them in their dormitory. There is one, I trust?"

The man's head bobbed up and down. "Yes, of course, but Mr. McRae prefers you carry out the exam in here." He pointed to a nearby door. "If you please, Doctor. And Miss...?"

"This is Miss Bevan, my nurse and assistant."

"Follow me, please." Mr. Meeker opened the door and sunlight flooded the darkened room. A cluster of children standing close together flinched at the bright sun, as if not used to it.

"Doctor, why don't we examine the children here, in the out-of-doors? It is a beautiful day," Cristyn suggested.

"What a brilliant proposal, Miss Bevan." Paris gave her a wink.

Mr. Meeker's cheek twitched. "I'm not sure we should." He glanced nervously at the second story window. The owner was no longer there.

"Nonsense, Mr. Meeker. I only need a table and chair set up by the door. Assist me, will you, please?" Paris crossed the threshold. "Good afternoon, children. I am Dr. Middlemiss. Please, come and stand by Miss Bevan."

They tentatively stepped outside, and Cristyn did a quick head count. Twenty-one children, but it was hard to ascertain their ages due to obvious malnutrition. They were pale and thin, their clothes patched and tattered. Their faces and hands were dirty. Her heart filled with sympathy.

Once the table and chair were in place, Paris turned to Mr. Meeker. "There is no need for you to stay, as this may take some time."

"Mr. McRae specifically ordered me to witness the examination, then bring you directly to his office. Only you, not Miss Bevan. I am sorry."

The man didn't sound the least bit sorry. Cristyn fought to keep her distaste for this sycophant from showing on her face.

"Nevertheless, I ask you give my patients a modicum of privacy, at least the girls. Return in fifteen minutes."

Mr. Meeker frowned, then glanced at the window once again. "I will return in ten minutes." The man turned and hurried away.

"Quick, Cristyn. Help me move the table and chair behind this open door. It will act as a barrier from any prying eyes," Paris whispered.

"You saw the man in the window, too?" she replied, then she helped him drag the table.

"Yes. Mr. McRae himself. Come, children, over here."

They seemed to gravitate toward an older boy, staying close to him, as if for protection. He was a good-looking lad with brown hair and eyes, his cheeks and nose covered by an abundance of freckles. He gave them both an assessing gaze, and his eyes displayed intelligence and a deep distrust.

Paris must have also noticed that the boy was the leader, for he pointed at him. "What is your name?"

He wiped his nose with his tattered sleeve. "Carter Rokesmith, guv'."

"A good, strong name. Will you assist me with the children? I brought slices of bread and apple; I thought they might like a bite of food before the exam."

"Aye," he mumbled. Carter snapped his fingers and the children immediately lined up in front of Cristyn. She handed out the sliced apple and bread, and the children greedily grabbed at the food and gobbled it up. Before she knew it, the bag was empty.

"Carter, will you answer a couple of questions?" Paris asked.

"'pends."

"Are the children given a dormitory to live in? A place with actual beds? Proper bedding? Healthy meals and—"

Carter shook his head. "No questions. Ain't answerin'. And neither will this lot be answerin'. Master said not to talk to ye. Got to do wot Master says."

Paris and Cristyn exchanged looks. "The Master being Mr. McRae?" Paris murmured.

"Aye. That be 'im. Do yer examinin'. Make it quick, 'fore that weasel comes back." Carter pushed a younger boy before Paris. "Do 'im first, 'is leg be hurtin' bad like."

Paris snapped into action, and the boy lined up the children in order of maladies. A small girl with curly golden hair stayed close to Carter, as if looking for protection.

They worked efficiently, cleaning and treating various wounds and cuts, examining mouths for sores and rotting teeth, which they found in abundance. "Make a note, Miss Bevan. Next visit, we will bring cheese with the fruit and bread. We will have to procure plantain for the irritation of the lungs, and vaccinations against smallpox."

"Yes, Doctor."

"And you, Carter?" Paris asked.

"I don't need no examinin'," he grumbled.

"Are all these children from the Union Workhouse?" Paris asked.

"The Bastille? Aye, some. Others be from an orphanage. 'Tis all I be tellin' ye." The little golden-haired girl slipped her hand into Carter's and tugged on it. "'Tis all right, Lottie." He leaned down and she whispered in his ear. "'Tis no more bread," he told the girl sadly.

The children were still hungry—how heartbreaking. "We will bring more the next we come," Cristyn said with a shaky smile. She felt like crying at the abject misery before her.

Carter scoffed. "If Master allows ye to come back. Aye, bring bread, apple, cheese. Anythin'. For the little 'uns."

Mr. Meeker arrived, giving Carter a stern look. "What have you been saying, Rokesmith?"

"Nuffin', Mr. Meeker, sir. The doctor be askin' about me chest, 'tis all." Carter coughed for good measure.

"Rokesmith, take the children to the spinning room. Dr. Middlemiss, if you will come with me. Mr. McRae awaits. He can spare you ten minutes."

"Miss Bevan, please take a seat. I will not be long," Paris said.

Cristyn sat and watched the children head toward the mill. Though the sun was out and the air was warm, she shivered. Something was not quite right about this mill, though she couldn't pinpoint exactly what. Giving another quick glance at the door the children had passed through, she impulsively jumped to her feet and hurried along in the same direction.

Opening the door, she stepped inside. There was a long hallway—which way to turn? Cotton dust floated in the air, similar to a gentle snow falling on Christmas Eve. Almost immediately she began to cough. Machinery noise was to the right of her—that was also where the greatest concentration of cotton dust was coming from. Cristyn followed the trail; the air grew thicker with the floating powder the farther she ventured into the mill. Cristyn waved it away from her face as she walked. The air was stiflingly hot, the humidity enough to seize her breath. She came upon a large sliding door. Dare she open it?

With both hands, she slid it open and was greeted by a huge room filled with equipment that hissed and clacked at a deafening rate. The dust was thicker here; she could barely see. It was mostly women working the spinning machines, methodically moving part of the mechanism to the front and back as if weaving, which, Cristyn supposed, was exactly what they were doing. A few men walked up and down the aisles, and to her horror, she caught a glimpse of some of the children they had treated scurrying along on their hands and knees under the apparatus, clearing away clusters of cotton fluff. My God, how dangerous!

She looked up, and out of the corner of her eye, a dark shadow moved through the white dust. It was a tall, dark-haired man, walking along a raised platform, wearing a black frock coat with his hands clasped behind his back. His perfect profile was a stark contrast to the depressing surroundings of the factory.

No. She must be hallucinating. It could not be *him*.

Cristyn backed up several steps, her heart pounding in her chest. Her insides tumbled, roiling and churning, the lunch she had consumed earlier came close to making a reappearance. *This* can't *be happening.* But the combined dread and thrill at looking at this man was proof it was him, ready to haunt her all over again. And break her heart.

Aidan Black.

Here in Earl Shilton.

It made no sense. Why was he here, of all places? All at once a coughing fit overtook her, and she reached in her bag and drew out a cloth to hold over her mouth. The air was foul, and making her physically ill.

She was about to turn and make her escape when a booming male voice called out, "Halt, you there!" She could barely hear it above the noise of the machines, but hear it she had. What choice did she have but to run?

Lifting her skirts while still holding the cloth over her mouth, Cristyn bolted through the door and down the hall.

# Chapter 9

Aidan could not believe it. His mind must have gone. Cristyn Bevan? His heart banged furiously against his ribs. Every nerve ending came alive, and because of it, he had to know if it was her. "Miller!" he called to a man walking between the machines. Aidan took the steps two at a time until he stood before Miller on the factory floor. "Keep watch until I return," he yelled in the man's ear. Not waiting for a response, he vaulted through the door into the hallway.

He grabbed the arm of a woman passing by. "Did you see a young lady with dark hair?" he demanded.

The woman shrank at his harsh tone, but his undertaking here was not to be polite. "Aye, sir. She went through that door."

Aidan ran outside, scanning the surrounding grounds. Found her! Her head peered around the door of the warehouse, then disappeared. He sprinted toward the stone structure. Once there, he grasped the door and slammed it. God, it *was* her. Cristyn had flinched at the sound, and stared up at him, her beautiful violet-blue eyes blinking rapidly. All he wanted was to gather her in his arms and kiss her. Hold her tight against him, and savor her softness and warmth.

His heart soared as he stepped closer. Blood rushed to every part of his body as he inhaled. That damned scent of violets had never left him, not in all these weeks since they had said goodbye. But to hell with showing his vulnerability. "Why are you here? Are you following me?" he demanded.

"What? Of all the arrogance!" Her eyes narrowed in anger. "I could say the same for you, for I've been here more than three weeks. And you arrived…when?"

"Three days past." Damn it all, he couldn't think straight around her, and because of it wound up blurting inane statements or denying his feelings—which at this moment burned with an intensity to rival the sun above.

"Why are you working in that mill for that horrible man? Have you seen the children?" she cried.

Children? Did she mean the scavengers? He didn't like the term given to the children employed to work under the spinner machinery, clearing away dust and oil and gathering the cotton that fell to the floor. God forbid McRae let any cotton go to waste. In truth, he hadn't had time to investigate anything thanks to the never-ending meetings that McRae insisted he attend. Today was his first full day in the spinning room.

Cristyn could ruin his covert operation before it even had a chance to begin. It wasn't that he didn't trust her, but Aidan had sworn to his family he would keep his true identity hidden. "It is only a temporary position; I'm assisting my father." Well, at least *that* wasn't a lie.

"I thought you bred horses," she snapped, clearly exasperated with him. "If you're so blasted wealthy, why are you working in a cotton mill?"

Hell, he loved it when blue-violet fire ignited in her lovely eyes. "I never said that I was a horse breeder; I said my family was. My uncle, with whom you are acquainted, is the horse master." He took another step closer, and a whiff of her evocative violet scent made him dizzy with desire. Aidan had to touch her. Reaching for a wayward strand of her hair, he gently tucked it behind her ear, then trailed the tip of his finger across her cheek.

Cristyn gasped, obviously affected by the contact. The touch of her was electric, and though tempted to caress and stroke her silky skin, he dropped his hand.

"Stop trying to distract me," she murmured, "and answer my question."

"I told you, I'm assisting my father. He is involved in factory work, and he asked me to step in and assist one of his industrial compatriots. I needed the distraction."

"Of all the places in England," she muttered crossly, rubbing her forehead. Her eyes widened. "You have to go. Paris is coming."

His eyebrows shot up. "Who in the hell is Paris?"

"He's the reason I'm here." Cristyn pushed him. "Please leave."

Aidan clutched her upper arms, holding her tight against him. He whispered hotly in her ear, "Not until you agree to meet me. Tonight. In the rear yard at the Dog and Gun Inn on Keats Lane. Seven o'clock."

"I will not meet with you!" She struggled in his grip, clearly annoyed.

He released her. "Then I will stay and meet your Paris."

"Fine. Seven o'clock. Now please, go!" Cristyn gazed up at him, her eyes pleading.

Aidan gave her flushed cheek a gentle brush with his fingers, then slipped around the corner of the warehouse and stood against the wall.

"How did the meeting go with Mr. McRae?" Cristyn asked.

"As I surmised, it was a complete waste of time. He would not hear of any scheme that would cut into his—as he called them—'meager profits.'"

Aidan nearly scoffed aloud. McRae bragged he was making pots of money despite the fact the mill was not that large. But beyond such, who was this Paris to Cristyn?

"I tried to explain that installing the wheel would lessen the lung infections and diseases many of his workers have, and that healthy employees would increase his profits," Paris continued. "He wasn't having any of it."

"I'm sorry. We should head to your office," Cristyn said, a little too loudly and insistently.

"Are you all right, my dear? You seem agitated."

*My dear?* Cold fury traveled through Aidan and he clenched his fists. Is this what jealousy felt like? For he'd never experienced it before. Disturbing.

"No, no. I'm fine. Please, let us leave this depressing place," Cristyn pleaded.

With the sound of retreating footfalls, Aidan chanced a glance around the corner. The tall, slender man took Cristyn's hand and slipped it through his arm.

Well, he would find out tonight who in hell this Paris was. Once they were out of sight, he headed into the mill, feeling dejected. A foreign emotion, for he'd never allowed any woman to get close enough to put his heart at risk.

The truth was Cristyn continued to reside in his thoughts, day...and most especially night. More than once he wondered if these muddled and intense emotions were due to the fact that she'd been instrumental in his recovery. If his feelings of gratitude had moved into an inappropriate infatuation. But Aidan had been infatuated before, however briefly, and the fever had soon dissipated. What he was feeling toward Cristyn lay beyond a passing fascination.

Regardless, he should keep his distance, keep her at arm's length in order to protect her, not only from this dubious and possibly risky situation, but his abject past. How to achieve such a thing when they were in the same damned village? And why suggest a clandestine meeting?

The answer was simple: because he couldn't stay away. Aidan had to know why she was here and who this Paris was to her. He would be damned if he would allow any man to touch her, to breathe the same air she did. He rubbed his forehead. Christ, his wits must have gone begging, for he was acting as if she were his. How unlike him.

"Mr. Black. The master wants you to come to his office right away," Mr. Meeker declared loudly. Already he could not stand this simpering slave of McRae's, always lurking about, taking copious notes.

"Thank you, Mr. Meeker." He headed upstairs, with the secretary hot on his heels.

Aidan knocked on the half-open door, then entered. "You wish to see me, Mr. McRae?"

The man looked up, and Aidan fought to keep revulsion from his face. The middle-aged man had a cold, imperious look, and the straining waistcoat buttons showed his gluttony and egocentric nature. He had disliked McRae at first sight, then outright despised him once he'd spent a couple of days in his company, listening to his smug ramblings. But the man was shrewd; he hadn't revealed anything that could be construed as illegal. *Yet.* It was obvious he was wary and distrustful, even though Aidan had been recommended by a close acquaintance of McRae's—a viscount no less.

"Meeker has informed me you left the factory floor," McRae said.

"I put the run to a strange woman who entered the spinning room. I followed her outside, and made it clear that she was not to enter any part of the mill again without permission." Aidan cast a side-glance at the self-righteous Meeker. He would bear watching.

"Good. Leave us, Meeker. I will handle this from here."

"As you say, sir." The secretary departed and closed the door behind him.

"Take a seat, Black." Aidan did. "My wife is holding a small dinner party in two weeks." McRae slid an envelope across the desk. "We wish for you to attend. You may bring someone with you if you like. But since you are new here, I assume you will be coming alone."

Aidan gave him a sly smile. "Not necessarily."

McRae chuckled, then sobered. "As I informed you on your first day here, I live on the two floors above this one. My wife and young son are to be protected. It is your duty to ensure none of the workers come near my home."

"Consider it done, sir." Leave it to McRae to live on the premises—easier to keep watch over his enterprise, and save valuable coin on a separate residence.

"I also want you to keep an eye out for any agitators. Many workers in the larger mills farther north are unionizing. I want none of that rabble-rousing here. It will be a cold day in Hell before any workers dictate terms to me."

"I will let you know at once, sir," Aidan stated firmly.

"Good man. Keep things running smoothly, and we will get along fine. The workers might try to convince you they're entitled to longer breaks according to law, but I set the hours here. I am the final word. Nothing or no one matters here at the mill but me and my profits. See that that continues to be the case, and I will see you well rewarded."

"Yes, Mr. McRae." Aidan's insides twisted with disgust. He'd been offered a bribe to go along with the status quo, but all it had managed to do was make him more determined to bring this autocrat down.

\* \* \* \*

Aidan paced in the rear yard of the Dog and Gun Inn, waiting for Cristyn to appear. He had checked his watch, and already it was past seven. Would she show up? His angel would not forego the chance to tell him exactly what she thought. How in hell had they wound up in the same small village? What had Riordan said about fate? That it often takes a hand, whether we want it to or not. How true.

All at once, he came alert. *Cristyn.* She scurried into the yard, wearing her shawl over her head.

Meeting her halfway, he took her arm and pulled her toward the gardening shed.

"What are you doing?" she sputtered.

"Finding a private place for us to talk," he murmured. Opening the door, he assisted her across the threshold, then closed the door. There wasn't much room among the many gardening implements.

"How dare you manhandle me in such a—"

Aidan pulled her close, and already his treacherous body responded. "Who. Is. Paris."

"Why do you care?" Cristyn grumbled.

"Because I do, more than I should."

"Blast you for saying that," she whispered. "You left, without an explanation. You pushed me away. Instead of owning your feelings, you denied them. Why?"

Damn it, he was hard. Aroused. Aidan's heart banged out a fierce, unrelenting beat, as if it would burst from his chest. "Tell me who this Paris is to you, and I will answer your question."

Cristyn huffed out an exasperated breath and took a step backward. "He is old enough to be my father. In fact, he's a friend of my father's, and has become a friend to me as well. His name is Dr. Paris Middlemiss. I'm here to assist him in his charity medical work until the middle of September."

"There is nothing romantic between you?"

"I'm not answering such an absurd question." Her eyes glistened with an obvious sadness that arrowed straight to his black soul. "Why did you ride away? Never had I felt so rejected, as if I wasn't worth anything at all—"

Aidan kissed her, something he had been aching to do for months. It was forceful, but when she tentatively returned the kiss, he gentled it, luxuriating in her taste. He was completely devastated by the potency of it. A soft moan escaped her luscious lips, giving him an opportunity to slip his tongue into her sweet mouth, which in turn ignited his insides. He wanted to devour her. Inhale her essence. Possess her totally and make her his.

The kiss grew fierce again. As he cupped her cheek and caressed it, taking the sizzling kiss deeper, his free hand trailed upward to grasp her breast. His fingers brushed across her nipple, which hardened under his touch. Aidan hungered for her. *Ached.* He backed her up against the wall and their bodies came together, his hard cock rubbing against her thigh. God, he was ready to explode. It was as if they weren't wearing layers of clothes, because searing heat flared high and hot everywhere their bodies touched. His hands trailed down her arms, then he cupped her arse, bringing her in tighter. A desperate moan of yearning left his throat.

Cristyn abruptly pulled her lips from his. "Stop. Don't."

It was as if she had poured cold water over his head. Aidan moved three steps in reverse, his entire body quaking with need. Losing control with a woman was not in his nature. But then, since his downfall, he wasn't the same man. "I apologize. Try to understand that I was doing the noble thing in riding away; I was sparing you from the chaos I had made of my life."

Her breathing was still ragged, as was his. The burst of desire still sparked between them. "Isn't that for me to decide? I'm weary of men making decisions for me. My father told me you admitted to being attracted to me, but the both of you decided that it was for the best if you departed." She stood up straight and exhaled. "And noble? You work for that awful man; have you not seen the state of the children?"

How in hell had they gone from emotions and desire to the cotton mill? *The children again.* Aidan mustered a look of indifference; he would have to act as if he didn't care at all. "What are they to me? I've hardly taken notice of them. Besides, today was my first day on the mill floor. I don't know what you're on about."

"Then perhaps you should investigate. I saw the children scrambling under the machines—isn't that dangerous? They're malnourished and dirty. Speak to the older boy with brown hair and eyes; he looks over them. His name is Carter Rokesmith. He will tell you what you need to know."

"The position I have is temporary, and Mr. McRae made it patently clear I was not to interfere with the running of the mill or disrupt it in any way. I will heed his warning." Aidan took a step closer. He had to breathe her evocative violet scent, taste her skin, and hold her close. Yes, he had lost his mind—and he might have lost his heart in the process. "Enough about the mill. What are we going to do about us?"

One of her perfectly shaped eyebrows arched in question. "Us? There is no 'us.' You said as much by riding away."

Would she ever stop rambling on about him leaving? For it had been one of the hardest things he'd ever done. "You would have us live and work in this tiny village for the next two months and pretend we do not know each other?"

Cristyn jutted out her chin. "Yes, exactly that."

He scoffed. "You're punishing me for hurting you, and I deserve it. To be completely honest, I don't know what my feelings are, beyond lust, because lust is the only emotion that is familiar to me. The rest?" He frowned. "You, more than anyone, know the condition I was in. What I went through. I did not exaggerate when I told you I am not a good man. There are things you don't know...."

Cristyn stepped before him, giving him a pleading look. "Then tell me. Be completely honest."

"What would it serve? Besides, I'm not going to dissect my nefarious past in a gardening shed."

"Then when? And where? If you want there to be an 'us,' I need to know everything."

Hell, he couldn't tell her everything, not while he was involved with the mill. Revealing everything would involve divulging his true name and family background; Aidan couldn't do that. Beyond such, he didn't want to see the look of repugnance on her sweet face. Yet he had the distinct feeling Cristyn would not judge him too harshly, for she was his angel of mercy. "Not while we reside in this place."

"What? Why not?" she bellowed.

"Hush, we don't want to be discovered." She frowned at his admonishment. "We both have duties to perform; I suggest we remain focused on them."

"Coward," she whispered, giving him a scathing look.

Now he was getting angry. "Damn it, I'm being practical."

"Take your devastating kisses and go. Or better yet, I'll leave." Cristyn moved toward the door, but he halted her.

"Devastating? You say that, yet want us to ignore what exists between us? When all I want to do at this moment is kiss you again? Tunnel my hand under your skirts, slip my fingers between your swollen folds to find you wet and wanting?"

Cristyn raised her free hand as if to slap him, but he clutched her wrist. "I thought you said we should be practical. Let me go," she demanded through clenched teeth.

He whispered in her ear, "You want me. But it cannot be half as much as I want you."

"It doesn't matter, for I will not act on it. Not until you can be honest about your past and your present, Aidan Black."

Aidan released her and stepped away. "Then you had best depart."

"Gladly." Cristyn pushed past him and marched through the door, slamming it behind her.

As tempted as he was to go after her, he didn't. He splayed his open hand against the wall and lowered his head, trying to regain control over his rampant emotions. He had no idea if he was doing the right thing. Why not tell her the truth, and reveal why he was in Earl Shilton? He may even be able to ask for her assistance in gathering incriminating information on McRae. Surely this doctor had records on those he had treated from the mill.

No. Damn it, *no.*

His first and original instinct was correct, to protect his angel at any cost. Even at the peril of his heart—and hers.

# Chapter 10

Rage or cry. Cristyn was determined to do neither. Perhaps, she conceded, she had not handled their meeting well. Emotions ran high on both sides. But she was hurting and had lashed out. She had almost slapped him. But then, what he'd said was entirely inappropriate. Yet beyond the shock and annoyance, she had been intrigued and excited.

It was likely that her emotions were muddled as well. His kiss merely muddied the waters. Cristyn brushed her lips with her fingers. The kiss was everything she'd hoped it would be: wild, tender, and completely overwhelming. Unless he kissed all women with such fervent passion—a disturbing thought.

But beyond that, it was the first real kiss she'd received. There was no comparison to the couple of sloppy kisses from boys in Standon. Cristyn wasn't so innocent that she was not aware what hard part of him had pressed insistently against her thigh. Despite her inexperience, she'd read plenty on the subject of physical relations between men and women. The prospect did not frighten her.

*Bother. Blast it all!* He was correct: she wanted him. But another obstacle stood in their way, besides his reluctance: his secrets, and their mutual jumbled emotions. The fact that he was working, however temporarily, for McRae at Morris Mill. No, she had never met the man, but she'd heard plenty from Paris, and from what little her patients had revealed. He was a cruel taskmaster.

Twilight had settled across the horizon. Cristyn picked up her pace toward Mrs. Trubshaw's home on Church Street, pulling the shawl about her face. While passing the narrow lanes, she noted that many of the villagers gathered around fires burning in barrels, cooking potatoes and other foodstuffs. Many warmed their hands, even though it was July. Others washed laundry in huge tubs, and hung them on lines high above the narrow alleyways.

This sorrowful place was nothing like Standon, with its idyllic country setting, fresh air, and abundance of flowers and shrubs. There she felt safe, comfortable, and protected. Cristyn experienced none of that here. She pulled her shawl closer about her and hurried toward Mrs. Trubshaw's.

Once she arrived and opened the door, her landlady stood before her, hands on her hips. "Miss Bevan, imagine my surprise when Dr. Middlemiss asked me to fetch you from your room and you were *not* there. He's about to go out and find you." The older woman shook her head. "It is going on eight o'clock. If you had stayed out any longer, you could have been robbed, or worse—"

"Mrs. Trubshaw, I believe you have chastised Miss Bevan enough," Paris said as he took Cristyn's arm.

"I overstepped, only I worry. It's not safe," she replied, not unkindly.

"Allow me to apologize, Mrs. Trubshaw. I merely wanted a breath of air, and I did return before darkness descended."

"While you stay under my roof, I feel responsible for your safety. I know of what I speak regarding the crime rife in this village. Well, enough about that. Doctor, why not take Miss Bevan into the small parlor? May I make you both a cup of tea?" the landlady asked.

Paris looked to her, then shook his head. "No, thank you, we will be fine."

Once inside the parlor, Paris closed the door as Cristyn removed her shawl, laying it in her lap once she sat on the settee.

"You must forgive Mrs. Trubshaw. She is worried for your safety. Mr. Green, the grocer's assistant, was robbed on Mill Lane not three nights past. He suffered blows about the head and lost ten shillings. Unfortunately, the threat is real."

"Yes, I understand. In the future, I will inform her if I decide to go for a walk. However, she is much like a guard at the palace gate. I cannot be a prisoner in my room."

Paris smiled. "Truly, she means well. You are forthright, Cristyn; if she impinges on your privacy, tell her." He paused, his expression turned serious. "And speaking of impinging on privacy, this is none of my business, but I shall ask it anyway: Did you meet the young man from the mill?"

Cristyn's blood froze in her veins. What to say? She remained silent, trying to craft a reply.

"I only ask because what little I witnessed appeared emotional. You know this man."

"Yes," she replied. "But it is my business." Cristyn spoke in a pol but firm tone.

Paris sighed. "I shouldn't interfere, but your father mentioned you v nursing a broken heart and asked me to look out for you. Don't be an he did not mention any details, only wrote of it because he knew I would be empathetic."

"I see." She tamped down her growing annoyance, for Paris's tone was conciliatory and kind.

"There is an age difference between us, Cristyn. But I have come to care for you. You are bright, kind, capable, and unfailingly honest."

"Thank you, Paris. I have come to care for you as a beloved uncle. Is that possible in three short weeks?"

He nodded. "Absolutely. People make connections in many different circumstances."

"Why is it you have never visited us in Standon?"

A melancholy look crossed his striking features. "Ah. You're young. I probably should not be discussing it with you, for it is a delicate matter. No one wants to be judged."

She laid her hand briefly on top of his. "I would never judge you." Yet she'd judged Aidan quickly enough. Regret covered her for allowing her hurt feelings to come spilling out during their conversation.

"The truth is your mother forbade me to visit. After she passed, I had become too caught up in my own heartbreak drama. Hence my charity medical journey across the country. At any rate, I was not in the right frame of mind to visit old chums."

"You knew my mother?" How surprising.

"Yes. We all met when your father, Elwyn Hughes, and I became fast friends at university. Gethin was courting your mother then." Paris paused; his mouth formed a taut line. "I am not quite sure how to say this except to reveal the truth: Your mother wanted nothing to do with me when she found out that I prefer…men." He gazed at her, as if waiting for her response. But Cristyn kept her astonishment hidden. "Thankfully, both your father and Elwyn did not shun me when they learned of my proclivities. We continued to correspond, and when they traveled to London, we met up for a meal. However, I respected your mother's wishes and stayed clear."

"I'm sorry. I would have liked to have known you sooner." She gave Paris a warm smile.

"I also regret us not knowing each other before this. But we do now, and will remain good friends, I'm sure."

"I agree. But in what way did Father believe you would be empathetic to my plight?"

Paris sat back in his chair. "I had a serious love affair with the oldest son of an earl. It was ill-fated from the start; we could never be together. He was the heir, and was expected to marry and see to the next heir. When you fall in love, you open yourself up to all sorts of vulnerabilities. I could not and would not deny my feelings. I plundered forth. A smashed-beyond-repair heart ultimately was the result." He laughed cynically. "The tragic thing is he returned my feelings. Alas, life is hard enough without complicating it with an illicit, and, dare I say, illegal romance. Hence my journey. Anything to forget. It's why you came here, is it not? To forget your broken heart?" he asked, his voice soft with understanding.

Tears formed in her eyes, not only for her own plight, but for Paris's tragic tale. Cristyn nodded. "Yes. What are the odds that he would be in the same village? It makes no sense. He's at the mill temporarily. I couldn't stay away. I had to know...I had to see him. Oh, this is terrible. I don't know what to do."

"Does he return your feelings?"

"He says he is not sure what his emotions consist of. You see, I met him at the sanatorium. He was my patient. Scandalous."

"But the heart knows," Paris whispered.

"Yes."

"I am not as studied in addiction as your father, but I will concede I've witnessed what havoc it can wreak, not only physically, but emotionally, in a few of my patients. Even among the upper classes. If he is still on the other side of recovery, I would have to agree he would be unsure about many things, feelings most of all."

Cristyn bit her lower lip. "I know this, but selfishly wallowed in my heartbreak instead of...oh, blast. We argued before he left Standon; we argued again tonight."

"Passions are running high," Paris said.

She laughed brokenly. "Is that what it is?"

"My dear, what will you do?"

"When next we go to the mill, I will apologize for my childish tantrums. Then I will ask him to agree that we not see each other while we're here. Act as if we are strangers. It is the only common-sense solution. What comes after that, I do not know. Go our separate ways, I suppose."

"There is no rush to cut ties with the young man yet. Believe me when I tell you, to find someone with whom you can share all manner of intimacy is a rare gift. Do not be eager to toss that aside until you're completely sure he is not what you want."

Cristyn met Paris's steady gaze. Good advice. "Does it still hurt?"

He laid his hand flat on his chest. "My heart aches constantly. But it has been more than six years since we parted, and time does lessen the pain. I doubt I will ever love again. For a few years, I had it all. It's more than some poor souls experience in their wretched lives. I am thankful."

"What happened to the heir?"

"Oh," Paris sighed. "Last I heard he married an appropriate diamond of the first water and had his heir. Apparently he and his wife are leading separate lives."

She placed a hand on his arm. "Then you could still find happiness." Was she suggesting an affair? How improper.

He shook his head sadly. "No, my dear. He chose duty over love, above all else. The break is permanent. I am nearing the end of my journey; I will no doubt settle in the country to set up a practice. Continue to fight for medical reforms. But I will never return to London. My oldest brother has three sons. I will never inherit my father's viscountcy, which is entirely fine with me." He patted her hand. "Enough about me. I should leave you in peace. Tomorrow, we throw ourselves into our work and put heartache behind us." Paris stood. "Good night, Cristyn."

Once he departed, she made her way to her room. The conversation with Paris gave her plenty to consider. *The heart knows.* Sitting at the small desk, she placed paper, ink, and pen before her.

*Dear Cyn,*
*You will never guess who is in Earl Shilton…*

\* \* \* \*

Once Aidan returned to his room, he tore off his clothes and immediately lost himself in his routine of calisthenics. Sweat dripped off him in rivulets, as if he were a block of melting ice.

Fate had certainly taken a hand. When Cristyn had appeared in the spinning room, time had stood still. She looked ethereal standing in the cotton fluff falling all about her, as if she stepped out of a wintery otherworld where fairy princesses resided. The mere sight of her sent his world spinning out of control. Never had a woman upended his life in such a spectacular manner, or shaken him to his core.

Their meeting had rocked him: a devastating, soul-shattering kiss followed by a heated argument. The kiss was like nothing he had experienced before. How could it hold such emotion and intimacy? Cristyn had departed in a huff, leaving him hard and aching. The rogue still existed within him considering he'd suggested touching her in intimate places. Truthfully, he didn't like feeling unrestrained, for he'd had more than enough of it during his fall from grace.

As for examining his feelings, how could he? He must remain focused on his task and not become distracted. But with her in the village, how could he avoid acknowledging the fact that he wanted her like he had wanted no other woman? Cristyn had seen him at his absolute worst and had still offered tea and sympathy. Hell, she had offered him more than that; she had gifted him with the most precious of commodities: her heart. And he had turned from her.

With one last exhale, he stood, then dumped the cold water in his basin over his head. He was making a damned mess of his life, as well as his room. Glancing at the pool of water at his feet, he realized he couldn't leave it there all night. Reaching for his trousers, he slipped them on, along with his shirt and boots, then went in search of the innkeeper.

As he walked along the hallway, a woman exited one of the rooms. When she turned and met his gaze, she squeaked with surprise. "Mr. Black, sir. I was…that is…" She blushed furiously, then her expression changed to that of a seasoned seductress. She sashayed toward him, giving a thorough inspection of his casual state.

"Do we know each other?" he asked, his tone indifferent.

"Aye, I work at the mill. In the spinning room. My name be Tessie."

Did she? It had only been one day; he wasn't able to recognize any of the workers, even if they had been lined up in front of him. "And I should care…why?"

"A few of us earn a shilling or two on the side. You get my meaning?"

"Quite." In other words, she acted as a prossie. Not his business. "If you will excuse me." He moved to dart around her, but she grasped his arm with her dirty hand. "I had an agreement with the other overlooker." Tessie brazenly cupped his genitals and squeezed gently. "Ah, you be responding already. I can suck on your pipe for a shilling."

Dear God, accosted in the inn. But he didn't push her hand away… not yet. The previous overseer? The man with the wife and five children? Unbelievable. "You did this for him regularly? Anything else? What about the master?"

Tessie gripped his semi-erect cock. Blast his rampant libido. Unfortunately, he would respond to anyone grabbing him. He fought his body's usual reaction.

"Ooo, you be a thick 'un. Wonder if I can shove it all in me mouth?"

Well, that thought killed his inappropriate sexual instincts. Fighting not to roll his eyes at the ridiculous statement, he gripped Tessie's wrist and halted her inapt actions. "Answer my questions first; if I like the answers, I'll give you three shillings."

Her eyes grew wide, and he could see feral hunger in them. A roll of compassion enfolded him. To think she had to debase herself in order not to starve. A pox on the men who would take such advantage of her grim circumstances.

"Aye, the overlooker would put an extra shillin' in me pay packet if I sucked him twice a week. As for Master...don't ask me, sir." True fear registered on her face.

"Has McRae ever harmed you?" he asked. "It's all right, Tessie. I will tell no one. I merely wish to know what manner of man I'm working for."

Tessie tried to pull away from him, but he held her still. "I can't. Not here in the hall."

"Then come into my room. I will not hurt you. You do not have to do anything for the money except tell me the truth." He guided her toward his door.

"No. No!" She pulled away, lifted her tattered skirts, and ran down the stairs, disappearing outside. He wouldn't chase after her. No use causing a scene. But the fright in her eyes had told him plenty. Aidan wouldn't let this pass. Next he had an opportunity he would make it clear that the three shillings was a standing offer. There was no mistaking that she needed the money.

One way or another, he *would* get to the bottom of this.

# Chapter 11

Three days had passed, and in that time, Aidan kept a close watch on the workers in the spinning room. He finally had it narrowed down to which youth was Rokesmith. Since the boy was too tall to be a scavenger, he did odd jobs, carrying pails of water from the well to pour on the spinning room floor to keep the area damp. He also swept up cotton fluff or delivered baskets of bobbins or cotton from room to room. All the while, Rokesmith kept a sharp eye on the younger children scurrying under the machines on their hands and knees.

The shift tonight was ending at seven, and Aidan was determined to follow the children to wherever it was they slept. According to the law, a suitable area must be provided for child workers living on the premises, including proper meals and bedding. It was mentioned in more than one factory or apprentice law that some modicum of education must be provided, of which he had seen no sign of at Morris Mill. These children often toiled fourteen hours a day, regardless of age. Aidan made note of it all. He had already started writing a report to send to his father and grandfather.

As for Tessie, she purposely ignored him. How to make her talk? If she needed the money badly enough, she would tell him anything. Hopefully, that would include the truth. He would approach her again in a few days.

The steam whistle blew and the machines at last grew silent. If he came out of this with a hearing problem, Aidan would not be surprised. Or he could develop a lung ailment from all the bits of cotton floating through the air. The adult workers filed out, heading to their homes. Once they left, the children climbed out from under the machines and gravitated toward Rokesmith. What was he, a pied piper? More like a big brother, for the children all gazed up at him adoringly. Aidan followed them, staying well behind. They headed toward the cotton warehouse. Rokesmith lifted a cellar door, and the children climbed down the stairs into a pit of darkness. Hearing someone approaching, Aidan ducked out of sight, but his gaze remained on the open door.

"Rokesmith! Come get the pies," a man barked. Rokesmith's head popped up and he reached for the basket. The man closed the door and sauntered away. A cellar was not a proper dormitory, as spelled out in the laws.

Aidan marched toward the door, flung it open, and descended the rickety stairs. A collective gasp rose from the children. There were two lit candles sitting on a long table. It was hardly adequate lighting for this dismal crypt. The children sat around the table on rough-hewn benches, all clasping their pies with their grimy hands.

Rokesmith stood, a wary expression on his face. "Wot do ye want, Mr. Black, sir?" His accent was thick, and Aidan thought it counterfeit. It didn't sound genuine.

"I've come to see your living conditions." He took a pie from the basket, broke off a piece, and popped it in his mouth. After chewing it for about a minute, Aidan immediately spat it out. That wasn't beef, pork, or mutton, and it damn well wasn't chicken. The few vegetables swimming in it tasted old. It was mostly flour paste and mystery meat with a greasy crust. Not a proper pie at all. "What are you served for breakfast?"

"Wot do it matter?" Rokesmith answered with an insolent tone.

"It matters to me. Answer the question."

"Gruel and water," a little girl piped up. Aidan turned in the direction of the voice and the child gave him a sweet smile. Despite her unkempt appearance, she was a pretty wee thing with long, curly, golden hair. She waved at him, then shyly ducked her head. God save him from precocious brats.

"Lottie, hush now," Rokesmith admonished gently.

Gruel: a thin, watery porridge to give the children energy, but a tasteless and bland diet nonetheless. And cheap. The food of the workhouse. It hardly constituted a proper meal. According to the law, boys and girls were to have separate sleeping areas. Not here. He glanced about the dim area, anger tearing through him when he saw that wooden pallets littered the floor, acting as beds. No blankets or pillows. A few of the children were obviously underage, including the girl who had spoken up. No child under the age of nine was to work in a factory, and those aged nine to thirteen were only to have a nine-hour day with an hour lunch break. Again, he had witnessed none of this. Multiple violations. It turned Aidan's bile.

"Rokesmith, I want to speak to you outside."

With a surly look on his face, the lad reluctantly followed him up the stairs. Hell, it was brighter out-of-doors than it was in that damned cellar prison.

He grasped the boy's arm and pulled him around the corner to shield them from any prying eyes. "I want you to be completely honest with me. You don't know me at all, but I am *not* the master. Not in any way."

"I don't know nuffin'."

"I appreciate it, truly I do, but I can be trusted. Where do those disgusting pies come from?"

The lad cocked a disbelieving eyebrow at him. "Why? Wot's it to ye?"

"That pie isn't fit to give a mongrel dog, that's why. I want to help, but we must keep it between us. How often does the management inspect your living quarters?"

Rokesmith didn't answer. Instead, he stared into Aidan's eyes as if trying to ascertain if he could be trusted. "They don't. Twice a year they scour it with lime. They feed us gruel for breakfast and lunch, and these pies for supper."

Ah, the accent had been exaggerated. But Aidan wouldn't comment on it now. "Again I ask: where do the pies come from? Are they made here?"

Rokesmith shook his head. "No. A man from the village brings them every night. Sometimes he wears an apron like a baker."

"Listen to me, lad. I want to assist you. But we must keep it secret. As far as the master is concerned, I'm on his side. When I can arrange it, I will bring extra food. Might manage some clothing, extra water for washing…"

Rokesmith shook his head. "No. Washing and different clothes will be noticed. The food? Aye, I'll take it. The younger ones are hungry all the time. And it must be small bits of food, easily hid."

*Clever.* "I will see what I can arrange without causing comment. If anyone asks about me, I'm of a like mind with McRae. But you and I will know differently."

"Why do this?" The lad gave him a wary look.

"When we know each other better and trust begins to build between us, I will answer your questions—and you will answer mine. Do you accept this compact between us?" Aidan held out his hand.

"I must be barmy," the boy muttered as he took Aidan's hand and shook it.

"Do you have enough water? What about the necessary?" Aidan asked.

Rokesmith pointed to a small wooden structure leaning precariously against a large oak tree. "Privy is there. Water buckets are delivered in the morn and for supper. No cups, but we have a ladle. Enough to drink, but not to wash, if ye get me meanin'."

The lad was laying on the thick accent again. "Yes. Loud and clear. We have an understanding. I take it there is no schooling of any kind? Can you read?"

Rokesmith frowned. "No schooling. And I don't trust you enough to answer the other."

"Fair enough. If you ever need me after hours, I'm staying at the Dog and Gun Inn. My name is Aidan. Top floor, room fifteen."

The boy gave him a dubious stare. Aidan couldn't blame him. With a salute, he turned and headed for the village. At the inn he sought out the innkeeper's wife, Mrs. Atwood. She had been receptive to his harmless flirting since his arrival; he could use that to his advantage.

"There you are, Mrs. Atwood. I was wondering if I could ask a favor. I find the food at the mill, what little there is, entirely inadequate. Perhaps you could supplement me with your astounding cooking?" He smiled, showing all his teeth, batting his lashes for good measure. "I would pay extra, of course."

The older woman's eyes twinkled. "What did you have in mind, Mr. Black?"

"Well, I'm not long recovered from a lingering illness." *Not a lie.* "I need heartier fair, but small enough that I may carry it for when I become peckish or feel weak." His smile widened. "And to share with my fellow managers, if so inclined."

She rubbed her chin thoughtfully. "I can make an oatmeal biscuit that melts in your mouth. It has rye, mullet, beetroot, as well as a little sugar and cut-up cherries. Robust ingredients to build up the blood. Sugar is dear, mind. But you *are* willing to pay."

He bowed slightly. "That I am."

Mrs. Atwood became animated, clapping her hands together. "I also make a lovely cheese roll loaded with onion, watercress, and tiny bits of ham."

Aidan gently took one of her hands and laid a kiss upon it. "You are entirely kind. And I am eternally grateful."

"Oh!" She blushed. "Shall we say two dozen—"

"Three dozen, three times a week. Same with the biscuits. I will pay you three pounds each week."

She tore her hand from his. "Three pounds? That's unheard of."

"Then let us make it four pounds, and ask you to keep this agreement between us. Call it a special order."

"It is far too much."

"Nonsense. You are worth every penny. Do we have a contract, Mrs. Atwood? Do you agree to the terms?"

"Well, I would be a fool to say no. A special order it is. I'll have the first lot ready for you tomorrow morning."

Aidan gave her another dazzling smile. "Brilliant. Now, a bit of information: Is there a pieman in the village?"

She frowned. "Yes. There is a loathsome man who takes advantage of those too poor to cook their own meals. Most of those horrid flats and rooms have no stoves; many also have no fireplaces. Tattle has it he uses whatever dead animal he finds along the road."

Aidan had tasted the proof. "His name? And where can I find him? Again, this is to stay between us."

"Of course, sir. He is William Michaels, over High Street way. Has a small shop. Can't miss it."

Aidan gave Mrs. Atwood an elegant bow. "My thanks, dear, dear lady."

She tittered and giggled as she headed to her kitchen. As for Aidan, he had to think how he was going to approach this disgusting pieman—if at all, for he couldn't tip his hand. Meanwhile, he would include this new information in his first report. Eventually he might use Rokesmith as a messenger, but he needed to build trust first.

Building it between him and Cristyn would not go amiss. But how, when he had to keep his identity and his operation secret?

\* \* \* \*

In the ten days since Cristyn had last seen Aidan, she'd sufficient time to reflect on their conversation. She admonished herself for the way she had handled it, and decided amends had to be made.

Was she asking too much of him? As he'd stated, he had barely moved beyond his recovery. How unfair of her to demand he admit his feelings, when, by his own admission, they were unknown and confused. She more than anyone understood the harrowing experience he had suffered. Though she was not aware of the circumstances that led him to be admitted at the Standon Sanatorium, Cristyn was sure it was worse than anything she could imagine. Being a nurse, she should have shown compassion and understanding.

Her core concerns remained: What about his past, and the horrible events that led to his stay at the sanatorium? Why wouldn't he discuss his background and family? And something about his explanation for being in Earl Shilton wasn't resonating. He obviously wasn't here because of her. The only one who could have told Aidan of her plans was her father, and since he believed they shouldn't be together, that scenario was rejected outright.

Regardless of her statement that they should ignore each other, Cristyn had to apologize. Hopefully she would be better able to keep her errant emotions under tight rein.

There was no better opportunity than today. Back at Morris Mill for another appointment with the orphan children, she and Paris followed the same routine as their previous visit. Along with the apples and bread, they brought slices of cheese. Paris had told her Mr. McRae would only allow them to care for the children if he abandoned all talk of a wheel, or any other concerns about the running of the mill and the health of the workers. Paris had reluctantly agreed.

As they concluded the examinations, Cristyn motioned toward young Rokesmith. Once he stood before her, she pulled him around the corner of the cotton warehouse.

"You know who Mr. Black is?"

He cocked an eyebrow at her, a cautious expression on his face. "Aye, he be the head overlooker."

She slipped a note into Carter's hand. "I need you to give this to Mr. Black. Can you manage it? Will you do this for me?"

"Aye. Only 'cause you and the doc be kind, with the food and the like."

"Dr. Middlemiss is an honorable man. Perhaps we can alert the authorities about your care. It is shocking how you all are—"

"Nay. Don't," Carter whispered fiercely. "Things would go worse. You'll do naught but muck it up. We'd all be separated. Or worse besides." He held up the note. "If ye wish me to deliver the note to the toff overlooker, keep yer nose out. And ye can tell that toff doctor and all."

Cristyn could see real fear and anger in the young lad's eyes. They burned with an intensity she'd never seen in one so young. "Very well. We will hold off. For now."

"Good. I'll slip the overlooker the note, never fear." The boy turned on his heel and marched away.

In the note she'd asked Aidan to meet her in the gardening shed at half past seven this evening. Her insides fluttered at the prospect of seeing him again. Yes, she yearned for him. But it would be prudent to keep her desires in check. But how, when the slightest brush of his fingers sent ripples of heated awareness through her entire body? When her heart ached for him to kiss her again? When his innate sadness and vulnerability touched her soul? Not that she thought him weak—far from it. One doesn't recover from an addiction unless they have discipline and courage. She had seen both in Aidan. If only he could see it.

By early evening, her quivering insides had abated enough for her to school her features into polite indifference. As she hurried toward the rear yard of the inn, she reviewed in her mind how she would handle this. Apologize, but be firm in her conviction they must act as strangers if their paths should cross in the village. As for the future, that would be up for discussion after they had both departed from Earl Shilton and her inquires were satisfactorily addressed. *Excellent.* It would take no more than five minutes to say her piece, and she would be back in her room before dark.

She opened the door and slipped into the shed, only to find Aidan already there. At the sight of him, her heart skipped a beat. The subtle scent of his cologne filled her senses. Lord, he was a incredibly handsome man, with the most glorious cheekbones.

He stepped before her, his masculine presence making it hard for her to concentrate. "You wished to see me?" His voice was low, husky. Sensual.

*Remain calm.* "Yes. I wish to apologize for my fit of temper the last couple of times we've spoken. I did everything but stamp my foot. Though the feelings I relayed to you were honest and just, I allowed my hurt to steer the conversation."

"I have apologized, but allow me to say once again that I'm sorry for riding away without a word. Though it is no excuse, I believed you would be better off without becoming involved in my wreckage." He took her hand; neither of them wore gloves. The contact was searing. "Nigh on eight weeks later? I'm not sure what to think. Not when you stand this close to me."

*Oh, blast him! Stay focused.* "I believe we—"

"Shh," he whispered urgently.

Men's voices were drifting closer.

"Get the hoes from the shed, Stan, along with the bone meal," one of them said.

Aidan pulled her close to his chest, as if to shield her. His cologne was even more enticing with her nose buried in his shirt. Mixed with the woodsy and bergamot scent was laundry soap and clean skin.

"The bone meal is out front, stored under the veranda," the other man replied.

"We'd best fetch it then. Come."

The voices trailed away, and Aidan took her hand, opened the door, and pulled her outside.

"What are you doing?" she whispered fiercely.

"I am endeavoring to find us a more private place to continue this conversation. If we run for it, we can make the back entrance to the inn before they return."

"I can't go into the inn with you, why—"

"I have it on good authority that Mrs. Atwood, the innkeeper's wife, is toiling in her kitchen, while Mr. Atwood is pulling pints in his tavern room. No time to argue." Aidan peeked around the corner of the shed. "All clear. Lift your skirts, my sweet, and run."

Aidan bolted forward, pulling her behind. Cristyn hardly had time to draw breath, let alone lift her skirts. It was difficult to keep up with his long-legged stride. Before she knew it, they were inside. "The stairs are directly to your left. Go, I'm right behind you. Room fifteen."

Perhaps she was wicked, for she could walk away and head to Mrs. Trubshaw's without casting a fleeting look Aidan's way. Instead, she was going to his room.

Cristyn grabbed fistfuls of her skirt and petticoats and ascended the stairs as quietly as she could. They both stood before his room. As he slipped the key in the lock, Cristyn glanced about the hallway to ensure they had not been seen. A thrill coursed about her spine. *Wicked, indeed.*

As she stepped inside his room, Cristyn was taken by the luxuriance. It must have been the best room at the inn—correction: *rooms*. This was a large suite. Of course, he *was* wealthy. The interior was decorated with dark hardwood walls with fancy trim and cornices. A mixture of green and light brown colored the curtains and bedding. The four-poster bed was huge, and she pictured Aidan lounging naked among the expensive sheets and silk bedspread. She flushed and looked away.

Aidan locked the door, then strode toward her. "Will you take a seat?"

"I will not be staying long enough to sit. Allow me to finish what I came to say, then I must take my leave before the sun sets."

"The floor is yours."

"I believe after tonight, if we should cross paths while in this village, we should act as strangers." *There.* She'd said it in a firm tone to punctuate the point.

"May I ask you to attend McRae's dinner party next week as my guest?"

Cristyn shook her head. "No. Absolutely not." She paused and gazed up at him. "How can you entertain the notion of breaking bread with that horrid man?"

"For as long as I am here, I must stay in his good graces."

"I don't understand, but I've no time to discuss it. You said during our last meeting that you lust after me, while your other emotions are muddled. Until you can see clearly, I believe that is reason enough for us to act as strangers." She stared into his lovely blue eyes. "I, however, own my feelings. I am not ashamed of them. I have fallen for you, Aidan Black. Against all common sense and propriety, and whatever professionalism exists between a nurse and her patient."

"I adore you." Aidan cradled her face in his hands, his thumbs stroking her flushed cheeks. "You are the reason I found the inner strength to recover. If not for you, I would be lost, wandering alone in this cold world with no purpose. Do not think these feelings are born from gratitude for your compassionate care, though I'm grateful. My emotions are muddled because I have never experienced them before, for any woman. Ever." He nuzzled her neck, laying gentle kisses along it, then across her jawline.

His tenderly spoken words touched her heart, causing it to speed up and thump rapidly. "While I'm flattered, do not place your recovery at my feet. You alone are responsible; if I assisted in a small way, then I'm glad. And I've never felt this way toward a man. Ever." Slowly, and in increments, he nibbled softly on her lips, coaxing her to respond. Cristyn could not find the inner strength to tear away from him. Instead, she tentatively nibbled on his, causing a deep-throated moan to escape him.

Aidan took the kiss deeper, exploring every part of her mouth. Daringly, she touched her tongue to his, causing another husky growl to reverberate through him. Aidan pulled her close, and had her distracted enough that she had not felt his hand slowly trailing down her torso, until he clasped her rear and brought her in against that hard part of him.

"God, what was I thinking?" he murmured in between kisses. "I never should have brought you to my room. The temptation is too great."

"I'm not sorry," she replied.

He pulled back and gave her a dubious look. "No?"

"I'm not some trembling virgin."

Aidan's shocked expression caused her to smile. "You are telling me you're not a virgin—" he began.

Cristyn stepped out of his arms and immediately missed the heat of his hard, solid body. "Oh, I am most decidedly a virgin, but not a trembling one." She held up her hands for his inspection. "See? Not a tremor or shake of any kind. I've read plenty on the subject of carnal relations. A man's body holds no trepidation or fright for me. I'm a nurse; I've seen plenty of men naked. I've seen you completely bare."

"Though I was not exactly at my best."

"Most people aren't when they are sick—or naked."

Aidan snorted. "You're supposed to say, 'Aidan, that's not true. You're a stunning specimen.'"

"I think not. Your ego is healthy enough without my compliments."

He laughed, and the rusty sound of it warmed her insides. "Nothing fazes you, it seems."

She shrugged. "I've even dissected a man's corpse."

His mouth dropped open. "What?"

"When I was studying anatomy, my father procured a cadaver from the hospital in Watford. It was most enlightening. The male body holds no mystery to me."

His expression showed admiration, and something more heated that Cristyn could not determine. "As I said, I absolutely adore you."

"Enough to do as you suggested last week?" My, how entirely audacious of her. The words slipped out before she could think. But Aidan stating he adored her had temporarily cast aside her rules of engagement—at least at this particular moment.

His eyes took on a fiery heat. "And what did I suggest, my sweet?"

Cristyn took a step closer. "You said that if you tunneled your hand under my skirts and slipped your fingers between my swollen folds, you would find me wet and wanting."

"And will I?" His voice rasped, his gaze sultry.

Oh, she *was* wicked. And not the least bit ashamed. Society claimed women should be above such desires. Complete nonsense. The moment he suggested they hurry toward his room, she'd had every opportunity to depart, but chose not to. For deep in her heart, no matter how much she spoke of keeping her distance and all the good reasons why she should, Cristyn longed for him to touch her in the most intimate of places.

"Yes," she whispered huskily. "You most certainly will."

# Chapter 12

*Jesus.* His heartbeat pounded in his head and blood rushed to his cock, making it stiffer than when he had kissed her. If he were a decent, honorable man, he would escort her to wherever it was she was staying and not look back.

But at his core, despite his downfall and his eagerness to redeem himself, he was still that notorious rake. To seduce her thoroughly would be a sweet victory. But conquering Cristyn was not his objective. He would not force her into anything—not that he had ever forced any woman.

Cristyn was special. Not at all like the women in his dissipated past. What set her apart? Her fresh beauty? Their shared experience of his addiction nightmare? Her compassionate nature and innate intelligence? It was all of that, and more.

Aidan spoke the truth when he said he adored her, though he suspected his feelings ran much deeper than mere adulation. But that was all he was willing to acknowledge today.

She was correct: She was no trembling virgin, but he wouldn't take anything from her that she was not freely offering. Cristyn asked him to touch her. *Yes.* Stepping before her, he grasped her shoulders and walked toward the wall. Once she rested against it, he lifted her leg and draped it across his hip. Her breathing came in short breaths, her chest rising and falling with each exhale. Cristyn's beautiful eyes were bright and filled with passion. With slow purpose, he trailed his fingers under her skirt, caressing her leg, reveling in the feel of her sheer stockings until he reached bare skin on her upper thigh.

Aidan moaned. *Skin as soft as silk. Warm to the touch.* He continued his exploration while nuzzling her neck and found she wore a type of undergarment that was flared enough for him to tunnel his hand inside of it. As his fingers brushed by her curls, she gasped, then sighed.

Passionate, as he knew she would be. He kissed her while he parted her folds and growled when he found her wet. Their kiss grew ferocious, and he wasted no time plunging two fingers inside her. Cristyn gasped again, and the sound of it urged him on. Moving in and out of her, simulating sex, his thumb pressed on her swollen clit. His mouth slid to her neck and he nibbled on it, savoring the taste of her flushed skin. "Yes, Cris. Let it happen. Come for me, sweet."

"Oh, my God," she panted.

"You've touched yourself, haven't you? Tell me."

"Yes."

"How often? Do you think of me?" he commanded, increasing the speed of his finger thrusts.

"Aidan..."

"Answer me."

"Nearly...every night."

*Fuck.* Her breathless confession had him ready to explode. "And?" he gruffly urged.

"I think of you. It has only ever been...you."

Those words sliced his heart in two. In the next breath, Cristyn cried out with her release; her inner muscles clamped down on his fingers as she shuddered. Resting her head on his shoulder, Cristyn struggled to catch her breath. As did he. He was close to coming himself, ready to spill into his trousers like a callow schoolboy.

"I've got you," he murmured. Aidan held her close, her heart beating as rapidly as his. If only they could stay like this.

They remained motionless while their breathing regulated. He was still hard, and yearned for more. But he willed his arousal to deflate, at least somewhat. Cristyn lifted her head and glanced toward the window. She stood upright, smoothing her skirt into place. "The sun is all but set. I must go. I only intended to stay a few minutes."

"Allow me to escort you."

"I can find my own way."

"We're still to act as strangers after the intimacy we have shared? How do you propose we do that, exactly?"

"Everything is complicated. What happened between us only makes it worse. I need time to think." She gave him a tremulous smile. "And I do not regret what happened, Aidan, but surely you must see we cannot be alone together again. At least until we are done in Earl Shilton."

Damn it all! No, he did not see it—nor did he wish to. Not when he wanted to strip each layer of sensible clothes from her lush body and taste, lick, and nibble every part of her skin. And that would only be the beginning. "I'll not argue the point. But I will follow you at a distance until you are safely at your residence. When we are out in the hall, go down the stairs at a normal pace, and head out the front door. I will slip through the rear entrance and follow. Where is it you're staying?"

Cristyn opened her reticule, took out her gloves, and slipped them on. "I suppose it doesn't matter if you know. I'm renting a room on Church Street."

"Then let us depart."

Cristyn hesitated at the door. "Aidan?"

"Yes?"

"What about you? I found release, but you..."

He lifted her chin in order for their gazes to meet. "What you confessed, about nearly every night? I do the same. I will find my release when I return." He cupped her cheek, the pad of his thumb slowly caressing the warm softness. "It is you, Cristyn. Since we've met, I only think of you." He groaned. "We had best leave, or I will lose all control."

Her lovely eyes glistened. "I'm not sure I'm strong enough to stay away from you, regardless of what I proclaim," she whispered.

Her candor humbled him, a sensation he was not used to. Honestly, he felt the same, but dared not admit it aloud; he had revealed too many of his feelings as it was. He opened the door and glanced out into the hallway. "No one is about. Be as nonchalant as possible. Do not hurry, but don't dally either." He kissed her forehead. "Go."

Cristyn slipped out into the hall. He waited. Two minutes. Three. Then he hurriedly descended the rear stairs and entered the yard. The men working on the landscaping had apparently finished and were no doubt nursing a pint in the tavern room. The sun was setting; it must have been well past eight. Walking at a brisk pace, he followed far enough behind Cristyn that she was in his line of sight without seeming as if he were following her. Watching her hips sway as she walked had him thinking of what had occurred in his room. She had allowed him to touch her. That brief intimacy overshadowed all his past assignations. Such silky skin, and—

Out from one of the alleys, a young lad dressed in rags ran toward Cristyn, pulling Aidan from his erotic daydream. The beggar pushed her to the ground, snatched her reticule, and vaulted away. Red fury clouded his vision. He sprinted toward her, and was about to follow the boy when Cristyn called out, "No, Aid—I mean, no, sir! Don't chase after him!"

A crowd had congregated around them. None of the citizens bothered to pursue the boy. It was clever of Cristyn to recover quickly and act as if they were unknown to each other.

He held out his hand. "Are you all right, miss?"

She slipped her hand in his and he assisted her to stand. "I am fine. Thank you for coming to my aid, sir." His admiration for her grew. "There was nothing of value—a few hairpins and a lace handkerchief. If the poor boy can fetch a few pennies for the items, he's welcome to them."

"How magnanimous of you, Miss...?"

"Bevan."

"I am Aidan Black."

Yes, there was no escaping their acquaintance now, considering how public this was. It would be the tittle-tattle of the village by morning. Aidan scanned the crowd. "The show is over," he bellowed. "Off with you." A few people sauntered away, but most stayed. "Get out of here, you cowards!" Aidan thundered. "Not one of you bloody bastards came to this young lady's aid!" Grumbling, the crowd moved off. Some of the men, a few he recognized from the mill, gave him a dirty look.

Aidan turned his attention to Cristyn. "Are you sure you're uninjured?" he whispered.

"Just my pride. I thought Mrs. Trubshaw, my landlady, exaggerated the possible danger in the streets. It appears not."

"Take my arm and I will escort you home. My coming to your rescue will undermine my authority at the mill."

She slipped her hand through the crook of his elbow and they started walking toward Church Street. "How?"

"The last thing I wish to be thought of is a hero, even a poor excuse for one." He had revealed too much, but Cristyn was too preoccupied to notice. "After all, I did not recover your property."

"There really wasn't anything of value. I admit I'm a trifle shaken. I've never been robbed before. Growing up in Standon spoiled me. I had no idea how others live. How they scrape and labor in order to survive. Even resort to stealing."

Aidan certainly could have told her ghastly stories, for he had lived it during those last months of his infamous downfall. They turned onto Church Street.

"The red brick building there. Number five. You don't need to escort me to the door," Cristyn said.

"From what I know of villages, your Mrs. Trubshaw will know the story from others by luncheon. Best to be honest. And I *will* see you safely delivered." He patted her hand briefly. "Now that we are publicly acquainted, you can accompany me to McRae's dinner party."

"No. I won't sit in a room with that wretched man. I still do not know why you would—"

"Ah, here we are."

The door opened before Aidan could knock. An older woman, with a formidable expression, looked them both over with one eyebrow arched in question. "Miss Bevan? Who is this?"

"Mrs. Trubshaw, this is Mr. Aidan Black. He came to my rescue, as it were, when my reticule was stolen."

"Good heavens! Are you all right, my dear?"

"Thank you, yes."

"Mr. Black, will you not come in?" the landlady asked.

"Alas, I have another appointment, but if I may call about this time tomorrow night? To check on how Miss Bevan is doing." Cristyn shot him a brief, stern glance, but he ignored it.

"Of course, sir. You're more than welcome. Come at eight o'clock, and I will have tea and cake at the ready."

He bowed, then faced Cristyn, taking her hand and placing an air kiss above her knuckles. "Until tomorrow evening. I am gratified you were not seriously harmed." As he walked away, he heard the landlady say as she closed the door, "So that is the much-talked-about handsome overseer..."

He did have another engagement. There were yesterday's ham rolls to deliver to the children. Once he stopped by his suite to gather up the canvas bag, he hurried toward the mill. Aidan smiled with amusement when he reached the area behind the cotton warehouse. Rokesmith had heeded his suggestion of allowing the children to stay outside when the evening was warm. To see a couple of the smaller children running and playing warmed his little-used heart, but he made sure his expression remained disinterested.

"Rokesmith. Come here." He thrust the bag in the young lad's hands. "And the pies?"

"I tried one; I think it was chicken for once. I gave it to them."

"In the bag are the oatmeal biscuits and the ham rolls. Remember to remind the children to keep it secret or all this ends."

The little girl, Lottie, skipped toward them. She stopped in front of Aidan, then slipped her hand in his. "Hello, sir." She looked up at him expectantly, as if silently pleading for attention—and no doubt affection, for these wretched children had been deprived of both. His heart lurched at the sight of her sweet face. Every time he had been here the past ten days, the girl had latched on to him. He should have pushed the child aside to keep up appearances, but he couldn't do it. "Good day, Lottie."

She beamed up at him and squeezed his hand, which in turn squeezed his heart. "You brought us biscuits, sir?"

"Yes. I want you to eat them all." Hell, she was far too young and innocent to be toiling away in a cotton mill. Usually children held no interest for him. When had he ever been around any? The few he had any interaction with were the pampered, spoiled spawn of the peerage. They usually were squawking about one thing or another, making demands, throwing tantrums, or stuffing their faces with sticky toffee.

But glancing down at Lottie, he wanted nothing more than to give her a hug—he had the feeling they both needed it. As if reading his mind, Lottie threw her arms around his waist and hugged him tight. Moved, he patted the girl on the shoulder.

"Leave the overlooker alone, Lottie." Rokesmith snapped his fingers, then motioned her to rejoin the others. She skipped away, but then turned and gave Aidan another wave. He returned it.

"Why are you doing this?" Rokesmith asked, his tone suspicious.

Aidan folded his arms. "Answer questions for me first."

The boy shrugged. "Fine."

"Can you read and write? Where are you from? How old are you?"

Rokesmith snorted. "In other words, you want me to tell you all. Only if you will tell me all."

"Agreed. To a point."

"Yes, I can read and write, but no one here knows that. I recently turned fifteen, but am passing myself off as thirteen. Not sure how much longer I'll be able to get away with it, I've grown three inches in the past few months. Your turn."

All pretense of a working-class accent was gone. This young lad was acting a part as surely as Aidan was. "My name is not Aidan Black. I am heir to an earl."

Rokesmith chuckled. "I had you pegged as a toff. What in hell are you doing here?"

"I cannot say, but regardless of what I may say or do, I am not on the side of McRae. I am collecting information. That is all I'm willing to reveal."

Rokesmith gave him a contemplative gaze. "Fair enough. I'm from Dover."

"You're a long way from home."

"Not by my choice. When my father died, my uncle had me committed to a boy's home, claiming I was incorrigible. He no doubt took my father's money, what little there was. I've no other family. As soon as I'm old enough, I plan to get my revenge."

"Jesus," Aidan muttered. "How long ago was this?"

"When I was ten. I've been moved around since then. I met most of these children at the orphanage in Leicester. We were sold to the master here at the cotton mill two years past."

"Sold?"

"It happens. More than you think." Rokesmith kicked at the dirt near his worn boot. "You're here to collect information. You're one of those do-gooder nobs. All you're going to do is cause trouble. I know it." The lad pointed at the children. "I look after them, see they come to no harm. They look up to me."

"I can see that," Aidan replied quietly.

"I won't help you."

"No? If you want to help those children, and keep the food coming, yes, I believe you will. Until trust builds between us, we'll start slow. I will need letters delivered to my man in Hinckley. I'll pay. The first letter is to be delivered shortly. Are you allowed off the mill property?"

"Yes, since I'm thirteen, and I get two hours off on Sunday."

"For religious studies? Or church?"

Rokesmith snorted. "Hardly."

Aidan shook his head. "You're entitled to two sets of clothes, two shillings a day wages, at least a few hours a week of education, separate dormitories, and proper beds. And proper meals." He pointed to Lottie, who was laughing and chasing another girl. "Children under nine are not permitted to work in mills. Those between the ages of nine and thirteen are not to work more than nine hours a day. Children aged fourteen to eighteen, no more than twelve hours a day."

"So?"

"None of that is happening here. Already there are enough violations to close down this mill. But I have the feeling there is more going on. Something hidden and ominous. Am I wrong?"

Rokesmith's eyes narrowed. "If you start kicking over stones, you're going to ruin everything. I've an agreement with the master. I keep quiet, he lets me watch over the children and keep them in line. That weasel Meeker arranged it. Speaking of which, he's onto you. He lurks about in dark corners, watching. Taking notes. You're going to have to yell at the workers more." The boy hesitated. "Maybe in the courtyard tomorrow, under Master and Meeker's eye, we should stage a fight."

Aidan gave Rokesmith a dubious look. "In what way? I'm not going to hit you."

"You know, grab me by the scruff, shake me, and threaten to clout me in the head. I'm used to it. That miserable overlooker before you did it. He was a right bully. And worse—at least to the women and children. He didn't have the guts to take on the few men in the mill."

"And I suppose none of the men tried to stop it."

"Not if they wanted to keep their positions. Besides, most of it took place off the mill floor." Rokesmith frowned. "I've told you too much already."

Aidan recalled Tessie saying she performed sex acts for extra money in her pay packet. When he'd mentioned McRae, there had been true fear in her eyes. He had a feeling there was much she could reveal. He should do as Rokesmith suggested: call her out as the former overseer would have. "Disciplining you for them to witness is a shrewd plan. You have a devious mind. I like it."

"Do it around three. Master usually stands in the window, watching the deliveries."

Aidan grabbed Rokesmith's arm. "You had better be on the level with me. No going behind my back to Meeker or McRae. I have the power to bring this place down around your head, and I won't be crossed. Work with me, and I will protect you and the children."

Anger flashed in the boy's brown eyes. "You're a toff sure enough; you think that you're above us all. To hell with your threats."

Obviously the wrong tack to take, but he had to make it clear there would be ramifications if he was betrayed. He released Rokesmith. "I am merely making it clear where we stand."

"How are you going to protect us?" he grumbled, rubbing his arm.

"I will not see you all separated and sent to another workhouse or orphanage, or sold to another mill. I will find a place for the younger children so they can stay together. It will be a place you approve of. As far as yourself, I will find a good apprenticeship. Then, when you're able, you can travel to Dover with your head high and coin in your pocket. I will even assist you in pursuing your rightful inheritance."

"It's not all that much money, Black. Not like you're used to."

"It's the principle of it. Your uncle stole from you, locked you away. You deserve justice. He deserves to be punished."

Rokesmith stared at him. "I can't bloody make you out."

"I have enough trouble trying to sort through it myself. Do we have a pact?" Aidan held out his hand.

Hesitating, Rokesmith stared at the outstretched hand, then met Aidan's determined gaze. "I want one more guarantee: Lottie stays with me. She's like a little sister. Family, you understand? I want to protect her."

"How old is she?"

"Six. She thinks. She's all alone. I'm all she's got."

"I will see to it that she stays with you."

"As I said before, I must be daft, but all right. Pact." He shook Aidan's hand.

Good. Things were starting to fall into place. Now he would have to step up his evil overseer role, even though he found it distasteful.

# Chapter 13

All the next day, Cristyn found it difficult to concentrate on the tasks at hand, knowing Aidan would be coming by the rooming house that evening. Perhaps she should send word for him to stay away, but she yearned to see him again. For all her supposed strength, she had none whatsoever as far as Aidan was concerned.

As for the sensual familiarity between them? Cristyn was not the least bit embarrassed, but she was astonished at her swift reaction to his intimate touch. Heavens, no wonder people risked all for such doings. And his breathless confession of thinking of her while he saw to his own pleasure…. The image of it haunted her dreams the entire night. It was easy enough to conjure, seeing as she knew what lay under his clothes.

"Cristyn. Where are you? Have you found the antiseptic?" Paris called.

Daydreaming once again. It was important she gain command of her wayward emotions. She located the glass bottle on the shelf and brought it to Paris in the outer office. "Sorry."

"Thinking of your rescuer?" He gave her a teasing smile.

"How did you hear about that?"

"I have had three patients inform me of your robbery. How the dashing Mr. Black, overseer at Morris Mill, gallantly came to your aid, though he did not chase the thief."

"I asked him not to bother, as it wasn't worth the pursuit. I was knocked to the ground. Nothing injured but my pride. I was going to tell you."

Paris crossed his arms. "I promised your father I would look after you. I am tempted to write and inform him Mr. Black is here. I should also mention the robbery."

"Please don't. It will only complicate matters, more than they are already. He would insist I leave, and I can't. Not yet. I'm accomplishing something here, doing good work, and I'm not finished."

Paris nodded. "I understand. For the time being, I will not mention Mr. Black or the thievery in my correspondence. You met with him last night, am I correct? Hence why he was close by to come to your aid?"

Cristyn sighed. "I cannot stay away. He is temptation incarnate."

Paris rubbed his earlobe. "I understand that particular sensation. But this is a small village. People talk. With decided frequency."

"He's coming by Mrs. Trubshaw's this evening. She invited him."

"Do you wish for me to be there?"

With Paris in attendance, she would not be tempted to find a few minutes alone with Aidan. She could publicly state he need not bother calling on her again. But the memory of his evocative scent, devastating kiss, and searing touch overrode all common sense and propriety. "No, Mrs. Trubshaw will be there. I will make it plain to Aidan he's not to call again."

But, later that evening, all thoughts of avoiding him flew from her mind when Mrs. Trubshaw showed him into the main parlor. Immaculately groomed and wearing an expensive black coat and neatly tied silver cravat, he exuded wealth and privilege. Mrs. Trubshaw tittered as he bent over her hand. When Aidan turned to Cristyn, she held out hers for him to shake—not to kiss. Aidan gave her a sly smile, took her hand, turned it, then pressed his lips across her knuckles. "Miss Bevan," he murmured sensually, "I do hope you have recovered from your ordeal."

Cristyn pulled her hand from his, flustered. "I have."

"Do take a seat, Mr. Black, and I will fetch the tea tray." Mrs. Trubshaw scurried from the room, leaving them alone.

Aidan did not hesitate. He swept Cristyn up in his arms and kissed her. Push him away? No. Never. She took the opportunity to clasp the sides of his head, meeting his tongue with hers, aggressively plundering his mouth as he had hers last night. Her fingers dove into his thick midnight-black hair, and Aidan growled in response, pulling her tight against him.

His hand moved to her breast, and a squeak of surprise escaped her lips. His thumb stroked her erect nipple, sending shocking waves of pleasure along her spine, settling in her feminine core.

The sound of footsteps broke them apart, and Aidan opened the door wider for the landlady. "Allow me to assist you, Mrs. Trubshaw." He took the large tray from her. "Where would you like it?"

"There, on that table will be fine, sir."

Once seated, Mrs. Trubshaw poured the tea and passed a cup and saucer to each of them. A knock sounded at the door. "Oh, one moment." Aidan gave Cristyn a questioning look, and she shrugged. "Why, Dr. Middlemiss! I was not expecting you tonight. Come in. We have company, but you're more than welcome to join us."

Aidan frowned. Cristyn was truly puzzled, for she had made it clear she would handle this situation—perhaps Paris had come for an entirely different reason.

Aidan stood when Paris entered the room. "Dr. Middlemiss, this is Mr. Aidan Black, head overseer at Morris Mill."

Paris pulled off his gloves and held out his hand. "Ah, the hero himself. Come to cover yourself in glory?"

Aidan's mouth twitched in annoyance—Cristyn knew the guarded expression intimately. "Well, tea and biscuits, at any rate." Aidan gripped Paris's hand and gave it a brief shake before retaking his seat.

Paris handed his cloak and gloves to the landlady. "Morris Mill. Is it to be a permanent position?" Paris knew it wasn't; what was he playing at? "I've never seen such a speedy exit. Mr. Hanson, wife, and children, all bundled into a wagon and disappeared in the dead of night. It was mysterious, to be sure. Then you arrive."

Aidan calmly sipped his tea. "I assure you the position is indeed temporary. Hence the reason I am staying at the inn. I've no plans to settle in this village of misery. No offense, Mrs. Trubshaw."

Paris crossed his legs and took the cup and saucer offered. "But I am sure Mrs. Trubshaw *is* offended, Mr. Black. After all, this is her home. Many villagers have fallen on hard times, the situation exacerbated by the cruelty of the masters who run the mill and rent out the stocking frames at exorbitant prices. But, as you say, your residence is a temporary one. Not long enough to impact anyone's lives. Or assist those in need."

Mrs. Trubshaw looked from one man to the other. "I'm not offended, truly—"

"There is a Mr. Muggeridge who frequents this village. He's here as agent for Queen Victoria, and due to arrive within two weeks to conclude his report. I can introduce you," Paris continued, his voice haughty. "The dire poverty here has reached the queen's ear; I'm sure you can fill in the agent on the doings at the mill."

"This village and its occupants hold no interest for me. I do not wish to become involved. I will do as I was hired, then, when the term is at an end, I will leave, and think on this place no more."

Cristyn gasped. Is this how Aidan truly felt? The ice-blue coldness of his eyes shocked her, as did the indifferent tone of his voice. Perhaps she did not know him at all.

"Well, not all of us are unaffected by the desolation. Isn't that correct, Cristyn?"

She murmured in agreement, not sure what to say.

"I would like to come tomorrow morning and visit the children." Paris turned toward Mrs. Trubshaw. "If you were not aware, Mr. McRae has allowed me to treat them. Gratis, of course. It was the only terms he would agree to. I have the smallpox vaccine, and would like to inoculate the children. Will you agree to such?"

"Why ask me?" Aidan said.

"You are the head overseer. Are you not permitted to make such decisions?"

"I find it prudent not to overstep my bounds as far as Mr. McRae is concerned. I suggest you take it up with him."

"I will. Now, as to why you are here."

"Dr. Middlemiss!" Cristyn exclaimed. What was Paris doing? The tension in the room was palpable.

"I am looking out for your interests, my dear, as I promised your father." Then he said to Aidan in a firm voice, his jaw determinedly set, "Miss Bevan is not available to be courted."

Mrs. Trubshaw cleared her throat, evidently uncomfortable by the icy tone of the conversation.

Aidan placed the cup and saucer on the table. "Is it not for the young lady to decide? Are you her guardian? Unless you have other justifications for protecting her."

Paris shrugged. "Perhaps I do. I esteem Cristyn greatly. We would make a formidable couple, considering our mutual interest in medicine and assisting those less fortunate." Paris gave her a heated look that, frankly, shocked her. Why was he spouting this nonsense?

Aidan stood, his expression dark. "Thank you for the tea, Mrs. Trubshaw. If you wish to examine the children, Doctor, make an appointment with Mr. McRae. For I care not. Good evening, Miss Bevan." He bowed and left the room.

Cristyn could only stare at Aidan's broad back and shoulders as he departed. What had happened?

"Doctor, I must say, I have never seen you act so rudely before," Mrs. Trubshaw huffed. "Excuse me."

When she left, Paris blew out a breath. "Are you angry, Cristyn?"

"Yes, I am, rather. I said I would handle this. Now Aidan believes you have designs on me. Mrs. Trubshaw as well."

"I apologize for being facetious. I had no right to interfere. I purposely baited him to ascertain his character and his motives, toward you and the mill. It appears he is the same manner of man as McRae. Surely you see this."

Heavens, could it be true? Aidan had said it plainly: He cared not for the children. But there had to be an explanation.

Paris met her gaze. "I do care for you, my dear. I don't want to see you hurt. That is a man with a cold, dark soul—I would bet my life on it." Paris stared at the door. "As far as your landlady, I must make my apologies. Do you accept mine?"

Cristyn frowned. "Only if you do not interfere again. I am more than capable of making up my own mind. If only everyone would stop interfering in my life." Her voice had a hard edge to it, for she was trying to keep her fury and frustration under control.

"I am suitably admonished, and deservedly so. But do not dismiss Mr. Black's words and actions here tonight." Paris stood, briefly touched her shoulder, then left to seek out Mrs. Trubshaw.

Left alone in the parlor, a tear slipped down her cheek, and she quickly dashed it away. Surely Aidan wasn't as cold and dark as he had been moments ago. How could he not care about what was going on at the mill? The state of the children, the grinding poverty all around them?

Yes, perhaps she had colossally misjudged a man, who, because of his handsome face and stunning build, had blinded her to his true nature. Was she that shallow? It was a sobering thought. Cristyn was deeply disappointed and hurt. Perhaps she should rethink her feelings about Aidan—or perhaps she needed more proof. She was not one for brooding or jumping to conclusions. One way or another, she would get to the truth of it, even if she had to confront him head on.

\* \* \* \*

By the following day, Aidan had managed to tamp down the potent mix of anger and jealousy, but it simmered under the surface nonetheless. What in the hell had the doctor been trying to prove? Obviously, Middlemiss wanted to damage him in Cristyn's eyes because he had designs on her himself. Now that he had met the man and seen him up close, it was obvious he was years older; the many lines fanning out from his eyes and the threads of gray at his temples placed him at mid-forties, at least.

Far too old. But when had that stopped most men from pursuing younger women? It was predatory, and churned Aidan's insides.

Enough of this. He had to concentrate on the task at hand: playing the overbearing overseer. Once he left the raised platform, he strode along the rows of spinning machines, glaring at everyone who dared to meet his eyes.

Aidan focused on a child coughing furiously. A woman was holding her close and rubbing her back. "You there!" he thundered. "The child is sick. Too sick to work. It is yours?" he asked the woman, who held the little girl closer, as if to protect her.

"Aye, sir."

"Send her home. Immediately. I'll not have the other workers catch her disease."

"We can't afford to give up her place, we need—"

"Not my concern. Escort her home, and if you are not back here in fifteen minutes, I'll replace *you*."

The woman took the child's hand and scurried away. Those nearby were watching him, dislike plain on their faces. *Good.* "Get back to work!" he roared. Out of the corner of his eye, he spotted Mr. Meeker taking notes. He might as well continue to play the role of the hated overseer.

With hands clasped behind his back, he continued on his journey up and down the narrow aisles, barking orders, admonishing those not working fast enough. He came upon Tessie, who was trembling and would not look his way. Aidan grabbed her arm and dragged her away from the machine. He pointed to a man repairing the leather band on the machine next to it. "You! Take her place."

Tessie nearly tripped, but he pulled her along regardless. The fright on her face made his insides clench, but this had to be done. There was no way in hell he could stay the full two months and act this way. It would destroy him utterly. Damage his already shriveled soul beyond all repair and redemption.

Tessie was crying openly now. He pushed her into the small storage room and slammed the door, but not before he glanced at the spinning room floor. Most workers had kept their heads down, but some glared at him with looks of hatred.

"Please, sir, don't hit me. I'll do anything." She dropped to her knees. "I'll suck you here, now..."

He gently grasped her arms and brought her to her feet. "Why would I hit you?" he asked, his voice hushed. "Did Mr. Hanson or Master ever strike you? Tell me the truth."

"Y-y-yes."

A fresh roll of indignation moved through him at the thought of these loathsome men bullying and assaulting this young woman. Oh, they would pay. "My offer stands: three shillings for information. It must remain between us. Now, when Mr. Hanson brought women into this room, it was for sexual favors for extra coin, correct?"

She nodded as she wiped the tears from her cheeks.

"These are the kind of questions I will be asking you tonight. You know where I'm staying. Room fifteen. Be there at thirty minutes past six. As far as that lot out there is concerned, I'm the same as Hanson. If they ask, you say as such. Understand?"

"Yes, sir," she answered, sniffling.

"Do not tell me any lies."

"Aye, no lies. It's just me mother and me younger brother. I'm all they've got. I need this job; I'm the only one making any money." Her expression hardened. "And I'll do anything to protect them. Keep them fed."

"If you give me truthful information, I'll make sure your family does not starve. You will not have to debase yourself again for money, you have my word." Aidan's voice shook on the last sentence, for it was a reminder of the depths he had plummeted into in order to buy opium. The memory made his hands shake. All this drama and turmoil had him craving oblivion with the pipe, an easy escape from reality. He closed his eyes briefly as he fought the temptation. With a raspy exhale, he opened his eyes and stared at Tessie. "Do not repeat any of this, or there will be no agreement between us. Will you trust me? I don't wish to hurt you."

Tessie gave him a dubious look. "Aye, I'll try to trust you, sir. I'm that desperate for coin. I'll come to your room."

"Good. Now, how long would you be in here with Hanson?"

"A few minutes only; he was a quick 'un."

Aidan bit back a smile. "When you leave the room, wipe your mouth and look disgusted. Allow the others to draw their own conclusions."

"Aye, sir." Tessie composed herself, then flung open the door and gave a performance that would have been applauded enthusiastically if she were acting on stage. Aidan closed the door, then pulled out his watch. Close to three o'clock, and time for the next phase of his dramatic routine.

Later tonight, when he finished his report, he would write to ask his father and grandfather if there was enough to bring McRae to justice, and if not, what else would be required, for as he surmised earlier, he hadn't the stomach to keep up this charade any longer than necessary.

A nagging thought would not leave him: What would become of these poor and desperate people if there was no mill to employ them? They would have no choice but to take employment from those cruel men who had firm control of the stocking trade. He would have to spell out his concerns for his family. Make them understand. What was the point of shuttering the mill, even temporarily, if it left these villagers in worse condition than when he'd arrived?

Projecting a self-satisfied air, he opened the door, then adjusted his trousers. His gaze slid across the mill floor, and many of the workers looked away with revulsion. In the dark corner Meeker stood, his rat eyes glowing, his face twisted with what appeared to be lascivious satisfaction. With the nub of his pencil, he wrote in his notebook as he turned and disappeared into the shadows. *Miserable bastard.* Aidan made a note to ask Tessie about McRae's secretary.

Rokesmith must already be out in the courtyard. Once he found Miller, the machine supervisor, he motioned for him to keep an eye on the spinning room. The man gave him a curt nod.

Stepping outside, the acrid odor of coal smoke and horseshit slammed his nostrils. Aidan nonchalantly scanned the courtyard, taking note of McRae standing in the window, acting as if he did not see him. Rokesmith was transporting two large buckets of water across the courtyard, spilling more than he carried.

"Rokesmith, you clumsy idiot!" Aidan yelled as he ran toward him. The men unloading the cotton wagons looked up at the disturbance.

Rokesmith cringed, looking appropriately frightened. Aidan grabbed the scruff of his neck and shook him hard, causing more water to splash over the sides.

"Push me to the ground," Rokesmith whispered.

Aidan did, and the lad sprawled across the cobblestones, dropping the buckets, the contents spilling across the ground. "You brainless dolt. Look what you've done. Stand up."

Rokesmith covered his head. "Please, don't hit me, sir!" he cried loudly.

Aidan grabbed him by the collar and brought him to his feet. He made a show of pulling back his hand, as if he were about to strike. "You sniveling little bastard! I should hit you—"

"Oh, my God!"

The familiar feminine voice halted him. He turned. There stood Cristyn with Middlemiss. The shocked and hurt expression on her face tore him in two. Damn it! When they had not arrived during the luncheon break, their usual time, he assumed they were not coming. There was no choice; he had to play out this farce. Aidan strode toward the mill, dragging Rokesmith behind him.

Any goodwill or warm feelings Cristyn may have held for him had just been destroyed. The expression on her face was unmistakable: shock, anger, and abhorrence. He felt sick to his core. The thought of losing her before they even had a chance to begin hurt far worse than he had expected. How could he make her understand? He couldn't—not without telling the truth.

# Chapter 14

Cristyn stood absolutely still, watching the shocking scene with disbelief until Aidan and Carter Rokesmith disappeared into the mill. Then the overwhelming need to cry overtook her, but she blinked away the tears. Everything became surreal, for she could not process the cruelty on display. Not from Aidan. Not from the man she had held in her arms while he cried and trembled. Not the man who, through sheer courage and determination, pulled himself out of the mire of opium addiction. Not the man she had fallen...in love with. How could she have misjudged him? Because she had been blinded by love. And desire.

But Aidan Black was everything Paris had said he was.

Cold. Dark. Soulless.

And it broke her heart.

Yet a stubborn part of her rejected what she had witnessed. It made no sense whatsoever. *Aidan would not act this way.* But he had.

Paris laid his hand on her arm, but she shook it off. She did not require comfort. "I'm fine. See McRae about the vaccines. I'll wait here." Her voice was flat, devoid of emotion.

"I am sorry Mr. Black is not what you had hoped." Paris sounded sorry, but she didn't want his pity.

Cristyn paced the courtyard, tempted to follow Aidan into the mill and confront him, but it would serve no purpose—and it would jeopardize their treating the children.

Paris returned within minutes. "He said no special appointments. But we can give the inoculations during our regular visit next Monday, as long as we do not go over the allotted time." Paris scoffed. "Can you imagine the gall of the man? He invited me to his dinner party Friday night."

"Did you refuse?"

"No. I wish to see this animal in his natural habitat. And I wouldn't mind a formal dinner. He said I could bring a guest. I suppose I could ask Mrs. Trubshaw...." Paris rubbed his chin, as if mulling it over.

"I will go with you."

"You think it wise under the circumstances? Mr. Black is sure to be in attendance."

She cocked an eyebrow at Paris in reply.

"And you wish me to mind my own business," he said.

"I do. Allow me to handle the situation with Aidan."

"I will contrive to keep my nose out in the future. But do know I am here if you wish to converse about any of it."

As they made their way back to the office, Cristyn decided she could not let this pass. She *must* hear from Aidan. Allow him to explain his abhorrent behavior toward the child. Crying and sulking alone in her room was not an option. Most shifts at the mill ended at different times throughout the week. Tonight's was six o'clock. As soon as she was finished at the clinic, she would head immediately to the Dog and Gun Inn. Blast proprieties. Time to demand answers.

It was close to thirty minutes past six when she headed to the inn. Still plenty of daylight. To ward off thieves, she did not carry a reticule, but made sure a hat pin held her straw hat in place—she could readily use it as a weapon.

Following the same path she'd used before, Cristyn stealthily made her way through the rear yard. She slipped through the inn's back entrance and started when she discovered Tessie from the mill standing at the bottom of the stairs.

"Tessie, you startled me." Cristyn stared at the dirty bandage on the young woman's arm. "You never came to have the dressing changed."

"I got no money, Miss Bevan."

"It was included in the original payment." Cristyn gently peeled aside part of the tattered binding. "These stitches should be removed."

"I'll come tomorrow." Tessie pulled her arm away. "I'll have money then. I'm here to earn coin."

How exasperating. Why couldn't she understand that Cristyn would treat her for free? But then, regardless of their poverty, many of these people had their pride. She couldn't fault Tessie for that. "I'm not sure I follow. Earn coin?"

"I do what I have to do to feed me family."

Oh. *Oh*.

"I only tell you so you know I'm earning the coin, not stealing it like others," Tessie continued in a low voice. "I know what happened to you. That were wrong. You're doing good here. But when one is desperate... when all is hopeless..." She shifted from one foot to the other, plainly uncomfortable.

"When you come to the doctor's office tomorrow, we can talk more. There are rinses I can give you. It will help avoid pregnancies, and disease. Promise me you will come tomorrow." Cristyn clasped Tessie's oil-stained hand. "I worry about you."

The young woman's look softened. "I've never had anyone worry about me, outside of me mother and brother. I'll come tomorrow, I promise. Now, I've business upstairs." Tessie patted her hand, then released it.

No. Not Aidan. Surely not. Her stomach plummeted with the thought.

Tessie ascended the stairs, and after a moment Cristyn followed, far enough that she could see where Tessie was heading. She stopped in front of Aidan's room and knocked. Cristyn's heart seized, then it started to ache. Not only bullying his workers, but now buying sexual favors from a vulnerable young woman. The door opened and Tessie was pulled across the threshold. Cristyn ducked out of sight, but not before catching a glimpse of a familiar perfect profile.

Aidan.

Grabbing the banister, she descended, her legs trembling, bile clawing its way up her throat. She covered her mouth with her hand and swallowed hard. How could she have been so wrong about him? She wasn't one to shrink away; she should march up the stairs, bang on his door, and demand an explanation. But not with Tessie there. She couldn't make a scene, as much as she was tempted to do exactly that. If she were a young lady of society, she would probably run to her room and sob her heart out. Take to her bed and nurse her broken heart for days.

But Cristyn was made of sterner stuff. When the opportunity presented itself, she would demand answers from Aidan Black. Then she would tell him exactly what she thought of his shameful behavior. But her heart ached regardless. The disappointment was acute.

Once she stepped into the yard, she lifted her skirts and broke into a run.

\* \* \* \*

Aidan laid three shillings on the table. "This is yours if you tell me what goes on at the mill."

Tessie eyed the coin greedily, then met Aidan's gaze. "Like what?"

"The dark secrets."

"You want tattle? Gossip?"

Aidan crossed his arms. "It's a good place to start. Are any of the children caught up in this? Are they preyed upon for sexual purposes?"

Tessie gave him a shocked look. "I've heard nothing like that. The masters like young women, but not children. Lord, I hope not."

*There's a mercy.* "How young?"

"Seventeen, eighteen. Not children; I'm pretty sure of it."

"Take a seat, Tessie."

She glanced at the finely upholstered chair and shook her head. "Me clothes are dirty, and me hands, from the machine—"

"Please, sit."

She did, though she looked thoroughly uncomfortable. Aidan pulled up a chair next to her. "How often does this happen? Being taken into the storeroom? Or called to McRae's office? What about Meeker; is he involved?"

Tessie exhaled shakily. "I can't speak for others, but when I was sent for I were told it be for discipline, for not working fast enough. Meeker brings the women to Master. He knows what goes on. Master, well he... said I deserved to be punished. He asked if I would accept his punishment. I had to say yes. Said he don't like what Hanson likes, the sucking and such. Then he...bent me over his desk."

*Jesus.* "How often?"

"Once a month. Sometimes twice. I've seen others taken upstairs. Young, like me. Some were crying when they come back to the spinning. One called Peg disappeared real sudden three months back. I heard she be pregnant, and Master shipped her away."

*Miserable bastard.* But from what his father and grandfather had stated, there were many like McRae and Hanson, taking advantage of their positions of power.

"Others...have gone missing," she murmured.

"Who?"

"Children. Some get sick. Then they're gone. New ones come in. He buys them, like they be goods. I heard he only let the doctor look at the children because it was becoming too costly to keep replacing them. I hear he starves them. Keeps them in the cellar like rats. No one dares to say anything."

Tessie was becoming braver, more talkative. Aidan remained silent and allowed her to continue.

"The machines ain't maintained proper. They're dangerous. They break down too much. Mr. Miller, he tries to do what he can."

Aidan had noticed.

"We aren't paid enough. Not given the proper amount of breaks. They work those children too hard. Someday there is going to be an accident...."

Tessie bit her lower lip. "I've said too much. And not only to you."

"What do you mean?"

"Miss Bevan came in the back way and I..." Tessie gave him a sheepish look.

Aidan vaulted to his feet. "She was here? When?" he demanded.

"Before I came upstairs—"

Aidan ran to the door, flung it open, and dashed into the hall. Damn it all! She'd come here, probably to talk to him. Or tell him off. Or both. His blood ran cold as he rushed outside. Cristyn was long gone. Had she seen Tessie come to his door? *Fuck.* Banging his fist against the wall, he returned to his room. Tessie was still sitting in the chair—surprising, as she could have taken the money and disappeared. He slammed the door in frustration and slumped into his chair. "You spoke to her?" he asked wearily. He knew the answer.

"Aye, I did."

"And she is under the impression you came here to service me as a prossie would service her customer," he murmured, his tone flat.

"Well, aye. I wanted her to know I would be able to pay for my tending. And I couldn't tell I be giving you information. You said tell no one." She held up her filthy, bandaged arm. "See? She's a good 'un, treated me and my arm proper. Miss Bevan won't say 'aught anyway."

Aidan reached in his pocket and tossed three more shillings on the table. "Take your money and go. Make it last. If you have information, I'll pay. How old is your brother?"

"He be twelve."

"I'll see if I can get him on at the mill, as a piecer. That should be enough money for you to cease prostituting. As for anyone taken to McRae's office, you tell me immediately. But all this goes away if anyone finds out. That includes your family. They cannot know any of this. Understand?"

Tessie stood and quickly scooped the coins into her pocket. "Aye, Mr. Black, sir. I understand. Thank you, sir." She bowed and bobbed as she scurried toward the door. Without looking back, she quickly slipped out into the hall.

Aidan banged his fist on the table in frustration. He was tempted to head to the boarding house and have it out with Cristyn. Tell her everything.

But he couldn't—not yet. He was close to discovering the deeper, darker secrets of this miserable mill. Once he sat at the small writing desk in the corner, he pulled pieces of paper from the drawer. Dipping the pen in the ink, he began to write:

*Dear Riordan,*

*I have been here barely three weeks and already I have discovered I am in over my head. Perhaps I'm not up to the task after all. Beyond what lies in my report to our father and grandfather, fate, the exact apparition you have spoken of, has made an appearance in this dismal village. Cristyn Bevan is here. Of all women! I could hardly believe my eyes. She has been here for more than a month, working as nurse to the village doctor, a friend of her father. Dr. Middlemiss is a supercilious man of middle age with poor eyesight and equally poor manners. God above, I am jealous of all the time he spends with her.*

*Needless to say, seeing Cristyn has torn me from my moorings and cast me adrift. We have met, in private, and more than once. It seems we cannot stay away from each other. Each meeting jeopardizes my covert mission (as it were), for she has seen me at my worst in my role as the cruel overseer.*

*I cannot bear that she is out there thinking the worst of me. It is slicing at my guts and my hollowed heart. Might as well throw my blackened soul into the bitter sauce. You were correct, as you often are: I am falling for her.*

*By God, what a rush these feelings are. All at once exhilarating and devastating. All I want to do is protect her. From the harshness of life. The cruelty of the world. From...me.*

*She is strong, Riordan. I admire her steel and adore her compassionate nature. Her willingness to help others. Her selflessness, intelligence, and honesty. If it sounds as if I am placing her on a pedestal, perhaps I am, but I'm aware she is a woman, not a statue. So real. So...soft.*

*I sound mad. Drunk with desire.*

*Here is my dilemma: Father and Grandfather said I am to tell no one. That won't work. Not in this situation. Not with Cristyn, who demands with every steady gaze of her beautiful violet-blue eyes that I be better than I am.*

*I need your advice, my brother. I need your calm and steady wisdom, along with your innate ability to always do the right thing. You, who know me better than anyone, what do I do?*

*Should I confess all to her, including my feelings?*
*Help me, Brother.*
*Love,*
*Aidan*
*Lord Nothing*


Aidan laid his pen aside. Releasing the stopper on his hidden emotions was not something he did often, but since his recovery, everything had changed. No wonder he felt strange in his own skin. He *was* a different man. In the dark days, he would call for a bottle of scotch or gin and drink away his troubles. If that didn't work, his demons would urge him to delve deeper. Women. Opium. Oblivion.

With a shaky exhale, Aidan stood and slipped on his coat. He would head downstairs to the tavern room. Order a meat pie. No alcohol. Tomorrow he would find an excuse to check on Nebula, then have Rokesmith deliver his letter and the report to Samuel, who would then ride with all haste to Wollstonecraft Hall. A reply would take at least three days.

While he waited, he would question Rokesmith about these missing children, for Aidan had the distinct feeling not much got past the lad.

As for Cristyn? He wouldn't see her until he decided if he would tell her the truth—all of the truth, no matter how wretched. His past, his downfall, his real name, and why he was here. But most of all, he would humble himself before her. Ask her forgiveness for not being truthful.

And tell her he was falling in love with her.

# Chapter 15

Friday arrived, and Aidan was not keen to attend a dinner with McRae and men of a similar disposition. But he had to keep up appearances and act like-minded with these greedy, ambitious men.

Before attending the dinner, he stopped to speak to Rokesmith, as he'd not had a chance since their theatrical performance in the courtyard. He might as well see the lad since he was on the property. Aidan handed him the bag filled with biscuits and rolls.

"Look at you," Rokesmith snorted. "A toff, to be sure, in your fancy coat."

"I am to attend a dinner. Up there." He pointed toward the upper floor residence of McRae's. "But three days past, I had information come my way concerning missing sick children and pregnant young women. You're holding back. You know more than you have revealed," Aidan accused.

Rokesmith gave him a dismissive shrug. "We need to build the trust, remember? And if I'm keeping quiet, it's to protect them." He pointed to the children.

"You *will* be telling me. For I have a distinct feeling this will come to a head sooner than I had first believed."

Rokesmith frowned. "I tossed the meat pies. What are you doing about that?" Changing the subject, shrewd of the boy. Obviously, Aidan would not be given any information tonight.

"What do you suggest? Confronting the pieman? Though I am tempted to pound him into a bloody pulp, he would run to McRae quicker than I can blink. For now, continue to test them; if they are inedible, toss them. I will try to bring different food, as well as the biscuits and rolls." Aidan met the lad's intense gaze. "Sooner or later, we will have to trust each other."

"Maybe."

Lottie skipped up and stopped in front of him. "Hello, sir." She gave him a shy smile.

Seeing this lovely child immersed in this horrific situation made his heart ache. Without thinking, he crouched down to her level. "Hello, sweet girl." He grabbed the bag from Rokesmith, reached in, and brought out two biscuits. "For you, a special treat. It will be our secret."

Her eyes lit up, and all at once, he wished he could gift her with more than biscuits. A better future. A decent life. The girl threw her arms around his neck and hugged him tightly.

"Here, Lottie. You'll get Mr. Black's coat all dirty," Rokesmith scolded.

A lump formed in Aidan's throat. The child was aching for affection, and it tore him in two. He hugged her back. "It's all right," he murmured.

Lottie kissed his cheek and whispered in his ear. "Thank you, sir."

Thanks for what? The biscuits? The hug? He should be thanking *her*, for allowing him to see what the world was truly like beyond the borders of Wollstonecraft Hall—and beyond the borders of his own selfishness. When it came down to it, all people wanted was a little love in their lives. Some humanity. A warm bed and a full stomach. It shouldn't be too much to ask for.

Lottie released him, bit into the biscuit, and skipped away. Aidan stood, handed the bag back to Rokesmith, and with a nod headed toward the residence. Time to prepare for his performance. He could not be distracted by adorable orphans—not tonight, at any rate.

In his three weeks here, he had not laid eyes on McRae's wife or son. Were they prisoners in the tower? The entrance to the residence was located in the rear, and, he'd heard, usually locked. But as Aidan rounded the corner, a middle-aged man in fancy livery stood in the doorway. As a guard, no doubt. "Mr. Black?"

"Yes."

The man checked the list. "Welcome, sir. Directly up the stairs."

Gaslight wall sconces illuminated his way. McRae had modern lighting in his home, but not in the mill. *Typical.* As Aidan stepped into the upper hallway, he had a look about. Wood walls with fancy trimming. Directly ahead were open, frosted-glass French doors. When he stepped across the doorsill, it was as if he had entered one of the fancier rooms at Wollstonecraft Hall, complete with chandeliers and gold silk wallpapers—though not as large, of course.

Already a group of men were deep in conversation, clasping glasses of some sort of punch. Off in the corner were three women sitting on chairs, whispering furiously. He did a quick head count. Eight people so far, excluding the host and hostess, the men outnumbering the ladies.

Standing near the door was McRae. Next to him was a rather beautiful woman with a vacant stare. *Must be the wife.* After handing his long coat to one of the footmen, Aidan stood before the couple.

"My dear, this is Aidan Black, of whom you have heard me speak. My wife, Portia McRae, the daughter of Sir Michael Linton, baronet."

Aidan lifted the gloved hand of Mrs. McRae and bent over it, giving it an air kiss. "My distinct pleasure." Leave it to McRae to brag of his wife's connections.

She murmured something indistinguishable. Aidan stood straight and gave her an assessing gaze. Good God, was she drugged? For he was well aware of the dazed and fogged expression of those under the influence. It could be laudanum, the drug of choice for middle and upper class women.

"I wish to speak to you, Aidan, as soon as I am done greeting my guests." McRae had never called him by his first name before. "Of course."

"Help yourself to punch and mingle."

He moved to the sideboard and stared at the pink beverage in the silver bowl. Filling his glass half full, with no intention of drinking it, he stood to the side, his back against the wall, assessing the room.

Aidan supposed these other men owned businesses in the village—some were probably those greedy devils who ran the stocking industry. As his gaze slid across the room, Dr. Middlemiss strode in with Cristyn on his arm.

The sound of conversation soon disappeared, and a loud buzzing replaced it. It took all of Aidan's sparse self-control to keep from staggering at the sight of her, for it had the force of a blow to the chest. Cristyn looked exquisite, wearing a lavender gown of simple elegance, with white lace across her décolletage, giving one and all a glimpse of her magnificent cleavage. The color, of course, enhanced her beautiful eyes, alabaster skin, and glossy black hair.

Out of the corner of his eye, he could see McRae giving her a bold inspection when they were introduced by Middlemiss. Aidan burned with possessiveness. How dare that cretin even look at Cristyn? But his focus remained on her. She hadn't looked his way. Instead, she was being escorted to the punchbowl. *Look my way. Just once.*

"Do you know that luscious creature?"

Aidan had been caught up in drinking in Cristyn's stunning appearance, and as a result he had not seen McRae sidle up next to him. Thankfully the buzzing in his head had quieted. In an indifferent tone, he replied, "His nurse, Miss Cristyn Bevan. But I am sure you have already been introduced." He paused, raised the cup to his lips, the liquid barely touching them. The punch was nauseatingly sweet. "She is the lady who wandered into the spinning room a few weeks past."

"The one you put the run to? My God, if I had known she was such a beauty, I would have allowed her to attend the meeting with the doctor. She would have been a lovely distraction while Middlemiss droned on about treating the brats." McRae leaned in and whispered, "Imagine her spread over the desk, skirts thrown over her head." He chuckled lasciviously.

Aidan gripped his glass so tight it nearly shattered. It would be his distinct pleasure to see to this man's complete ruin. His blood boiled at a dangerous, high heat, an intoxicating combination of searing desire for Cristyn and intense hatred for McRae. Aidan thought it best not to reply to the disgusting remark. But, oh, how McRae would answer for his misogynistic, disrespectful statement. "You wished to speak to me?"

"Ah, yes. I must say, when you first arrived here at the mill, I was suspicious. Regardless of your recommendation from my acquaintance, Viscount Kerridge, I found it all rather strange. I mean, Hanson and his family vanished in the night. Then I received a curt note claiming he would not be returning to his position. Blasted ingrate. After all I've done for him."

"Hmm." Aidan had nothing to add, for he couldn't care less.

"I sent Meeker along to Hanson's residence this afternoon. The place had been emptied out. Well, good riddance." McRae snorted. "Come to my office tomorrow at three. I wish to discuss the possibility of making your temporary position a permanent one. You've proven your worth."

Aidan gave McRae a sidelong glance. "In what way, sir?"

"Meeker reports that you are a man after my own heart. Plus, I saw you disciplining one of the older urchins in the courtyard. Well done. They all have to be kept in line, regardless of age or gender."

"I am not sure I wish to make this permanent, as I have other commitments," Aidan murmured.

"Do you? We've tried to check your background. There wasn't much to find. You will need to fill in the blanks if you do decide to stay. But we will discuss it more tomorrow. I can make it worth your while. Come, and I will introduce you to the others. All upstanding men of business."

Hardly. But Aidan went through the motions, shaking hands, acutely aware of Cristyn in the room. When he glanced her way, she was not looking at him. But judging by the stiff set of her delicate shoulders, she was as aware of him as he was of her.

He waited patiently for his chance. Middlemiss barely left her side, damn him. But when the grocer pulled him away, Aidan made his excuses to the other men, placed his cup on the table, and headed toward her. The fresh scent of violets filled his nostrils. He stood in front of her and held out his hand. "Good evening." She looked away. "Take the hand, Cristyn, people are watching."

With a huff, she slipped her hand in his. Aidan gripped it; although he was not wearing any gloves and she was, a sizzling heat blazed between them. Slowly, he released her hand, his fingertips trailing across her palm, causing his heart to thump madly. "We need to talk."

"There is nothing to say. You've made your true self known to me. How deluded I've been all these months." Her beautiful eyes flared angrily.

"Am I deluded?"

"I know you were in the inn a few nights ago. You'd come to talk to me, hadn't you? Tessie informed me of your presence. Not everything is as it seems, Cristyn."

Cristyn opened her mouth to retort when Middlemiss appeared at her side. Blast the man for his miserable timing! The doctor clasped her elbow as if staking his claim. "Mr. Black, good evening. They are calling us to the dining room. Cristyn, allow me to escort you." She was swept away from him, and Aidan clenched his fists. When in the hell would he be able to speak to her again? He had to try. Hopefully, tomorrow, there would be a response from his brother. He needed his advice more than ever.

* * * *

What did Cristyn expect? That when she saw Aidan again she would feel completely apathetic? No, for one did not turn off the spigot of emotions immediately. At least, she couldn't. Not with him standing before her, resplendent in his black coat and silver cravat. He was by far the most handsome man at this event, and he drew the women's eyes—except Mrs. McRae, who did not appear to be aware of what was going on around her.

They entered the dining area—not overly large, but enough space to accommodate twelve people at the table. Cristyn was struck at the opulence of a multi-storied flat situated above a cotton mill. The table held lit silver candelabras, fine white-and-silver china, and crystal goblets of various sizes with matching decanters. A fruit centerpiece of sliced pineapple, grapes, and berries finished the elegantly set table. Two men dressed in fine livery and two maids in starched white uniforms commenced with serving the multicourse meal.

Cristyn was seated across from Paris, with Aidan farther along the table, one chair away from McRae. A watery bowl of broth was placed before her. All this money spent on fancy dishes and rich meals, while people in the village fought over a crust of bread. She suddenly wished she had not asked to attend this miserable banquet. Paris had warned her to keep her decided opinions about social injustice to herself, in order not to jeopardize their treating the children. Small talk broke out at the table during the soup course, which carried over into the salad, then the fish.

"Miss Bevan, have you recovered from your ordeal?"

The table grew silent; all eyes were on her. The woman asking the question was a stocking magnate's wife. Blast her for bringing up the robbery! "What ordeal do you speak of, Mrs. Tramble?"

"My word, how many have you experienced since arriving in Earl Shilton?" Polite laughter scattered between the guests.

"I've had a few, for witnessing such widespread and grinding poverty certainly is harrowing. Or do you speak of my reticule being stolen?"

Paris shot her a warning look, and Cristyn took it under advisement. But the woman's tone grated. The condescending expression aggravated her as well.

"The thievery, of course," Mrs. Tramble said as she shoved a piece of shrimp into her mouth.

"I was pushed to the ground. The young lad managed to get away with a lace handkerchief and a few hairpins—hardly worth the bother. I was not injured," Cristyn replied.

"But then, someone came to your rescue." Mrs. Tramble turned her gaze to Aidan. "How gallant you are, Mr. Black. What a discovery."

Murmuring broke out around the table.

"Gallant?" Aidan sniffed haughtily. "Hardly. I merely assisted the young lady to her feet."

"You offered to chase the young rogue, Mr. Black. That is a gallant gesture to me," Cristyn replied, giving him a cool but dismissive smile.

Aidan met her gaze. His sensual mouth was twisted in a cynical smile, his eyes alight with blue fire. "And you bade me not to. I acquiesced to the lady's wishes."

"Why ever not?" Mr. Tramble bellowed. "The thief should have been brought to justice. We have a village constable, and an adequate jail."

Cristyn cut into her herbed sole. "The lad was dressed in rags, no doubt starving. If my meager possessions can fetch him a few pennies for food, I'll not pursue it."

Mr. McRae cleared his throat, then frowned. "You do the thief no favors by allowing this crime to fall to the wayside. It will only embolden him to further illegal acts. I would suggest, Miss Bevan, you report this crime with all haste."

Murmurs of assent rounded the table, a few of the men adding, "Quite right."

Paris shot her another look of caution. How tempted she was to call out these reprehensible men on their lack of compassion for their fellow man. "Perhaps if there was a charitable organization in the village, the destitute would not have to resort to illegal acts to buy bread. I'm surprised to find the church does not provide something as basic as a bowl of soup for those in need."

The silence in the room was awkward. Boldly, she glanced about the table. A mixture of disdain and anger. Paris shook his head. Aidan, however, gave her such a heated, admiring look her insides quivered.

"We have adequate poor laws. Anyone in need can go to the Union Workhouse in nearby Hinckley," Mr. McRae replied, his tone frosty. He then turned to the man next to him. "Now, as to the price of cotton..."

Cristyn's cheeks flushed in annoyance as she turned her attention to her meal. No doubt Paris would admonish her in his gentle tone later. She had said far too much, and may have damaged their plan for caring for the mill children.

Mercifully, eventually, the meal came to an end, and as was standard for such formal meals, the ladies rose and headed to the parlor for tea while the men stayed in the dining room to partake of brandy and cigars. As she entered the hall, Cristyn found herself swept into a nearby alcove—and into Aidan's embrace.

"Are you mad?" she whispered fiercely.

"Mad for you," he replied, giving her another heated look. "We have only a few minutes. I want us to meet. Tonight. We must talk. As I said, not all is as it seems. Allow me to explain."

She arched an eyebrow. "Explain what, exactly? How you bullied a child? How you are taking advantage of a poor young woman in your employ?"

He grasped the sides of her head, staring at her with such an intense gaze it made goose bumps raise on her flesh. "You truly believe this of me?"

"I believe the evidence of my own eyes," she retorted.

"Even a condemned man is given a fair trial." Aidan nuzzled her neck. Then he stepped away from her, his chest rising and falling. "Tonight, Cristyn."

He turned and headed in the direction of the dining room, leaving her dizzy. She would not be slinking out in the dark of night to go to his room—that must end. But deep down, she wanted to hear what he had to say. Could there be an explanation? A small part of her believed that there must be. For five months they were in daily contact; they'd gotten to know each other. Despite his dismissal that they were friends, she had *liked* him, regardless of his mistakes and his past—whatever it was. Perhaps they *should* talk.

A few stolen moments in his arms and already she yearned for more. Sighing, Cristyn walked toward the parlor.

\* \* \* \*

When the evening concluded at ten o'clock, Aidan tried to speak to Cristyn once more, but the doctor kept her well away from him. Glancing at the night sky as he headed to the inn, he made note of the heavy gray clouds that had all but engulfed the full moon.

Upon entering the inn, Mr. Atwood called to him. "A young man delivered this for you an hour past." The innkeeper passed him a large brown envelope. Judging by the weight, there were a couple of letters inside. Only the name "Aidan Black" was written on the front of it. He recognized Riordan's handwriting. Samuel had been by. The young man must have ridden all day and part of the night.

"Thank you, Mr. Atwood."

"I lit the fire in your room, sir, as there is rain coming tonight, I'll wager. And it is a cool evening. Thought it would take the chill off. Would you like a brandy or whiskey?"

Hell, it was tempting, for it would tamp down his frustrations. Aidan slid a couple of shillings across the counter. "No, thank you. For your trouble, Mr. Atwood."

Once in his room, he shrugged out of his coat and waistcoat, tore off his cravat, then rolled up his sleeves. Getting comfortable in front of the fire, Aidan ripped open the envelope, and two letters tumbled out. One was from his father. He read it first.

*Dear Aidan,*

*I am aghast at what you have reported, but sadly not entirely shocked. I agree with your assessment that this particular operation will not take the full two months. I also understand your concern regarding the fates of the workers and the village itself should the mill be closed because of the violations of various mill and factory acts.*

*The sad fact is, the mill may not close because of multiple violations. There would be legal chastisement, and perhaps fines, but ultimately*

*the law believes the owner is the captain of the ship, and he is perfectly
within his rights to mete out punishment.*

*This is what we are trying to change. There should be consequences,
and better inspections and laws. Children should not be used as slave
labor. I could go on, and I understand your dissatisfaction. Though we
may not be able to bring down this particular owner, we can certainly
make his life a living misery by using the laws already in place.*

*I have reached out to the queen's representative in Earl Shilton,
Mr. Muggeridge, and made him aware of the situation. He informed
me the factory system will be coming to Earl Shilton with regard to
the making of stockings, and will also affect the cotton mill as well.
No more working in the home for pauper wages. No more violations
of regulations at the mill. I have his assurances that Morris Mill will
be rigorously monitored. The wheels are in motion to make changes
for the better.*

*As for the children you spoke of, I am appalled at the conditions.
Allow me to inquire with regards to a reputable orphanage or school
where they can receive an education, proper meals, and training for
jobs in the future. But be aware: If we remove these children, McRae
can easily replace them with others.*

*But one thing at a time. We are moving forward. Be proud of your
achievements, for I am proud of you, Aidan.*

*All my love and admiration,*

*Papa*

*Postscript: July 29th will soon be here. If I do not see you before then,
happy birthday. We will celebrate when you return home.*


Aidan exhaled. Not exactly the news he had hoped to hear. But if the
factory system came to Earl Shilton, it could change everything. No longer
could Morris Mill operate in feudal obscurity.

Yes, it was a start, and a good one on which to build further reforms
and improvements.

The closing sentences touched Aidan. If anything positive came out of
his decline, it was the renewed love and respect between him and his father.

Setting the letter aside, he opened Riordan's next.

*Dear Aidan,*

*Do not make the same mistake I did. If you love Cristyn, reveal all.
No more lies, no matter how noble the intent behind them. I nearly lost*

*Sabrina because I was not honest with her about my background—I should have told her the moment I realized I was in love with her.*

*Love is exhilarating. And exhilaration is what you are feeling, Aidan, for you described it perfectly. But love can also make you feel adrift, as you stated.*

*From what Father told me of your situation in Earl Shilton, you have handled it well. He showed me his letter, and I know you will find it frustrating that there is only so much you are able to do. I found the same with my teaching. But whatever small and incremental changes you do construct, know you are making someone's life better. Outside of falling in love, I know of no other elation. Take pride in your achievements.*

*Take your Cristyn in your arms. Tell her ALL. Do not hold back, good or bad.*

*When you have the support and love of the woman you adore, you can conquer anything.*

*Love,*

*Riordan*

*Postscript: You are NOT Lord Nothing. Not to me. Not ever.*

Aidan sat perfectly still, taking in all he had read from his brother and father. He had made one decision: He would wrap up this enterprise immediately. He wanted to be there for Riordan when Sabrina gave birth, to support his brother and the entire family. Because even though none of the men had spoken their concerns aloud, the curse still lingered, reminding them of all they had lost. And could lose.

Riordan's advice echoed over and over in Aidan's head. *Tell her all.* He shot to his feet and ran from his room, slamming the door behind him. Sprinting down the stairs and exiting the yard, he walked briskly toward Church Street. A fat raindrop splashed on his forehead, then another. By the time he turned onto High Street, the skies had opened up.

He stood in front of the multistory brick home where Cristyn resided. He was soaked through, his white shirt all but transparent. What floor was she on, second or third? Did her room face the street, or the alley in the rear? This was utter madness. The ground floor lay in darkness. The widow must have retired. What was the time, eleven? Or later? No lights could be seen from the front of the house, so Aidan jogged to the alley.

There was an oak tree he could climb if he were feeling adventurous, but he grabbed a handful of pebbles. One light was visible on the second floor. He would have to make a hasty escape if it turned out to be the widow.

He tossed the stone, and it bounced off the windowpane. He waited, then threw another. At last, the window opened and Cristyn peered out.

Even through the rain and clouds, the moon managed to cast enough light for them to see each other—he hoped.

"Aidan?" she whispered.

"Yes, let me in."

*All the way into your heart.*

# Chapter 16

Aidan, here? His shirt was plastered to his finely chiseled torso, showing every taut muscle. Blinking away the rain, he brushed his wet hair from his face and gazed up at her. His expression was beseeching. And he was shivering.

She stuck her hand out, and the cold rain stung her skin. He would catch his death. What if he wasn't recovered enough to fight off a chill? "I'll stand here all night. Let me in, please." He didn't whisper.

Cristyn placed a finger to her lips to indicate he should be quiet. She considered slamming the window shut and heading to bed, but she knew that he was stubborn enough to stand there all night. Besides, her nursing instincts would not allow him to succumb to a possible fever. Exasperated, she pointed downward, drawing his attention to the back door. Aidan nodded.

Thankfully, Mrs. Trubshaw was often asleep before half past nine; with any luck she would be deep in dreamland. Cristyn slipped into her wrapper and, as quietly as possible, descended the stairs. Turning the key, she opened the door, and Aidan slipped in, water dripping from every part of him.

"Up the stairs," she whispered fiercely. Cristyn pulled off her wrapper and followed behind him, sopping up the trail of water left in his wake. She pointed to her room and he stepped inside.

His teeth were chattering. Locking her door, she turned to face him. Beads of raindrops clung to his long lashes. Her gaze followed an errant trail of water down his throat to the V of his sodden shirt. It drew attention once again to his sculpted chest and leanly muscled arms. Cristyn motioned to the chair before the small fireplace. "Take off your clothes." She tore her blanket from her bed and tossed it to him. "Wrap yourself in this. You're wearing smalls?"

Aidan nodded.

"Keep them on." She gathered up the wet clothes and arranged them in front of the fire.

"I like it when you look after me. It's as if you are concerned for my welfare." Aidan gave her a sensual smile, and her traitorous body responded, her heart thumping madly.

"I am a nurse, after all. Why are you here?" she asked, struggling to keep her voice even.

With the wool blanket resting on his shoulders, he rubbed his hands in front of the crackling flames in the hearth. "As I said, we have to talk. Allow me to explain. You had better sit down for this."

"Talk lower. Mrs. Trubshaw must not find you here." Blowing out a huff of air, she sat on the corner of her bed, facing him. "Say your piece, then you must go."

Aidan turned the chair to face her, then sat upon it. "My father is a Member of Parliament for the district of Kent. He is working with select members from the House of Lords on a new version of the Factory Act. I thought to do something meaningful—call it redemption, but I put myself forward to gather information my father can use to further his cause. I suggested a clandestine operation in a mill with a terrible reputation. It was decided that Morris Mill would serve." He stared at her intently. "Do you grasp what I'm saying?"

Cristyn bristled. "I am perfectly capable of following a conversation." *Keep calm.* "Redemption for what?" she murmured.

"Allow me to finish explaining this portion of my tale. As far as McRae is concerned, I'm his man. It's why you witnessed me shaking Rokesmith. It was a performance, for the master standing above, in the window, in order to prove that I am like him. It's why Tessie came to my room—I am paying her for information. Nothing else. I swear it."

This sounded like a plot from a convoluted fiction novel. Yet it held kernels of truth. Relief poured through her. "Not for sex?"

"No. My God, Cristyn. You truly believe I would take advantage of a desperate young woman? Beat on a defenseless child?"

"What was I to think? The performance in the courtyard was quite convincing. And Tessie told me that she earned extra coin by prostituting herself. Add that to your cold words at Mrs. Trubshaw's and it became all the more compelling." Actually, Tessie hadn't used that exact phrasing, Cristyn had merely assumed. Misjudgments all around. "Then I see Tessie knock at your door? What conclusion was I to draw?" Her voice rose to a shrill, and she shook her head. "Forgive me," she whispered. "I find this difficult to take in."

"Say you believe me. I am not a monster. At least, not anymore."

Cristyn stared into his sad but beautiful blue eyes. There were no lies in his earnest expression, no shield for once. "I believe you." A small part of her had believed he was better than what she'd observed, and it was a relief to find she had not been completely wrong.

"I don't know what I would have done if you rejected my explanation." He met her gaze. "I'm trying to convince Rokesmith to trust me. There is much he is hiding. I have been taking food to him and the children."

Cristyn chuckled. "Paris and I have been bringing food during our exams."

"Rokesmith is a sly devil, playing both ends at once. Good for him. The accent he puts on is entirely false. The boy is playing a role the same as I. My true name is Aidan Wollstonecraft. Black is my mother's maiden name; my brother and I use it on occasion."

"Wollstonecraft? Like the author?"

He nodded. "A distant cousin removed, I'm not sure how many times."

"You have a brother? You've never said."

"A twin, though not identical. There is much I haven't said."

"You could have told me what you were up to at the mill. I would have kept your confidence."

"I trust you, but I had promised I would not reveal my real name or purpose to anyone. That compact no longer matters, considering our situation."

"And what is our situation?" Cristyn whispered, her heart beating faster.

"Before I tell you more about my life, my past, and the wreckage that comes with it, it's more important that I reveal my feelings." He gave her a heated look. "You move me. You touch my damaged heart, and it terrifies me how much I feel."

He stood and walked toward her. Oh, but he was magnificently masculine. He was much more robust than he had been at the sanatorium. His emotionally spoken words still echoed in her heart. Gently grasping her arms, he brought her to her feet to stand before him. Wearing only a cotton shift, her body reacted immediately to his nearness. His woodsy scent mixed with the odor of fresh rain. A lock of damp hair fell forward across his forehead, and she could not stop herself from tenderly moving it away. Her fingers lingered, caressing his cool cheek.

Aidan moaned, then grasped her fingers, brought them to his lips, and kissed them. "I am falling for you, Cristyn Bevan. I'm weary from fighting it. Running from it. You see, I suffered under the belief I was not worthy. Perhaps I still believe that, for when I tell you everything, you will turn from me in abhorrence. I couldn't bear your rejection. It is why I left the clinic in such haste. The coward's way. But then, I've always been a coward. Afraid to live, to take responsibility. Afraid to...love."

Her insides melted. "Love?"

"I thought at first the unknown emotions were borne from my deep and abiding gratitude for all you have done for me. I've never experienced them before. I am still trying to work out what it all means." He cupped her cheeks, staring into her eyes. "You said you had fallen for me. Does it still hold true, despite my erratic behavior?"

Cristyn nodded, then stood on the tip of her bare toes and kissed him. Aidan slipped his arm about her waist and brought her in tight against him. With little clothing between them, she could feel everything. A groan that bordered on a growl slipped from Aidan as he took the kiss deeper, hungrily exploring every part of her mouth. As his lips trailed to her neck, he whispered huskily, "Touch me."

*Oh.* Dare she? Her hand slipped below the waist of his smallclothes. There was no mistaking the hardness that met the brush of her fingers. Cristyn gripped him and squeezed, causing another moan to reverberate though him.

"Yes, damn it all," Aidan rasped. He laid his hand on top of hers, rubbing them across his erection. He then guided her hand to tunnel under his waistband until she made contact with his arousal. The feel of it burned, causing her breath to hitch in her throat. She was curious. And excited. Not the least bit afraid. "Stroke me," Aidan urged. He showed her how.

Aidan clasped her breast, his thumb brushing across her pebbled nipple. "So beautiful—"

A sharp rap at the door broke them apart.

"Miss Bevan! Open this door at once! Who's in there with you?"

"Quick, get dressed!" Cristyn whispered fiercely. Mrs. Trubshaw must have the ears of a hawk. Aidan scrambled to collect his clothes and boots from the fireplace. Hastily dressing, Cristyn flung open her window. "Out on the roof, you can climb down the oak tree."

The pounding became louder. "Open up or I will fetch my master key!"

"Coming, Mrs. Trubshaw. You've woken me out of a dead sleep. Give me a moment!" Cristyn cried as she pushed a half-dressed Aidan toward the window. He had on his trousers and boots, clasping his shirt in his fist. It would have to do.

Before he climbed out, he gave her a swift kiss. "Come to my room at seven tomorrow night."

As soon as he disappeared through the window, she closed it partway and drew the curtains. Taking the blanket Aidan had discarded, she placed it about her shoulders. "I'm coming!"

Cristyn no sooner opened the door when the widow pushed past her, looking about the room. "I heard a man's voice. Do not deny it. Where is he?" She marched to the window and threw it open, and a blast of cold rain hit Mrs. Trubshaw square in the face. Sputtering, she immediately closed it. "Miss Bevan, I'm tolerant of many things, but a man in your room at night is beyond the pale." The widow sounded more disappointed than angry, and Cristyn felt a twang of guilt—especially for the lie she was about to tell.

"I fell asleep in the chair. I must have been dreaming, speaking out loud." Cristyn yawned and rubbed her eyes for good measure.

The landlady frowned. "If I come across as brusque and nosy, it is because I am concerned for you. You arrived here without a proper guardian, and I felt it my duty to take on the role. I understand your father wished for Dr. Middlemiss to act as such, but men, in my opinion, are inadequate for such a delicate task." Mrs. Trubshaw's look softened. "I speak from experience. Regardless of your social standing, a young, unmarried woman's reputation is everything. Do not make the mistake I made. Long ago, I was caught in a compromising position with a man far above me in station. I was in love, but he turned from me. I'm thankful that Mr. Trubshaw stepped forward to save me from complete disgrace. Do not allow it to happen it you," she ended on a fierce whisper.

No doubt Mrs. Trubshaw's disgrace came at a time when society manners mattered more than anything. They were still important, but not to the extent they had been thirty years past." I do thank you for your ongoing concern. But as I said, I was dreaming."

The widow cocked a dubious eyebrow. "Well, if you say that is what I heard. But know this: I have rules for any boarders. No visitors in your room, or I will have no alternative but to turn you out."

"I will certainly heed your warning, on all counts." Once Mrs. Trubshaw departed and Cristyn had closed and locked the door, she exhaled. First Paris with his sad tale, now her widowed landlady. But would she heed the warnings? She gazed at her hand. It still burned where she had stroked him. How bold of her. Aidan's husky plea for her to touch him had nearly made her knees buckle.

The attraction between them roiled at full heat, enough to scorch them both. If they kept meeting in secret, Cristyn understood where it would lead. Though she appreciated Mrs. Trubshaw's well-meaning admonition, her virginity was her business. When to give it up, and to whom, was always a choice she was determined to make, inside of marriage or out of it.

She yearned for it to be Aidan. But first, she must hear the rest of what he had to say. What possible debris in his past had compelled him to take on such a mission? Wollstonecraft: such an odd and rare name. If only Mrs. Trubshaw had not interrupted them.

Improper or not, she would go to his room tomorrow night. Not only to allow him to continue his narrative, but for his overwhelming kisses. Cristyn yearned to explore his hard, muscled body. To see that fiery look in his eyes once again.

The following day, a steady stream of patients filed in to the medical clinic. When Tessie entered the office around noon, Cristyn stepped forward and escorted her behind the curtain. Peeling back the dressing, Cristyn tried not to frown at the condition of the wound, nor would she admonish the young woman. There was swollen skin around the stitches, showing a slight infection. With quick efficiency, Cristyn bathed the wound in antiseptic, snipped away the threads, then redressed it with a smaller plaster.

"I share an acquaintance with Mr. Black," Cristyn murmured. "He tells me you went to his room for a specific purpose."

Tessie sighed. "Aye."

"You can trust me, Tessie, and, more importantly, you can trust Mr. Black. Why did you go to his room?"

"Not what you think," she replied, her voice low. "He wants to know about the mill. Hell's bells, he told me to say 'aught."

"I will keep your secret." Cristyn now trusted Aidan fully, but she was silently relieved to hear confirmation of the truth. "Tell him everything, Tessie. He will protect you."

Tessie bit her lower lip and nodded. "Aye, miss."

In a louder voice, Cristyn said, "Keep this clean. There is a bit of infection, but if you wash the scar twice a day, and brew this tea"—Cristyn thrust a packet of willow bark tea leaves into Tessie's hand—"it should heal properly."

"Thank you, Miss Bevan."

Cristyn gave her a smile of support. Once Tessie departed, Paris pulled aside the curtain.

"We have a brief reprieve. Mrs. Wilson, one of my patients, delivered a plate of raisin scones. Come, have one, along with a cup of tea. It's already brewing."

She followed Paris into the outer office and sat before his desk. Once he served the tea and scones, they ate and sipped quietly.

"I am not quite sure how to broach this subject; Mrs. Trubshaw claims there was a man in your room last night." He held up his hand to stop her retort. "I know this is none of my business. If anyone knows of surreptitious rendezvous, it is I. But Mrs. Trubshaw has a legitimate concern. It's her house." He peered at her over the rim of his mug. "Was it Aidan Black?"

Cristyn nodded. "Yes. He stood outside my window in the pouring rain. He wouldn't leave; he would have caught a chill, or worse." Paris's mouth quirked. "And yes, I wanted to speak to him. Be in his presence. Kiss him. That is all that happened. He also started to tell me what I have wanted to know since I first met him in January."

"What is that?"

"The story of his past, his family. What brought him to my father's clinic. Why he's in Earl Shilton. Unfortunately, Mrs. Trubshaw interrupted our conversation. He asked me to come to his room tonight."

Paris shifted in his chair. "You are attracted to each other. It was obvious at McRae's dinner party. If I noticed the intense yearning, I'm sure others did as well. Let me impart a little sage advice: No matter how careful you are, how well you plan your tryst, there is always a chance of discovery."

"I grant you we're playing a dangerous game. But I'm not a young lady of society. I don't have to protect my reputation as if it were a life-or-death prospect."

"Perhaps not. All I am saying is it should not be given up easily, for any young woman, regardless of standing." Paris broke off a small piece of raisin scone, chewed, and swallowed. "It is hardly fair, is it? Young men are expected to indulge in affairs, but young ladies are not. If you don't mind me asking, what is Aidan's name?"

She considered Paris a friend, but how deep did the trust go? Aidan hadn't sworn her to secrecy as such. Perhaps Paris had heard of the name. "I cannot reveal why he is using a different name, the few details I'm aware of have convinced me it is best not to say anything until I learn more." She paused. Curiosity had got the better of her. Paris was the son of a viscount. He would know of most wealthy families in England. "I must have your word, Paris; you will repeat this to no one."

"Absolutely."

"His last name is Wollstonecraft." Cristyn watched Paris closely for any sort of reaction. His eyes widened briefly, but then his features settled into complete neutrality. "Do you know of the family?"

"Beyond the author of *Frankenstein,* Mary Wollstonecraft Shelley, and her mother, Mary, the advocate of women's rights? Not really. Are they landed gentry? Tradesmen?"

"I'm not sure." Cristyn sipped her tea. Paris had reacted to the name. Why? Was it because of the author? Or was there more? "You said you knew all about secret assignations. How? The man you spoke of?"

Paris's eyes reflected a deep sadness. "Not only was our affair against the law, but it was doomed from the start. You see, heirs to the aristocracy are strange creatures. They are born, weaned, and raised on a steady diet of 'honor and duty.' When it comes down to it, no matter the utterances and assurances of love and devotion, they will ultimately choose duty and family."

Paris sighed. "His father found us embracing in the library. There was no dramatic scene, no screaming or cursing. The earl merely said he understood his son's sexual curiosity, but the choice must be made. My lover said, 'Well, of course I choose duty. Always.' I was hastily escorted from the premises, told not to contact the heir again. He wouldn't even look at me as I was all but dragged from the room. Foolish me, I pleaded, 'Do not reject our love,' but he did. Without blinking an eye."

"No wonder your heart was broken," Cristyn whispered.

"Smashed, really. But enough about me. Why not meet Aidan Wollstonecraft here, at the clinic, after hours? If discovered, you have a ready excuse with discussing the children at the mill. Meeting in each other's rooms is too risky. Besides, I will be right upstairs if you need me."

Paris had a point, especially in light of Mrs. Trubshaw almost catching them. "How would I get word to him?"

"Leave it to me. He's at the inn, correct? I will arrange a meeting for you tomorrow night. For I imagine you both need to discuss many subjects. That is, if you wish. It is only a suggestion."

Caution would be prudent. "Yes, tell him we will meet here, tomorrow night."

\* \* \* \*

Aidan couldn't wait for the day to end; his body thrummed with the anticipation of seeing Cristyn again. He couldn't wait to hold her in his arms. Kiss her. Touch her. Have *her* touch *him*. God, it still felt as if she were gripping his cock. His bold and beautiful angel.

During his meeting with McRae, he'd found it hard to focus on what the loathsome man was saying. He'd laid out a plan to keep Aidan on permanently, and had offered a perfectly adequate salary, one any man of modest means would covet, along with promises of bonuses if Aidan improved production while making cuts to advance profits. In other words, make life miserable for the workers. Aidan acted interested, only half listening, and when McRae began to ask probing questions about Aidan's family and background, he brought the meeting to an end. He promised to consider the offer.

Meanwhile, Aidan was making plans for his exit. He mailed a short note to Samuel in Hinckley to stand at the ready with the carriage. Aidan was missing his home and his family, and wanted to be there for Riordan.

After consuming a bowl of mutton stew in the tavern room, Aidan paced the floor, awaiting Cristyn's arrival. Hell, no woman had ever had him in knots like this. Not even during his most intense affair. If only the interfering widow had not interrupted them. He'd barely had enough time to explain. For all his supposed confidence and arrogance, the thought that Cristyn might look at him with repugnance after he revealed everything tore at his insides. His recovery stood on shaky ground. Because of his frail emotions, any rejection would send him reeling, and it concerned him. Briefly, he thought he should keep from revealing his feelings for Cristyn—but he couldn't. They were overwhelming, frightening, and utterly glorious.

A rap at the door brought him out of his troubled thoughts.

His anticipation plummeted when he opened the door to find Dr. Middlemiss. "Good evening, Mr. Black. A moment of your time?"

Standing aside, he motioned for the doctor to enter. "Come in."

Once he closed the door, the doctor turned to face him. "I know you're expecting Cristyn. She will not be coming."

Aidan could not contain his fury. Grabbing a fistful of the doctor's cravat, he growled, "You are interfering in a situation that does not concern you. I saw the way you hovered over her at the dinner. Cristyn. Is. Mine."

The doctor arched an eyebrow. "How territorial of you. Release me at once. I am not your enemy, nor am I romantically interested in Cristyn."

Reluctantly, Aidan let go. "Then, please, explain yourself."

"Shall we sit?"

"You will not be staying long enough to become comfortable."

Middlemiss straightened his cravat. "As you wish. Cristyn will not be coming tonight. It is far too risky. Surely you see this, Lord Wollstonecraft."

Disappointment covered him. Had Cristyn confided in this haughty doctor?

The look on his face must have been plain, for Middlemiss said, "She told me nothing of your brief conversation but your name. Obviously, you haven't informed her of the fact you are heir to the Earl of Carnstone."

"I hadn't the chance."

"Mrs. Trubshaw was quite irritated, but also concerned that there was a man in Cristyn's room. I assumed it was you. I am only here to suggest a more neutral meeting place to continue your discussion, for she deserves to know everything. If you care for her—"

"My feelings for Cristyn are none of your concern," Aidan snapped.

"Yes, as she has told me. But have a care with her reputation. Meeting in your rooms is not prudent. May I suggest my office, tomorrow night? When does the shift end at the mill?"

"Seven o'clock."

"Come straightaway to the office on Church Street, two doors down from Mrs. Trubshaw's. I have a shingle outside the door. You can meet alone, but I will be upstairs in my rooms. That way, if anyone sees you both, you can state you were meeting about mill health matters. My presence in the building will be sufficient for chaperone purposes."

Aidan's anger dissipated enough to take the words to heart. Hell, he didn't want Cristyn to be whispered about—and he should have thought about that before showing up at her window in the rain, and coaxing her to his room before that. And then there was the earth-shattering kiss in the garden shed....

"I will not listen in on your private conservation. I promised Gethin I would look out for Cristyn, but not to the extent that I hamper her independence. Despite our age difference, we've become friends. I think of her as a dear niece. Nothing more. But I will speak out if I believe there is sufficient justification."

Aidan clenched his teeth, holding his temper. "I will take you at your word. Seven tomorrow night."

"Cristyn is an amazing young woman. I don't want to see her hurt."

"Neither do I. We are in agreement."

"A truce, then?" Middlemiss held out his hand.

"Truce." Aidan shook it.

Middlemiss headed for the door, bowed slightly, then departed.

Damn. Hell. *Fuck.* After pacing the floor for over an hour, Aidan stormed out of his room. God, he needed...something. He hesitated outside the tavern room. *To hell with a drink.* It wouldn't be enough. Fuming, he walked toward the front entrance and stepped outside. A brisk walk would do it. His arms pumped, his breath coming out in short puffs. All of it was closing in on him. That heavy weight of anxiety. The stress of juggling multiple situations and emotions.

He stopped at the corner of the Keats Lane alley, leaned against the wall, and exhaled, closing his eyes.

"Guv. Care to chase the dragon?"

The gruff, raspy voice was immediately followed by the odors of cheap gin and stale tobacco. Aidan's eyes popped open and a weasel of a man, no taller than five inches over five feet, stood next to him. He wore a peaked cap pulled low over his eyes. The foul man opened his hand, and sitting in the palm of his fingerless glove was a clothed ball.

Opium.

His heart was beating so fast it could have easily leapt from his chest. That blasted buzzing noise he'd experienced at the Crimson Club, when he was last offered opium, had returned in full force. Even when he tried to be good—to do good—it all turned to rubble. What were the odds? Fate was indeed mockingly cruel.

Here was the answer to all his problems. The cure to the restlessness of his soul. The temptation was too great to ignore, and without further thought, he nodded. His throat was too dry and his brain too foggy to form a sentence.

The man held up two fingers. Two pence. Slightly cheaper than an apothecary shop. The price of a pint of beer. He'd be better off having a pint of bitter in Mr. Atwood's tavern room than going down this road. Disregarding the alarm bells clanging in his head, he thrust the coin into the man's hand and took the opium.

Fifteen minutes later, Aidan sat in his room, staring at the cloth ball on the table. He might as well have been staring into the abyss. As he wrestled with his demons, sweat covered his forehead. The buzzing in his head reached a crescendo. He reached for the opium, but froze when voices drifted in from through the open window.

"You're stealin' now for the thrill of it. It's one thing to do it when hungry—"

"Leave off!" the second man yelled. "I know what I'm about, and I can stop anytime. But why should I? Thieving gets me what I want. What I need."

"'Twill be your downfall. 'Twill ruin your life...."

The voices faded into the night. "I can stop anytime," the man had said.

Aidan pulled his hand away. A reprieve. For tonight. He should throw the opium away. But he would not. Perhaps he would save it for when he truly needed the blessed oblivion—or when he needed a stark reminder that, despite his supposed recovery, this struggle would stay with him for the rest of his days. With a shaky exhale, he took the handkerchief from his pocket and mopped his damp brow. *Exercise.* Standing, he tore off his clothes, hooked his feet under the footboard, and began his regimen.

# Chapter 17

With Wollstonecraft Hall constantly alive with activity, it was difficult for Julian to find a private moment to rest and reflect. The prospect of becoming a grandfather had brought his maudlin thoughts to the forefront of his mind. Which, of course, meant the curse had reared its ugly head once again. Despite the men's talk of embracing love, Julian watched the calendar with a stark fear borne from the debilitating loss of his wife more than twenty-five years past. Would Sabrina safely deliver? Would the child be sound and healthy? He kept his troublesome thoughts to himself, for he hadn't the slightest idea what he believed any longer with regard to the curse.

Since he and Alberta had first made love at the end of May, they'd had numerous trysts when they managed to find time alone together at her residence, usually when Jonas was at the hall.

There was no denying it: He was in love. With all the exhilarating and worrisome thoughts and emotions that came with it. Julian had been thinking of marriage. They could live at the small manor house.

Last night at dinner, his father had announced he and Mary Tuttle would be getting married in September. It would be a small affair at the hall, with only family in attendance.

Julian could wait on his plans. Besides, he hadn't even broached the subject with Alberta. Hell, he hadn't even said the words "I love you."

And neither had she.

The Wollstonecraft men were perhaps too cautious when it came to love. After suffering loss and living in grief, there were many who would not expose their hearts again. Julian never thought of himself as craven, but when it came to matters of the heart, it seemed he was.

Tonight, he would fight it.
Tomorrow? The next night?
Another battle to be won.

As he strode across the well-worn path between Wollstonecraft Hall and the Eatons' small manor house, he decided to wait until the birth of his grandchild to mention marriage. But love? It was well past time to reveal his true feelings to Alberta.

She met him at the door, looking absolutely stunning in a summer gown of pale yellow linen and cotton with a floral bodice. He couldn't wait to peel it off her. As Julian pulled her into his arms to kiss her, she turned her head.

"No kissing," she whispered. "We must talk. It's important."

Alberta sounded grave, her brows knotted in worry. Once in the parlor, he sat next to her on the settee. "What is wrong? Is it Jonas?"

She shook her head. "No, he is thriving. Jonas has completely embraced his training as a groom, and is doing well by all accounts."

"Garrett is pleased with his progress. That leaves you. Are you ill?" Hell, now he was worried.

"I don't know where to begin, except to blurt it out. I'm pregnant, Julian."

What? He couldn't have heard her correctly. The room started to spin. His whole world was caught in the vortex. *Pregnant. But how? When?* His lips moved, but no words came out. His throat had closed.

Alberta gave him an inquisitive look. "I've shocked you. I've shocked myself. I mean, I will be forty in three months. But Dr. Phillips confirmed my suspicions yesterday. How could it be possible? A stupid question. I mean, I am still having my menses. Obviously I'm able to conceive. But I never had with Reese. I assumed I couldn't. And then we...we..." She buried her face in her hands.

"But we used protection," he offered lamely.

She glanced up at him. "Not the first time, at the end of May. Remember?"

How could he forget? It had been one of the most erotic encounters of his life. And the sex that followed had only improved. God. He *had* spilled inside her. What were the odds of getting her with child on the first shot? Damn it all to hell and back, he was about to be a grandfather! He scrubbed his hand down his face.

"I could sell this house, move away," Alberta said, her voice shaking. "Or do what most women do in this situation: head to a secluded country spot, give birth, give up the baby, and return and act as if nothing had happened. Or I could have the child and damn society and its censure, but then the child would be forever tainted—"

Julian enfolded her trembling hands with his. "Stop, Alberta."

"I was rambling, wasn't I? And I've upset you. I could have kept this to myself and left without any word or explanation, but I could not do that to you."

"I'm shocked, and, yes, upset. My twins were born close to twenty-seven years ago. I am too old to be a father."

Alberta pulled her hands from his and frowned. "Well, I am not exactly in the prime of life. I'm frightened, Julian. Pregnancies at this age are fraught with complications. I don't want to go it alone."

"I've put you in danger." His heart lurched with worry. What had he done?

"Are you speaking of the curse?"

He nodded. "It is not to be dismissed."

"We must dismiss it, Julian. I'm not with child because of the ghostly specter of an ancient curse. We had unprotected sex. At our age, we should have known better. It's called *life*. It happens." Her voice had an edge, but he couldn't blame her.

Julian took her hand again. "You're right. It is time for me to say that I am deeply and irrevocably in love with you, my darling. I've hinted at it, and showed you physically, but I held back from speaking the words because, as I said, the scars run deep." He kissed her hand. "Would you believe me if I told you I was thinking of marriage on my way here? Father announced at dinner last night that he and Mary would be doing the deed come September. It appears we will be beating them to the altar—if you will have me, superstitions and all. If…you love me."

Alberta's eyes were moist. "Oh, you dear man. I think I fell in love with you the moment Poppy the llama spit on you all those months ago. The moment you were kind to Jonas, and didn't talk down to him or treat him as if he were damaged or unacceptable. I fell in love with your dedication to your social causes, how seriously you took your position as a Member of Parliament. How much you love your family. And yes, I even love your curse." She placed her hand on top of his. "I understand your hesitation, but we cannot allow the past to affect our future. We need each other, Julian. We love each other. And together, we can accomplish anything. Even the uncertain prospect of becoming parents at our age."

Julian leaned in and kissed her. Then their arms were about each other. When they broke apart, Alberta laid her head on his shoulder. He spread his hand and laid it across her middle. "A child. Our child. My God. What did Phillips say? Are you in fine health?"

She nodded. "If I take care, keep activity to a minimum, and eat well. I must say, I shocked him when I asked about sex. He said if I'm careful, there is no reason I cannot continue relations for the next few months."

Julian laughed, feeling lighter than he had in ages. Happiness washed over him. A cloud had been lifted from his soul, one that had held a tight grip on him for decades. "Will you marry me? Make my life complete? Love me until the end of our days?"

"Yes. Oh, yes."

He continued to caress her stomach. "There is much to do. I will procure a special licence immediately. We will be married within days."

"What about Aidan? Surely you wish for him to be in attendance."

*Right. Of course.* "I will send word. By the sound of his last letter, he is near the end of his task. When he gives us an approximate date of when he'll be home, we will plan. Two weeks at most. We can be married at the hall, or the chapel in Sevenoaks. Entirely up to you."

She cupped his cheek, and he reveled in the warmth of her touch. "Everything will be all right, Julian, I know it. Our baby will be born healthy, and I will survive the ordeal. You have my word."

He gently pulled her into his embrace. God, let that be the case. No more dwelling on the past or lingering on loss and grief—or a centuries-old curse.

He was being given another chance at love and life, and damn it, he was going to take it.

\* \* \* \*

Cristyn nervously awaited Aidan's arrival. It was past seven. Had he changed his mind? With the soft rap at the door, her heart sped up. She opened it and there he stood. He bowed slightly, and she stepped aside to allow him to enter. Once she closed the door she was swept up into his hot embrace and he kissed her, delving into her mouth with a scorching heat that ignited her insides. Cristyn couldn't help herself; she tunneled her fingers into his thick hair, hungrily caressing her tongue with his.

Breathing hard, they broke apart.

"Where is Middlemiss?" Aidan asked, looking about.

"Upstairs in his room. He promised not to disturb us."

Aidan stroked her flushed cheek with the back of his fingers. "He informed me he is not interested in you romantically."

"Believe me, he truly isn't. Shall we sit?"

He touched her forehead with his own. "The last damned thing I want to do is talk. I am selfish to the core, for I want nothing more than to lay you across this desk, lift your skirts, and lick and taste you until you scream out my name."

*Oh.* "How deliciously naughty. Have you done that with other women?" "Too many to count." Aidan laid hot kisses along her neck. "I have a bad reputation; you might as well know it now."

"Will you tell me of your past?" She took his hand and led him to the small settee on the opposite side of the room. Once they were seated, they turned slightly to face each other.

"My decline came over a number of years. You saw me at rock bottom. Even after all this time, I cannot quite puzzle out how it happened. Or why. I was rich, selfish, eager to experience all life had to offer. I make no excuses. I accept my failures. All I wanted was the next thrill, and it consisted of seedy venues and disreputable companions of both sexes. Until I disappeared, lost in the morass of utter depravity. Uncle Garrett and Mr. Seward located me and brought me to the sanatorium. I do not remember much of my last month, but I remember enough to be horrified and ashamed."

His sober words touched her heart, for she had seen the result. "The circle of burns on your back. What happened?"

"You will leave me with nothing?"

"I want to understand. Is it something to do with the man that showed up at the sanatorium? The brute who wielded a knife?"

Aidan's eyebrow arched. "You witnessed that?"

She nodded. "For a few minutes, he yelled at my father and me to leave."

"Ah," Aidan murmured. "I remember. Yes, it had to do with the brute. It is not a pretty story. But before I reveal that particular mess, I need to finish telling you about my family. The Wollstonecrafts do live in Kent; my uncle does breed horses. I told you of my brother, Riordan. He married last autumn and his wife, Sabrina, is expecting a baby in a matter of weeks. My father is a Member of Parliament. My grandfather is in the House of Lords."

Cristyn blinked. "Lords? Then he is a member of the peerage? Which makes you, what exactly? Are you the older brother?"

Aidan nodded.

*My God.* He was the heir. An aristocrat, though his posh accent should have been a clue. She merely thought it a result of his wealth and education. Her conversation with Paris pushed to the front of her mind, and what he'd said about his lover. *Heirs to the aristocracy are strange creatures. They are born, weaned, and raised on a steady diet of honor and duty. When it comes down to it, no matter the utterances and assurances of love and devotion, they will choose duty and family.*

What would an heir of the peerage want with the daughter of a Welsh country doctor? Except for a dalliance? An affair? A mistress? She gulped deeply. "And your grandfather is what, exactly?"

"An earl."

"I had no idea. You are Lord Wollstonecraft. Isn't that how the heir apparent is referred to?" she whispered.

"It's a courtesy, it means nothing. In fact, I often insist that it not be used, for it makes me uncomfortable." His mouth quirked sardonically. "I sign my letters to my brother 'Lord Nothing.' And I have been that for far too long. It's why I'm here. I wish to remedy my past mistakes."

Good God, a *lord*. Her mind was swimming to such an extent she couldn't form a response to his Lord Nothing remark. "I knew you were rich, but part of the aristocracy? This changes...well, everything." She frowned and shook her head.

"In what way?" Aidan demanded.

"How can there be anything of permanence?" Cristyn rubbed her forehead. "I am getting ahead of myself, for when has either of us mentioned a lasting relationship? Though we've been acquainted for months, what do we really know about each other? Why use the false name?"

"It was Garrett who gave the name of Black; I went along with it. I understood his way of thinking. Protect the family. Protect me. In light of the gossip, it was a wise move."

"Gossip?"

"Before my disappearance, I was called a notorious rake. Scandalous affairs. Dissolute company. Sinful parties. Indulgences of all sorts. I told you, I am not a nice man." He crossed his arms and frowned. "The burns on my back? Done by an aristocrat who wanted to inflict pain, not only on me, but my family." Aidan told her of the Marquess of Sutherhorne and his intense hatred for the family, his kidnapping of his brother's wife, the shooting of his uncle, and the gossip he'd spread.

Cristyn gasped. "That is terrible."

"The long discussions with your father have put much of what happened in proper perspective. I agree with him that addiction is a disease, even though everyone, including those in the medical community, do not. They say it is a weakness, a lack of character. Perhaps it is both. All I know is that I don't want to be that man anymore. The selfish, rich, heir apparent. Hence why I suggested this covert operation to my father and grandfather. They are working to amend the Factory Act. All the information I gather here will further their cause."

"I admire you for it; you've already proven you are not 'Lord Nothing,'" Cristyn said. And she meant it.

He bowed in response.

"The act certainly needs amending," she continued. "The plight of the poor here needs immediate attention. My reason for coming here? I wanted to do something useful with all I had learned from my father. But there was a selfish motive as well; I needed to distance myself from the sanatorium, and from the memory of you."

Aidan caressed her cheek, trailing the tip of his finger across her lips, causing her to shiver with desire. "As usual, I handled it in a ham-fisted manner. I should have explained myself better. I wanted...hell, I *needed* to discover if I was even worthy of your affection. Anyone's affection. To see if there was a decent man below the artificial surface."

"And would you have sought me out after your journey of discovery?"

Aidan dropped his hand. "The truth? I'm not certain. By the time I departed Standon I had convinced myself you were better off without me. Finding you here in Earl Shilton was fate. Who am I to argue with fate? But it also made me realize I was a fool for walking away."

Cristyn absorbed his words. Then she recalled what her father had said: *He is far above us in station. He's not for you.* Her heart sank. "Maybe you were right to walk away," she murmured. "My father said it would never work between us. That you are not of our class." She shook her head sadly. "Heir to an earl? You're expected to marry well. Society demands it, perhaps even your family. It is your duty—"

"Fuck duty! When did I ever give a hang about it?" Aidan cried. "You speak of something lasting. Damn it all, Cristyn, why can't we be happy?"

Her eyes widened at his vulgarity.

"Yes, my angel. I am profane on top of my many faults. Apologies. Believe me when I tell you that no one in my family holds with such strictures. In fact, my grandfather, the Earl of Carnstone, is to marry a lovely woman who happens to be an ex-lady's maid. The family couldn't be happier for him."

*Wait.* "Did you say Earl of Carnstone?" The conversation with Cyn flooded her mind. Disgraceful party. Orgy. Auction. Licentious lord. An heir to an earl. All the jagged pieces fit together to form a tragic picture. Aidan was the heir. The brute that had showed up at the sanatorium in February? Did he have something to do with the gossip? Was the lord the one that perpetrated heinous acts against his family?

*Oh, Aidan. How horrible.* Her heart swelled with compassion, hating the fact Aidan had come to such a degrading circumstance. "I heard the gossip from my friend, who heard it from her cousin in London. I had no idea it was you. Only that it was the heir to the Earl of Carnstone. I am sorry."

He blinked. 'What are you on about?"

"The auction at an orgy," she replied sympathetically.

"No pity, please. I can see it in your eyes," he snapped.

Cristyn placed her hands on her hips. "It's not pity. There is no need for you to be defensive about it." She huffed.

Aidan didn't have a chance to reply, for Paris walked into the room. Blast it.

"I am sorry to interrupt, but we have a medical call. Mrs. Barton's son came to the back door. I will need your assistance," Paris said.

"Then I will take my leave." Aidan bowed stiffly and departed before she had a chance to say anything. But this conversation was not over. Once the medical call was completed, she would tell him that she would never turn from him.

Cristyn would make him understand that she loved him in spite of his past, and, in turn, because of it.

# Chapter 18

Aidan marched toward the inn. Christ, she'd heard of the gossip in Standon. What were the odds? How far did the blasted tattle spread? Coast to coast and every point in between? Once he entered the inn, he vaulted up the stairs. Fumbling for his key, he grumbled and cursed under his breath until he located it, unlocked the door, and entered. Aidan halted in his tracks. The room was in darkness, as the curtains had been drawn. Someone was here, for he could smell stale tobacco and sweat. In the corner of the room, the red illumination of a lit cheroot glowed in the shadows.

"Hello, Aidan."

The gravelly voice was unmistakeable. *Delaney.* Aidan closed his eyes. Unbelievable. Why, at this moment, considering he had just discussed this disturbing episode with Cristyn? *Yes, I am cursed, and no mistake. Stay calm.* Aidan's eyes popped open and he glanced about the dim room, looking for anything he could use as a weapon.

Delaney dropped the cheroot to the wood-planked floor and ground it out with his boot. "I'm not here to harm you."

"Then why are you here?"

"To finish the conversation we started at that damned clinic." He turned the knob on the gas lamp by his chair and came into focus. His harsh looks were made all the more menacing by the muted light.

Aidan's past would follow him straight to the grave. It pursued and haunted him regardless of his good intentions. He couldn't even come to a small village in the middle of nowhere with an assumed name.

Delaney kicked a chair toward him. "Sit. You will hear me out."

Aidan took a seat, facing the man. "Have you been following me?"

"Aye. A bit. Wanted to make sure you're all right."

Aidan scoffed. "As if you care for my well-being."

"Listen up, my pretty pup. The world doesn't revolve around you. Or that damned marquess. Sutherhorne attended one of my fights. You see, he likes inflicting pain on men as much as he likes watching it. He offered to hire me as his protector. An object of his amusement, more like. I needed the coin. Not much to be made on illegal bare-knuckle fighting—at least, not for the fighter."

"Am I to feel sorry for you?"

"No. I'll bet you feel plenty sorry for yourself to have any sympathy left for me. But let me finish, and don't interrupt again."

Aidan shrugged, stinging from the brute's rebuke. The man was not wrong.

"I attended more than one of those toff parties; I know what goes on. When you were brought out for the auction, I figured you were a male prossie like all the rest, regardless of what they claimed. You hardly looked the part of an heir to an earl. You were a right mess."

Again, the man was not wrong. Aidan remained silent.

"Sutherhorne and I took you to a room, and I found out soon enough you weren't a prossie at all."

"What is your damned point? I am not going to sit here and have you describe in detail what happened between us. I don't remember most of it, and I would prefer to keep it that way. And you still haven't said why you have been following me. It's more than being concerned."

"You're interrupting," Delaney growled. "And don't act like you didn't enjoy it. You responded."

"I would have responded to anyone touching me, regardless of age or gender. I was out of my head, in a drug-addled fog. Now *you* listen to *me*: I am not horrified by what physical acts two consenting men get up to. I attended Eton and Cambridge. I've seen plenty, though I did not seek it out personally. What I am horrified by is the fact that I sold myself for money to buy opium. As I said, you were a means to an end, nothing else. If you have formed an attachment to me from our one brief encounter, the sentiment is not returned, nor shall it ever be." Aidan figured it had to be said.

The silence between them was deadly.

"Fair play. I hear you. Let me continue. Sutherhorne told me you really were an heir to an earl weeks later. The whole situation hasn't been sitting well with me. That night, I'd left the room for a moment to relieve myself. When I came back, he was holding a lit cigar to your back while he...Jaysus."

Aidan's stomach tumbled. "Enough. I do *not* want to hear any more of what happened in that room."

"Fine. But I'm not done. When the marquess sent me to Standon to investigate Mrs. and Miss Hughes, I saw you sitting outside a building in a wheeled chair. Found out the place was a clinic. Aye, I was concerned. Was it me that put you there? It's why I came to your room in February. Then your damned Scottish uncle burst through the door, mucking things up good and proper."

"And since? Why follow me?" Aidan demanded.

Delaney met his gaze. "To see that you were safe," he answered, his husky voice soft. "After February, I traveled around, taking odd jobs. In May, I watched your home. Saw you with your family. Then you left. Aye, I was curious where you were going. I recognized the man with you. He was in Standon with your uncle. I've been nearby these three weeks."

"Now that you see I am quite recovered, there is no reason for you to stay. What happened to me, my time in the clinic, had nothing to do with you. I hold you in no blame. Our acquaintance is at an end." Aidan's tone was firm.

Delaney shook his head. "I'll be staying a bit. I've taken a job collecting rent from stocking workers. I'll stay until I've got traveling coin."

Aidan sat forward. "I will give you fifty pounds to leave tonight."

Delaney arched an eyebrow. "Oh, aye? I don't take bribes. Or charity."

"Oh, this is most definitely a bribe. I will make it seventy pounds if you leave and never seek me out again." It was all the damned coin he had on him.

Delaney rubbed his whiskered chin. "It's tempting, but no, my lordling. I earn my keep."

"I can assure you that the position you have accepted will soon be gone. There are changes coming to this village, ones the masters will not like."

"Is that what you're doing at the cotton mill?"

Aidan exhaled. Why wouldn't this blasted man take the money and go? He supposed even a brute had a code of honor. "Never mind what I'm doing. The air is cleared. There is nothing between us. No hate—and certainly no affection. If you were led to believe otherwise, accept my apology. I was not myself." In speaking the words, a part of his dark soul lightened. It was time to allow the nightmares to fade and move on with his life.

Delaney sat back in the chair. "Well, that is clear enough. I wanted you to know I'm long done with Sutherhorne." He stood. Hell, the man was huge.

Aidan stood as well. "Sutherhorne has been banished by Prince Albert to a rocky island in the North Atlantic. He will never be heard from again."

"Good. You probably wish I was there and all. If we see each other out on the cobbles, I'll act a stranger. Goodbye, Aidan."

A sharp rap on the door interrupted their conversation. "Aidan! Open this door! I'll stand here all night if I must."

Cristyn. He ran to the door, flung it open, and pulled her across the threshold. "Are you mad making such a ruckus?" he admonished. "Why are you here?"

"You left before things were settled, an annoying habit of yours, and—oh." Her gaze settled on Delaney. "You. The man with the knife." Her gaze pivoted to Aidan. "What is going on here?" Her tone was even, not shocked, merely questioning.

"You're the woman at the clinic." Delaney looked between them. "Ah, it is like that, then? The air is fairly crackling between you. I came to apologize. It was accepted. Now I'll leave."

Delaney gave them a slight nod and departed. Aidan closed the door and locked it, then turned to face Cristyn. "Done with your medical call?"

"Mrs. Barton was experiencing false labor."

"We shouldn't be alone together in my room. Isn't that what was decided?"

"Blast it! We need to talk, and we'll do it here."

"As you have witnessed, my past is not pleasant."

She placed her hands on her hips. "I'm aware of it, Aidan. You're not the only young man with a dismal past to pass through the sanatorium doors." Cristyn stepped closer, tentatively, as if she were approaching a skittish horse—which he supposed he was.

"You sold yourself for money. I'm assuming to buy opium. That was not part of the tattle. When you mentioned your grandfather's name, the pieces of your past fell into place. I'm a nurse, Aidan. I've heard and seen things you would not believe. I'm not easily shocked." She gently laid her hand against his chest. As always, her touch scorched him, from his skin inward. "You must stop running when emotions overwhelm you. It's no doubt part of the reason you became lost in the dark."

Aidan marched to the bureau, opened the drawer, and grasped the opium. Once he stood before her, he opened his clenched fist. "Apparently the dark still beckons. I bought this from a shifty character last night, and spent the next several hours wrestling the demons that still clamor inside me." His voice shook. Admitting his weaknesses had his insides twisting into knots.

"But you didn't take it," she whispered, staring up at him. "You need to start believing in yourself. Look at what you're doing at the mill. You have a purpose in life. You can and will make a difference. The demons are part of your past. They don't have to be part of your future. Don't be ashamed of your struggle."

Cristyn cupped his cheek. "You don't have to stay in the dark anymore, Aidan. There are people who love you. Worry for you. Care if you live or die. You have the courage. I've witnessed it. You came back from the brink of destruction through sheer willpower. Do you realize how close you were to death?" Her words were tenderly spoken, and touched him deeply.

"Yes, but it was you, Cristyn. I wouldn't have made it if not for you." His voice cracked on the last few words.

She gave him a shy smile. "I may have assisted, but the decision to recover was yours to make. And this may be surprising to hear, but you are *still* recovering. It's why you're finding it difficult to handle certain situations."

"You speak the truth. Take this and dispose of it." Aidan handed the cloth ball to her and she tucked it away in her reticule.

"You will beat this, but it won't be easy. Remember to seek help from those who care."

"No more running?"

"Exactly. And don't run from what is between us, Aidan. If we're to have a brief dalliance, I accept the terms gladly. I wanted you to know it."

"I don't deserve you. I've called you my angel of mercy, and you are." He took her hand and kissed it. "You are wise and kind and I thank you for your compassionate counsel."

"And Delaney?"

"He followed me here because he was concerned. I offered him money to leave; he refused. He claims he doesn't mean me harm, but I remain wary."

"He cares for you," she whispered. "Perhaps more than he should."

"I told him in no uncertain terms there could be nothing between us." Aidan filled her in on Delaney's position collecting rent from the stocking makers, and the fact the job would be short-lived.

"Why short-lived?" Cristyn asked.

He took her hand and they sat on the edge of his bed. He told her of the contents of his father's letter. "My time here is near an end. I want to take another run at Rokesmith, see if he will reveal the secrets I know he is keeping."

Cristyn's expression was reflective. "I am in love with you, Aidan. I think I may have been from the beginning. No man has ever made me feel the way you do. Falling for a patient? It is against everything I believe in."

She loved him. It humbled him, but also made him anxious. How could he return the sentiment when everything was still unresolved, including his wayward emotions? For Cristyn had spoken the truth: He was *not* fully recovered. Aidan remained silent, but squeezed her hand gently. "I want to tell you what I remember of those last months. But before that, I want to tell you of the egocentric rake." In a firm voice, he told her of the numerous affairs, the drinking, and the parties. He held nothing back. To her credit, she listened, and did not judge.

"My. Quite the narrative," Cristyn said.

He released her hand. "Does it give you pause?"

"Do you live that life now?"

"No."

She stared at him, as if waiting for further clarification. He gave her none. "Do you have any intentions of returning to that lifestyle in the future?" she asked, one eyebrow raised.

"No," he answered, his voice firm. "Never."

"Where do we go from here?" she asked, her voice soft.

"What do you want, Cristyn?"

"For you to make love to me."

Aidan groaned. "You shouldn't even be in my room."

"I understand the ramifications. I've listened to the advice. But when, where, and why we meet is my decision."

He snorted. "I do not wish for you to be the subject of gossip. It is not something I recommend."

"Again, that is my decision. I don't expect anything in return, any promises or whispered words. Just us, together. I have yearned for it for so long."

How could he refuse such an open and honest declaration? "God, Cris. You have invaded my dreams for months." He tunneled his hands through her hair. A few pins clattered to the floor. He gently pulled her head back, exposing her neck. Her pulse throbbed rapidly. He nibbled on the vein, biting gently, licking and kissing until soft moans left her throat. "Damn it, I have no sheaths with me." He continued on his journey along the column of her neck. "My bleak past? Diseases? A possible pregnancy?"

"There are ways to avoid pregnancy. You've been with no one since January, surely."

Aidan froze. Damn. Hell. *Fuck.*

"Oh. I see." There was no censure in her voice, but there was no emotion either.

He sat back, then cupped her face, gazing into her eyes. "I stopped at a brothel in London on my way home. It turned out to be one of the more empty and meaningless experiences of my life. I thought it would erase you from my mind, but it was a dismal failure. I am not the same man. Those types of amusements no longer appeal. Regardless, it can be argued I am not worthy of you. Do you wish to give your virginity to the likes of me?"

"You truly are a bounder," she murmured.

He kissed her forehead. "Yes. A complete cad. And I've been with a man; let us not forget that salient proof of licentiousness. I am a lout, a scoundrel, a dissolute rascal, a—"

"Stop. I believe you when you say you're not the same man." She gazed into his eyes, as if searching for truth. Or decency. But if he had any decency, he would escort her to her room and say good night—apparently enough of the rake still lingered.

"I am not. But I want you, Cris, I ache for you. I used sheaths at the brothel, and enough time has passed that proves I do not have the pox. I was damned lucky, considering my earlier recklessness. But I give you my word I will withdraw. I will not come inside you. Do you believe me?"

Aidan waited; had he been too blunt? Cristyn was a nurse, and made of a strong substance. By her own admission, she'd heard and seen plenty. But he could not bear the fact she might think less of him because of his past. As for the future, he couldn't think of it here. All he wanted was her. For them to be joined. To hold her in his arms. To be...inside her. Aidan waited, and started to grow worried at her silence.

"Yes, I believe you."

He pulled her into his embrace and held her close to his rapidly beating heart. He was grateful. Elated. Aroused. And completely happy, for the first time in years. "A word of warning: I will not be able to go slow."

Cristyn gazed up at him. "No one asked you to."

His mouth crashed down on hers. From there, the room began to spin; how fortuitous they were sitting on the bed. The kiss deepened, grew fierce and hungry. Without verbalizing their wishes, both began to pull and tug at layers of clothing, kicking off shoes and boots. The rest of her hairpins rained to the floor as he tugged her raven locks free. Briefly burying his nose in her hair and reveling in her violet scent, he quickly shrugged out of his coat and waistcoat as Cristyn pulled his shirt from the waistband of his trousers. They laughed when they became tangled in various garments. But Aidan stopped laughing when her breasts peered out from the confines of her bodice. "Perfect, as I knew you would be."

Cristyn lay on the bed, her expression sultry. All he wore were his trousers. There was so much he wanted to do. Kiss and lick her skin. Taste her, suckle her breasts. But he was not a patient man. Aidan slipped his hand between her legs, found the ties to her drawers, and quickly removed them. Brushing past her curls, wetness coated the tips of his fingers. *Yes. Now.*

But easy. She was a virgin. For all her seductive looks and eagerness, he could not forget that salient fact.

"Now, Aidan. Put it in me."

*Oh, hell.* "Put what in you?" he teased, his voice husky.

"Your...cock. Isn't that what men call it?"

"Indeed." Once on his knees before her, he unfastened his trousers and pulled out his stiff and aching prick. Giving it a few strokes, Aidan kept his gaze firm on hers, for she watched him, licking her lips. He spread her legs wider. Grasping his shaft, he teased her wet entrance with its swollen head.

Cristyn moaned.

"Next time we are alone, I want you to show me how you touch yourself. How you make yourself come," he growled.

"Only if you do the same for me."

That sensual demand broke the last of any control he had managed to keep. He pushed into her. Cristyn's eyes widened as he seated himself. She was wonderfully, gloriously tight, and it caused spasms of desire to tear through his body. He stayed still, savoring the feel of how well they fit together. How right this felt. He caught her gaze. "Are you fine? Any pain? Shall I continue?" *Please. Please.*

Her breath came in shallow pants, matching his. "A slight pinch, but I'm more than fine. Oh, how I love the way you fill me."

"Whenever we do this, please, tell me what you're feeling. Demand what you want. I will give it all to you." *Including my heart.*

"Then show me how notorious you are."

"My sweet Cris, I cannot show you all that in one night. But I would love nothing more than to teach you all I've learned." He paused. "How unbearably conceited of me. But I do want to share this knowledge with only you."

Aidan pulled out almost all the way, then plunged back in, making her gasp. "More."

"More it is." Aidan started slow, building to rapid strokes, all the while encouraging her to raise her hips and meet his thrusts. Then he lifted one of her legs, tilting her enough that his swift thrusts stimulated her clitoris.

Cristyn moaned. "Yes, there. Oh, God."

All those faceless women he'd had dalliances with since the age of fifteen faded. He leaned forward, rocking back and forth, lost in complete and utter bliss.

Aidan was close, for he could feel that familiar pressure building in his ballocks. Taking his thumb, he pressed on her clit, rubbing vigorously. He wanted her to come first. Give her pleasure before his. "Come for me, Cris. Cry out."

She writhed and moaned louder. How passionate she was. Absolutely beautiful.

As soon as she shouted his name and trembled as her peak hit her, he pulled out and spilled on the bedding. Clenching his teeth, every cord in his neck strained as his entire body wracked with shudders. It went on for several minutes, as this climax was one of his most intense—ever.

How could he let this beautiful woman leave his side? He had fallen for her, and the emotions were as confounding as they were astounding. Aidan had no idea how to proceed; this was all new to him.

Tumbling down onto the bed by her side, he pulled her in close. After several moments, and once their breathing regulated, he asked, "Have I hurt you?"

"That depends," she murmured, "on what you decide you want from me."

Ah. And therein lay the heart of it all.

# Chapter 19

Aidan kissed her forehead, but said nothing. Damn it all, he couldn't commit to anything until this situation at the mill was settled, or at least addressed. He should give her the courtesy of telling her that much. The fact she actually loved him held him in thrall; he was still completely shocked over her heartfelt declaration.

All he knew was he'd had sex on more occasions than he cared to remember, but this was the first time he had ever made love. It made him yearn for more: unhurried exploration, mutual oral pleasure, and experimentation with the dozens of sexual positions he'd learned through the years. How he longed to make that connection again, the one that moved beyond the physical. The joining of hearts. And souls. For his blackened soul felt—lighter. It could have been his imagination, but Aidan wished to see if Cristyn was the one woman who would bring light into the dark corners of his soul. Hell, she already had—but he wanted more.

She stirred. "I must go. Mrs. Trubshaw locks the door by nine, and the sun is setting."

They sat upright. "This is not a sordid affair," Aidan stated. "I've had enough of them to tell the difference. But I must complete my...mission here, before I am able to tackle what is happening between us." Aidan grasped her chin and tilted it upward until she met his gaze. "There is something quite profound between us, my angel. And I swear to you, we *will* be discussing it. Do you regret what happened?"

Cristyn gave him a tremulous smile. "Not at all. It exceeded my expectations."

"Thank God. I promise it will only improve. We have much to discover." He kissed her on the tip of the nose. If he kissed her on the lips, he would be tempted to keep her in his bed the rest of the night—and all of tomorrow. "I will escort you to Mrs. Trubshaw's."

They hurriedly dressed; Aidan even assisted her in pinning her hair in place. With a quick inspection of the hall, they quietly descended the back stairs and exited through the rear door. Once on the street, Aidan offered his arm and they strolled along the cobbles toward Church Street. Once they neared the corner, Cristyn halted. "We should part here."

"God, I want to kiss you senseless. When can we meet again?"

"Shall we try for the clinic? Tomorrow night at seven?"

They were not going to his room. Though disappointed, he hid it. "Yes. Seven o'clock. I will arrive once I extricate myself from the mill." He bowed slightly. "Good night, my angel," he murmured.

"Good night, Mr. Black." In a quieter voice, she whispered, "My dearest."

The endearment warmed his heart, and like a smitten, love-struck idiot, he stood and watched until she disappeared into the widow's residence. Making his way toward the inn, Aidan decided he would head to the mill for one last pass at Rokesmith. The sun had all but set, and the darkness would hide their meeting.

Once he entered the inn, he strode into the tavern room. The innkeeper stood behind the bar, wiping glasses. "Mr. Atwood, what have you left in foodstuffs?"

"Four pork pies, some bacon. Two cottage loaves, rice pudding."

Aidan pulled out a couple of pound notes. "I will take it all. If you can spare any paper napkins, and cutlery, along with an old bowl and a few spoons you no longer need. Do you have any milk?"

Mr. Atwood's eyes widened at the money on the counter. "Aye, enough to fill a large jar."

Aidan slapped another pound note on the counter. "If you have any tin cups and plates you can spare, toss them into a box as well. I need it all right away."

"Aye, sir!" The innkeeper snatched up the bills and hurried off. Less than five minutes later, he returned with a large basket.

Aidan took it. "Good man. When I return in forty minutes, I would like a meal delivered to my room. I am sure you keep prime cuts of beef for your best customers—"

"Of which you are, Mr. Black."

"Thank you. A cut of beef and whatever vegetables you can muster."

"I will see it done, sir. Never fear."

Aidan glanced about the empty tavern room. "What I purchased here is no one's business. Understand?"

Mr. Atwood touched his forelock. "You can count on my discretion, sir."

Satisfied, Aidan carried the heavy basket outside, then walked briskly toward the mill. The rain had finally dissipated the night before, and it left warm weather in its wake. The moon cast enough illumination to light his way. When he arrived at the warehouse, many of the children were still outside.

When Lottie spotted him, her sweet face lit up and she ran toward him. "Mr. Black!"

She encircled his waist and hugged him close. No doubt the child was happy to see him because of the food.

Still gripping his trousers, Lottie gazed up at him, admiration in her eyes. "Are you a fairy-tale prince?" she asked.

Aidan wanted to laugh at the absurdity of it, and give the little girl a dismissive comment. But looking down into those innocent, wide orbs, he couldn't be cruel to her. "No, child. Not at all," he replied in a soft voice. "I will never be, I'm afraid. Go and fetch Rokesmith. There's a good girl."

She smiled, gave him another hug, then scampered away, leaving him wondering how the young girl could still retain any semblance of childhood wonder and playfulness in this dismal place.

Rokesmith emerged from the cellar. Aidan thrust the basket at him. "See the children are fed. The dishes and cutlery are to stay with you. Keep them hidden. I'll need the basket back. We need to talk. Alone. Dismiss everyone else." His words were clipped, because he was at the end of his tether in dealing with this stubborn youth.

Rokesmith motioned to an older girl and boy and whispered instructions to them. They disappeared into the cellar with the food, along with the rest of the children.

Rokesmith closed the cellar doors, then turned to face him. "What brings you here?"

"My time here is coming to end sooner than I thought. You have two days to tell me everything you know about the pregnant women and the missing children. In return, if the information is useful in my endeavors, I will keep my promise of suitable placements for the children and assisting you in finding justice for your situation."

Rokesmith curled his lip. "Sorry, the trust isn't there, Black—if that is your name. How do I know you'll keep your word?"

Aidan pushed Rokesmith against the warehouse wall. "You had better locate the trust, and swiftly, or I will be washing my hands of this place and leaving you and everyone at the mill to the fates. I promise you, the future will be a bleak one. Those children will be scattered to the four winds, and there will be no justice—not for you or anyone here."

Rokesmith frowned. "Go to hell."

"Last chance," Aidan forced out through his clenched teeth.

"All right. I'll think on it. Two days, you said?"

Aidan leaned down, meeting him eye-to-eye. "Do not think to use that time to try to double-cross me, boy. You do not wish to betray the Wollstonecrafts. Not an heir to an earl. Think on that." Aidan stepped back. "Go and bring me the basket."

Rokesmith growled, but did as he told. "I knew you were a toff. You walk like you own the world. Your hands are too clean. No old scars. I should have known."

"It hardly matters in this place." Aidan grabbed the lad's arm. "Enjoy the meal. Think of your Lottie. You want to protect her? Keep her with you as a sister? Then you know what to do." He released Rokesmith, then said in a gentle tone, "I will hold up my end of the bargain. And more. I give you my word."

Rokesmith mumbled inaudibly as he walked away.

Well, he'd tried. If the boy cared as much for the children as he claimed, then he would comply. Already Samuel was ready to move rapidly and alert the authorities in Hinckley when needed. It would depend how serious the news would be. Aidan had the impression the secret would be grim indeed.

Enough of this; he had a hot meal waiting for him. Things were coming together on all fronts. Once concluded, he could concentrate on living his life. He was more than ready to place the past behind him and live as an honorable man. And, with any luck at all, a man in love.

\* \* \* \*

Aidan would be a hard nut to crack. Since their first encounter at the sanatorium, Cristyn could tell he held his emotions in check. He was doing the same here. Though he may not wish to acknowledge it, he was vulnerable—perhaps he always had been. Men usually avoided such examinations, as if they made them less of a man. Not in Cristyn's mind. She sighed and sipped her tea. There was no fire in her room tonight; it was far too warm. She had the window open and was curled up in the chair next to it, taking advantage of the slight breeze wafting in from outside. The pleasing scent of Mrs. Trubshaw's prized roses filled the air.

Hard to believe it was the end of July. The past few weeks had passed in an exhilarating blur. Not only in her duties at Paris's clinic, but with Aidan. Cristyn thought that after losing her virginity she would feel... different. She certainly didn't mourn the loss of it. Except for a slight ache between her legs, and the fact that it felt as if Aidan were still inside her, no great transformation had taken place.

Never had she felt more alive. Her nerve endings still sparked. Her heart still thundered madly. A slow smile crept across her face. Considering the fact they had not removed all of their clothes, and that the act itself concluded in less than fifteen minutes, Cristyn had thoroughly enjoyed it.

Closing her eyes, she relived him moving in and out of her. How skilled. He varied the speed and depth of his thrusts to give her maximum pleasure. Dear heaven, such incendiary passion—on both sides. Cristyn had observed desire in his eyes as he thrust into her.

And to think Aidan claimed it would only improve. She opened her eyes and glanced at the open window with a wistful look, hoping he would appear. But they couldn't take the chance.

Beyond all the drama and the appearance of Delaney, the fact that she had told him she loved him had lifted a weight from her. Cristyn reasoned that being truthful with her feelings would spur Aidan into confronting his emotions at long last, but it appeared she would have to wait a little longer for him to say those all important words: "I love you."

And what about Aidan's confession regarding selling himself for opium? Shouldn't she have been horrified at such a scandalous act, and turn from him in revulsion? Many ladies of society would.

But Cristyn was not one of them, beholden to strict rules and codes of acceptable behavior. She was not a rich, coddled heiress living in a protected bubble of elite privilege and self-righteous axioms.

Though it could be said she lived in a protected bubble of her own. Born and brought up in an idyllic country village, what had she known of true suffering? Earl Shilton had given her an eye-opening lesson about those who dealt with poverty and sickness on a daily basis, doing all they could—legal or not—to survive.

She took another sip of tea, but paused when she heard loud arguing in the alley. Two men were fighting over a chicken, no doubt pilfered from a nearby farm. Yes, these were desperate people. It wasn't right that humans must exist in such conditions. It made her admire Paris all the more for his generous offering of medical care.

But the majority of her admiration was for Aidan. Perhaps he needed to cleanse his soul, seek redemption, whatever it would take for him to be the man that he truly wished to be. Though he was brutally honest in admonishing his own behavior, Cristyn more than anyone understood how difficult it was to admit, let alone do anything to turn one's life around.

Living in her own shielded cocoon, she had little experience with men. Oh, she had certainly treated many of various ages, had seen plenty of men naked in her duties as a nurse. But outside of messy kisses from neighborhood boys, no one had touched or kissed her like Aidan had.

Placing the cup on the table, Cristyn drew her legs up and wrapped her arms around them. Aidan was notorious, scandalous, a complete bounder—and she loved him anyway, because along with that love was a deep and firm belief that an honorable and heroic man lay at the core of his being. He was worth loving. Worth supporting. Worth the entire world.

Now it was time for Aidan to realize it. Only then could they move forward.

\* \* \* \*

Aidan had stayed up half the night writing out every violation he had witnessed the past month. In between his scribbling, he consumed his meal, and also completed a rigorous session of calisthenics. He had to work off his excess lust, turn his mind and body toward other pursuits besides a certain violet-eyed, innocent—but seductive—siren. It had been difficult, for the brief lovemaking had consumed his thoughts, scorching his heart and soul. It wasn't enough, not near enough.

Perhaps it would not be enough even for a lifetime.

Along with his sexual appetite, he found that his appetite for food had also increased of late. That was another good sign for his continued healing. But the best indication had been being honest with Cristyn, and handing the opium over to her. That crisis had mercifully passed.

Today, he was on a mission. If Rokesmith did not reveal the supposed secrets, then Aidan would need plenty of ammunition to bring official charges against McRae—and he had taken an abundance of notes.

As he strolled along the platform, watching over the factory floor, his mind drifted toward Cristyn, as it had done often since yesterday evening. God, he could not wait to see her again. Hold her close. Kiss her until those soft moans escaped her luscious lips.

His gaze slid to Miller, who walked the narrow aisles between the machines. The man was diligent in his work, kept the machines humming and in top working order regardless of McRae's neglect. Aidan would have to ensure the man was looked after once he made his report. Recommend him for a better position elsewhere should Morris Mill be shuttered—if that happened. Aidan found he had less and less confidence in fairness and proper government oversight.

A blood-curdling scream made Aidan freeze in his tracks.

"Stop the machines!" Miller yelled. "Don't move, girl!" The spinning room fell silent, except for a child shrieking at the top of her lungs. The woman who had been operating the machine covered her mouth and turned away in horror.

Aidan vaulted down the stairs and ran toward Miller. "What is it?"

"One of the scavengers, sir. Her hair got caught in the machinery. Good bloody thing I was right here when it happened, or her head would have been crushed."

Aidan lowered himself onto his haunches. His stomach tumbled with nausea when he saw it was little Lottie. Part of her scalp had torn away on the left side of her head. God, the amount of blood. It ran in rivulets down her shoulder. It was a wonder she was still conscious. "Hush, child. I will free you." He turned toward Miller. "I need scissors. Now." He could cut away the long hair trapped in the mechanism, for if they moved any part of the machine, it could tear her scalp off completely.

Rokesmith scrambled under the machine to get to the small girl, who was whimpering now, obviously losing consciousness. "Lottie!" he cried, frantically pulling at her tattered dress.

"Carter, we need a wagon. Go outside and fetch one. Can you drive it?"

He nodded, tears streaming down his dirty cheeks.

"We will head to Dr. Middlemiss. You know where it is?"

"Church Street?" he rasped.

"Yes. Go. Quickly now."

Rokesmith tore out from under the machine and ran for the exit. Miller returned and passed him the scissors. "Lottie, don't move. I'm going to cut you free."

She slumped, and Miller quickly held her upright and in place while Aidan sliced through the long curling locks. At last, she was free. Aidan stood and shrugged out of his coat, wrapping it about her head. He had nearly slipped in the blood pooling on the floor. He remembered hearing of Garrett's gunshot wound, how Abbie had kept constant pressure on it to stem the flow of blood. Her quick-thinking action had kept him alive until he could be treated.

"Take over, Miller!"

Aidan didn't wait for a reply, but sprinted outside. Lottie wasn't moving. She lay in his arms like a doll made of rags. He found Rokesmith arguing with one of the workers.

"Get out of the way; we are commandeering this wagon." The man opened his mouth to argue, but Aidan gave him a deadly look. "Stand aside, or I'll beat you fucking senseless."

The man backed up several steps, and he and Rokesmith scrambled onto the bench. Grabbing the reins, Rokesmith snapped them and yelled, "Hah!" The dray horses vaulted forward until they were out of the courtyard. "Is she...still alive?"

Aidan twisted his coat like a tourniquet over her head and face, leaving only her nose and mouth visible. His fingers felt for a pulse in her neck. Faint, but still there. "Barely. Faster, lad."

Blood had already seeped through the fabric of his coat. Head wounds bled more profusely than most other injuries. How in hell had he known that? Could Middlemiss even do anything for the young girl? What kind of training did he have?

Rokesmith was openly sobbing, and with his free hand, he patted the boy's arm. "Stay strong, lad. For Lottie. We will do all we can to save her."

Rokesmith quieted, sniffling as they headed into the village proper. "Out of the way!" Aidan yelled as they rumbled through the narrow streets. Once they arrived at the clinic, Aidan barely waited for the wagon to come to a stop before he was scrambling down with Lottie in his arms. He burst through the door. "Doctor!"

Both Middlemiss and Cristyn emerged from behind a curtain.

"Accident at the mill. Her hair caught in the mechanism of the spinning machine. Part of her scalp...God." His insides tumbled. How else could he explain it?

"Bring her through here." Middlemiss pointed. Cristyn followed. Aidan gently laid the young girl on the table. "You should wait outside." Rokesmith ran behind the curtain, making the small area more cramped than it already was. "Take the lad with you. Allow us to examine her."

Aidan seized the boy's shoulders and he struggled, not wishing to leave the girl's side. "Come with me," Aidan murmured. "The doctor and nurse will care for her."

"Wait in my office in the rear, Mr. Black," the doctor said as he unraveled the coat about Lottie's head.

Rokesmith's shoulders slumped, and he dejectedly followed Aidan into the small office. The lad was obviously devastated, and Aidan was at a loss as to how to comfort him. It was not something he bothered with, considering how egoistic he was. Or rather—had been. "Carter."

The lad sniffled and wiped his runny nose on his sleeve. "She was too young," he muttered, so low Aidan could hardly make out the words.

"Pardon?"

"She shouldn't have been a scavenger. I trained her best I could, watched out for her...I failed."

Aidan turned the boy to face him. "No, you did not fail her. Or the others. If not for you, the rest of the children would have been worse off."

"I could've done more." His lower lip quivered. He was obviously on the edge of tears again.

"We all could do more in this life, but often we don't. I certainly didn't. I lived for my own pleasures. Never gave a thought to anyone, not even my family. But I am trying to make amends." Aidan laid a comforting hand on Rokesmith's shoulder. "You, however, looked out for those children. Protected them. What happened to Lottie was not your fault. It was an accident, something completely out of your control."

"I tied her hair back, I know I did. I always do it for those under the machines."

"It must have come loose. Again, it's not your fault. She should have never been under there, for you're correct, she was too young to be working in the mill at all. That blame is on McRae."

Rokesmith blinked, his eyes swelling with tears. "I don't want her to die. She's all I have."

Aidan's heart swelled with compassion, and he pulled the boy against him, giving him a comforting embrace. Strange that he would do this, but it was instinct, a wish to console the boy. At first, Aidan thought Rokesmith would pull away. But he leaned against Aidan and began to cry.

"Let it out, lad. Let it out," he whispered softly. Aidan found his own eyes had filled with tears. In the midst of this tragic event, perhaps there was hope for his shriveled soul. But this wasn't about him. "I promise you, if she lives, I will see to her safety. And yours. And I will do all in my power to see nothing like this happens ever again. To any child."

Aidan meant it. By God, he would make it his life's mission to bring down every cruel master who mistreated children. What good were power and money if not used to better the lives of those in need?

And how would his family feel about him bringing two orphans back to Wollstonecraft Hall? Because, damn it all, he would not leave Carter and Lottie to the fates.

# Chapter 20

Cristyn had never seen such a horrible injury. Yes, she had lived a sheltered life, not only in Standon, but at the sanatorium.

"Fetch a basin of water, Cristyn, and cloths," Paris said, his tone even.

Right, focus on the patient. Once she returned, she laid the objects on the shelf next to the examining table. Aidan's blood-soaked coat had been tossed aside. The small child was unconscious. Perhaps that was a blessing.

As Paris cleaned away the blood, the extent of the injury became more apparent. The tear started on the left side of the forehead, near the hairline, and continued partway across her head—not as horrible as Cristyn had first thought. Large chunks of hair were missing, no doubt cut away to free her from the apparatus.

"This will take numerous stitches, but I believe we can close the wound. Whether she will survive the shock and the loss of blood is another question. Then there is the possibility of infection. I will need the razor; we will have to shave the hair close to the gash and begin stitching immediately."

Once Cristyn collected the items needed, they worked together to clean the wound with antiseptic, shave the hair, and begin closing the jagged tear. They worked on each end of the wound, meeting the in middle. Through it all, the child slipped in and out of consciousness, and did not scream once. *Brave girl.*

They had no sooner completed when the girl's eyes fluttered open. "Cristyn, some cool water with two drops of laudanum. She must sleep."

They sat her upright enough to take the drink. Coaxing the girl with soft words, Paris held the glass to her mouth and she swallowed. In no time at all, she was asleep.

After wrapping part of her head in a gauze bandage, Paris wiped his hands on a towel. "I do not believe blood will collect under the skin and place pressure on the brain. But I cannot be sure."

"Will she survive?"

"It is hard to say. You had better fetch Wollstonecraft and the boy."

Cristyn walked toward the rear office and came upon Aidan comforting the lad.

"Let it out, lad. Let it out," he whispered softly. Cristyn's heart squeezed with sympathy at the sight. "I promise you, if she lives, I will see to her safety. And yours. And I will do all in my power to see nothing like this happens ever again. To any child."

For all Aidan's talk of being a heartless rake, she was seeing none of it here. She was moved beyond words at him offering solace to the distraught boy. Any man who would protect children was not without a heart and soul, no matter what he claimed.

"Aidan."

He looked up questioningly.

"The doctor will see you now. Come, the both of you."

They followed Cristyn to the exam area. Their gazes slid to the sleeping child.

"Is she...alive?" Carter asked.

"Yes. But there could be complications," Paris replied.

"Such as?" Aidan asked.

"Pressure on the brain, infection, shock from the loss of blood. Because of this, I believe it best we move her to the hospital in Hinckley."

"And what can they do for her that you and Cristyn cannot? If she goes there, you know that because she's an orphan she will immediately be transferred to a workhouse infirmary and lost in the morass of a broken system. She is under my protection, and I will not allow her out of my sight."

Carter gazed up at Aidan with admiration, and he patted the boy's shoulder in reassurance. The sight made Cristyn's heart skip a beat. Aidan claimed that he was not a hero, but she would beg to differ. And so would the boy.

Paris met Aidan's gaze. "Well, I do have a bed in the rear she can use. What is her name?"

"She said Lottie, but I think she was given the name at one of the orphanages. She doesn't know her age, either. Maybe six or seven," Carter replied. "I want to stay with her. Can I, Mr. Black? Please, sir. Please, Doctor." He looked pleadingly between the two men.

"I don't see the harm," Paris said. "It is best if someone sits with her. The boy and I will take shifts. What is your name?"

"Carter Rokesmith."

"Carter, wait out front while we get Lottie comfortable," Paris said.

"One moment," Aidan interjected. "I will send for my man in Hinckley. He has a carriage. If the child takes a turn, we will transport her to the hospital immediately. It is a far better choice of vehicle than a ramshackle wagon. Carter, if I write a note, will you deliver it? You know where it is; you delivered an envelope to him before."

"Aye, sir."

"Unfortunately, I have to return to the mill. I will explain Carter's absence somehow."

Cristyn laid a hand on his arm. "Come, I will show you to pen and paper."

Once they moved into the front room of the clinic, Cristyn impulsively stood on the tips of her toes and kissed him.

"What was that for?" Aidan whispered.

"You were wonderful with Rokesmith. I heard you pledge your protection. I didn't think I could love you more, but..."

Aidan swept her up into a crushing embrace, kissing her hungrily, as if he were starving. Cristyn tunneled her fingers into his thick hair and he lifted her from the floor, holding her tight against him. The sound of voices broke them apart.

Reality caused the passion to dissipate as quickly as it had flared. Aidan sat at the desk, and Cristyn collected pen and paper and placed it before him. As she turned to leave, he clasped her wrist. "I need to see you. Tonight," he rasped.

"I'm not sure how that can be achieved," she murmured.

Aidan didn't answer, as Carter had walked into the room. Aidan scratched out a message, then folded the paper. "Stay there and return with Samuel Jenkins. Understand?"

Carter touched his forelock. "Aye, sir." He took the folded note and scampered away.

"I will have to acquire a room for Samuel. Hopefully there is a vacancy at the inn."

"If not, maybe Mrs. Trubshaw could spare a room." It struck Cristyn that Aidan's time in Earl Shilton was coming to a close. "You're nearly finished here, aren't you?" The thought of him leaving caused her heart to ache.

"Yes, sooner than I had thought. Much depends on what Rokesmith will tell me—if he tells me."

Cristyn gave him a sad smile. "I believe he will. He looks at you as if you were his hero."

"What nonsense," Aidan sniffed. He stood and walked toward her. He took her hand and laid it on the fall of his trousers. She found unyielding hardness. "See what you do to me? One passionate kiss and I am desperate for you. Tonight, Cris. Come to me. However you can achieve it." He dropped her hand, then departed. Cristyn stood in the window, watching him climb onto the wagon. Giving her one last sultry look, Aidan snapped the reins and disappeared down the lane.

Damn the warnings and sage advice from Paris and Mrs. Trubshaw, and even her father. Nothing would keep her away.

\* \* \* \*

Aidan had no sooner arrived at the mill when he caught sight of Mr. Meeker, his face flushed with anger and annoyance.

"Mr. McRae is beside himself. Taking one of the delivery wagons when it was needed to pick up bales of cotton? You've put us behind schedule with your foolhardy rescue mission." The man followed the wagon until Aidan brought it to a complete stop. "He wants to see you. He is livid. Leaving the mill floor in complete pandemonium…you should have reported to Mr. McRae first!"

Aidan jumped down from the wagon and strode toward Meeker, grabbing a fistful of the man's cravat. He squeaked in protest like the rat he was. "Shut your mouth, you miserable cretin. Or I will shut it for you."

"How dare you threaten me—"

Aidan slapped the man across the cheek, effectively silencing him. "Next time, there will be more. Now, I will go and see *the master*, and you will stay well clear." Aidan needed to contain his fury—at least until he knew the dark, undisclosed narrative of this blasted place.

"You struck me!" Meeker sniveled.

"I barely tapped you, don't go on. But I will do it again if you interfere with me." Exhaling a cleansing breath, he headed upstairs to McRae's office. His coat was gone and his waistcoat and shirt were soaked with blood. Let the bastard see it. He knocked and entered. "You wish to see me, sir?"

"Close the door. Sit." The words were curt, angry, as if he were speaking to a disobedient dog. "You dare show yourself in my office in this state?" McRae thundered.

A child had nearly died on the mill floor, and this was the man's main concern? "I thought it best to return here immediately." Aidan sat and crossed his legs, struggling to keep his voice and expression neutral.

"You've made a muddle of today's delivery schedule. Caused chaos in the spinning room, leaving it unsupervised. The machines didn't run for over an hour. So we are behind that schedule as well."

"I'm assuming Miller had to clean and recalibrate the machine. That takes time. Also, you cannot expect workers to carry on as if nothing happened. The blood had to be scrubbed away."

"You brought this mill to a complete standstill over some squalling little monster," McRae snapped.

"What would you have me do, stand by and watch the child expire? Her hair was caught, part of her scalp torn away. She needed immediate medical attention."

"I refuse to pay for her care. It would have been more prudent to have her replaced."

Aidan narrowed his gaze. "What are you saying, exactly?"

"That in the future, if one of the imbecile orphans is caught up in the machinery, then that is their fate. I can procure any number of poor law brats anytime. Where is the boy who drove the wagon?"

"He was injured trying to rescue the girl."

McRae frowned. "Now I'm deprived of two workers, and have gained nothing but inconvenience and extra cost."

Aidan's blood boiled hot. McRae would have let the child die. "I will take responsibility for both of them. And for their expense. You need not think on them again." Aidan stood, pulled out pound notes from his pocket, and tossed them on the desk. "In fact, buy more slave workers, on me," Aidan growled.

"There is no need to take that tone. You are under obvious duress, so I will allow it to pass…this once." Nevertheless, McRae gathered up the pound notes like an edacious cardsharp. "Change your clothes and return to work. Tell those on the floor they will be staying an extra hour tonight, to make up the time lost. You may go."

Aidan gave a mocking bow and left the room, before he said something he would regret.

As soon as his shift ended, he returned to the inn to pick up the food he had ordered. Luckily, he was able to secure a room for Samuel on the first floor. As he waited for the victuals, Samuel strode into the tavern room.

"Good evening, Mr. Black."

"Good evening to you, Mr. Jenkins."

He pulled Samuel aside. "You're settled in?"

"Aye, sir. I sent word to the earl and viscount that I've moved to Earl Shilton, same inn as you. I also can report that there are a couple of constables in Hinckley. But more importantly, there is currently a small army regiment in Leicester if we need them."

"Good man. Lay low until I have the information we require." Aidan pulled out pound notes and thrust them into Samuel's hand. "For your accommodations and meals."

Samuel took the notes and nodded.

Once Aidan collected the food, he headed toward Church Street. Walking along the cobbled streets, he admonished himself for revealing too much to Meeker and McRae. In the past, he never would have shown such volatile emotion. And what had possessed him, in the middle of a crisis, to kiss Cristyn and have her touch him? Yes, his control as far as she was concerned had been completely shattered. Yet he refused to mention or even think on that most elusive and earth-shattering of emotions—love.

But what he felt for Cristyn had to be love, for it went far beyond lust or temporary passion. He hadn't thought this would happen. He had already decided he would remain unmarried, for who needed such tangled turmoil in one's life? A small part of him used the curse as a motive, but he now wondered if he used it to avoid examining what lay in his heart? Damn his vulnerabilities. Damn his cowardice.

Aidan was still cross when he entered the clinic. The place was eerily quiet. "Hello?"

Middlemiss came out from the back room. "Wollstonecraft."

"How is the girl?"

"Still sleeping. I imagine she will slumber the rest of the night. There is no change; her pulse is still weak. If she lives until the morning, there is a good chance of recovery. Most of the scar will be hidden under her hair; there's a mercy."

"Then I pray she survives the night." Aidan thrust the sack of food at the doctor. "I brought pies from the tavern."

Rokesmith entered the room and stood next to Middlemiss. "I want to stay the night. With Lottie. Until she's better."

The doctor took the sack. "She will sleep the rest of the night, lad."

"I don't care." He pouted. "She needs me."

"What harm will it do? He should not return to the damned mill, anyway." Aidan met Rokesmith's gaze. "Is there someone who can see to the children in your absence?"

He nodded. "Aye, Sarah and Charlie know what to do. They're almost as old as me."

"Where is Cristyn?" Aidan asked.

"She has gone to her rooms, to refresh and rest," the doctor replied. That was all he needed to hear. "Thank you. I will check in on the girl later." Aidan departed before the doctor could respond. He'd no sooner stepped outside when he saw Cristyn walking toward him. His heart skipped a beat. Then another. He clasped her elbow and steered her away from the clinic. "Have you eaten?"

"No, I—"

"Excellent. Then you shall come and dine with me."

"At the inn?"

He lengthened his strides, and Cristyn struggled to keep up. "Yes. More specifically, in my room."

"Aidan…"

He pulled her into a nearby alley, away from prying eyes. With her back to the wall, he faced her. "What you make me feel terrifies me. I had plans, you see, to live a dissolute existence, only I went too far. All was in darkness until you came into my life. I was broken, like a rusty, neglected toy ready for the rubbish—until you. I thought the feelings to be gratitude for your medical assistance—what else could they be?" Aidan cradled her face in his hands, staring into her eyes. "I am still trying to puzzle it out. Please, be patient with me. I am a work in progress, as if a sculptor were shaping me and the clay is not yet set. Am I making any sense?"

Her eyes grew moist. "Yes. I understand."

God, he didn't deserve her. But for the first time, he was speaking from his heart. "I am a selfish being. I always will be, especially when it comes to you. We haven't much time; will you come to my room?" He nuzzled her neck and whispered hotly in her ear, "I need to be inside you."

"Oh," she whimpered. "I'm selfish, too. Yes. Now."

Her breathless words caused a torturous groan to escape him. Reaching in his coat pocket, he slipped his room key into her hand. "Go up the back stairs and wait for me. I will procure some provisions."

"I can't stay long. I told Paris I would return to help with Lottie."

"Food and sex, then I will escort you to the clinic. Or, better yet, sex then food."

Cristyn laughed, and his soul soared at the sound. She took the key, kissed his cheek, and hurried away. He waited in the alley until his arousal had dissipated enough not to be noticeable, then walked briskly toward the front entrance of the inn.

Mr. and Mrs. Atwood were busy serving customers. "Mr. Black. What can I do for you?" Mr. Atwood said.

"More food. What do you have available?"

The innkeeper chuckled. "You're certainly keeping my wife and me busy with your requests. I swear you're feeding the village."

"Not the entire village, surely."

"I have ham sandwiches. Would four suffice? And some cheese?"

Aidan tossed coin on the counter. "As soon as you can gather them together."

Standing by the counter, he glanced about the room. He recognized a couple of the men from the mill. They touched their forelocks in greeting, then turned their attention to their pints of bitter. The men had never acknowledged him before, and had never shown him any respect. Were they in the mill when Lottie was injured? He wondered if word had gotten around that he'd struck Meeker? That would make it all the more imperative he conclude this clandestine undertaking as soon as possible.

With the food in hand, Aidan wasted no time climbing the stairs. He turned the knob and slipped into his room. Cristyn stood by the window.

"I have food. It's not much, but enough to take the edge off any hunger pains. Shall we eat?" He locked the door, then met her at the small table. Handing her a sandwich wrapped in brown paper, he also produced a jar. "Hot tea. Not fancy." Giving her a smile, he unscrewed the lid and passed it to her.

"It's lovely. I *am* rather famished." She bit into the sandwich, and Aidan did the same, not taking his eyes off her. Even watching her eat caused his arousal to sizzle at full heat.

Once they completed their meal, Aidan stood and held out his hand. "It seems we can only collect moments alone here and there. Soon you will be in my bed all night, and we will take our time and savor."

"But not at this moment?" she teased.

"No." When she slipped her hand in his, he gathered her up in his arms and carried her to the bed. Cristyn laughed, her beautiful face reflecting pure joy. To think he was capable of providing the means of her happiness. It was humbling indeed.

Once he lowered her, they wordlessly removed their clothes. Aidan lay on the bed. He unfastened the fall of his trousers and pulled out his cock. "Sit here, sweet. And ride me."

# Chapter 21

Ride him? He gave her a sly, sensual smile as she tried to work out in her mind how that could be accomplished. *Ah.* The picture took form. Facing him. Straddling him. His shaft nestled deep inside her while she...rode him. Aidan was temptation personified—one she could not or would not evade.

Cristyn gathered her skirt and climbed atop him, knees on either side of his slim, muscular hips. The hardness of him rubbed against her wet core. Her bodice was open, her breasts all but spilling out. How she trembled with yearning.

Aidan still wore his shirt, but it was undone, giving her a delicious peek at his sculpted chest. With a satisfied sigh, she spread the garment farther apart, trailing her fingertips across his hot, silky skin. He truly was a beautiful specimen of masculinity. Her fingers moved upward, tracing his full lips, the deep lines bracketing his mouth. Her father had told her he was twenty-six. He looked older, no doubt a result of all he'd been through. The weariness and hard living were apparent in the creases on his face, reflected in his summer-sky-blue eyes.

But Cristyn also saw hope there. And though he had not spoken the words aloud, dare she say...love? Certainly desire.

"Put me inside you," he growled.

Reaching between her legs, she grasped him and rose up onto her knees, then slowly descended, taking all of him.

Aidan released another husky groan. "I will not come inside you. Take your pleasure. Move back and forth." His hands gripped her upper thighs and he demonstrated the rocking movement.

Oh, the friction was delicious. Laying her hands flat on his chest, she found the rhythm as Aidan thrust his hips upward. How absolutely *wonderful*.

"Touch yourself. Show me how you give yourself pleasure." His eyes burned with blue fire. "How you come when you think of me."

*Wicked, passionate man.* Cristyn did not hesitate; she found that sensitive little nub and gasped at the sizzling contact. She soon became lost in the sensations of riding his shaft and rubbing her clitoris. Soft whimpers turned into throaty moans.

"Yes, Cris. That's it. Come for me," Aidan urged.

The motions between them became frantic, then she shattered, crying out in an explosion of utter bliss. Aidan groaned, then lifted her off him as he shook and shuddered. He covered his shaft with his hand. "Hell," he rasped, "that was close. Nearly spilled in you."

Cristyn curled up next to him as their breathing regulated.

"We had best clean up and return you to the clinic," he murmured as he stroked her arm.

She caressed his chest. "I can manage."

He kissed her forehead. "You can more than manage anything you put your mind to, but I also want to check in on the child."

"What will happen to her...and Carter?" Cristyn whispered.

"I haven't come to a decision as yet. But I'll be damned if I see them returned to that miserable mill, or a workhouse."

They allowed themselves the luxury of laying in each other's arms for another five minutes, then rose, tidied, dressed, and were heading toward the clinic as the sun set. As she slipped her arm through his, she gazed at him adoringly, not caring if the villagers witnessed it. Most women—at least, women of the upper classes—would not be so patient with Aidan as he worked through his emotions. But she more than anyone understood the difficult journey he had been taking since he'd arrived at the Standon Sanatorium.

For all Cyn's talk of how reformed rakes make wonderful husbands, there was a darker aspect to it. What if the man became bored with marriage? What if he missed the adventure of his wild, dissipated life? What if he only sought out matrimony because he was temporarily exhausted? Would he take up his old habits, women and opium? Aidan had stopped at a brothel on the way home. For all his claims of it being empty and meaningless, would it remain as such?

Cristyn was not so blinded by love and desire that she couldn't see the pitfalls before her. Could they have a future? By his own admission, he was still being molded into the man he wished to be. Would the clay hold? Could he commit to one woman for the rest of his life? Instinctively and with surety, she understood she would not tolerate an aristocratic marriage, where the man led a secret life of sin while the woman was tucked away in the country, forgotten and alone.

Shaking away the horrid thoughts, she looked up at him. He *was* a good man; she felt it in her bones. If only Aidan would accept it.

Arriving at the clinic, he held the door open for her. Paris and Carter came out from behind the curtain to greet them. "The child?" Aidan asked.

"Resting, but fitfully. We will stay with her tonight," Paris said.

Cristyn removed her gloves. "And I will as well."

"Mr. Black...or, Mr. Wollstonecraft, I will tell you what you want to know," the boy murmured, looking down at the toes of his worn shoes. He then cast a quick glance to Paris and Cristyn. "You can stay and all." He took a deep breath and exhaled. "Not sure what happened to the women expecting babies. I heard they were sent to Scotland. But there's a grave on the edge of the mill property. There are...children buried there. Not sure how many. I only know of two since I got here."

The adults exchanged shocked looks. Carter bit his lower lip. "What you did for Lottie, getting her help, you're the first to do it. When the children got sick, or injured, he—the master, and Hanson—let them die. There was no real doctor here before Dr. Middlemiss came. They stopped feeding them. I tried to slip the sick ones food, but he took them away to some other part of the mill. Then I saw them no more."

Aidan laid a comforting hand on Carter's shoulder." How do you know about the grave?"

"I followed them. It was dark. There were bundles on a wagon. Hanson and a man I've never seen before dug in the dirt and buried the bundles. It had to be the children. They were the right sizes." He shook his head. "I was afraid to say anything. It made me want to protect the children who were left all the more. I...I stole. In the village. I stole food to keep them fed, for what the master gave us was never enough."

Cristyn was horrified. Glancing at Aidan, she could see the shock, but also the barely contained fury.

"The sun has set. You will show me this grave in the morning?" Aidan asked, his words clipped.

Carter nodded. "I don't want Lottie to wind up there. Or any of them. I should've told, but I was afraid."

Aidan slipped an arm about the boy's shoulders. "No one blames you, lad. Who could you have told? No one at the mill."

"I could have told Dr. Middlemiss," Carter sniffled.

"Yes," Paris said gently, "but I could have done more as well. I heard the whispers of mistreatment and neglect, and did not act quickly enough.

Mistakes are lessons learned; they are not meant to be lasting regrets. Try not to think on what if, but move forward from where you are."

\* \* \* \*

Aidan stared at Middlemiss, the empathic words resonating deep in his soul. *Mistakes are lessons learned, not lasting regrets. Move forward.* Isn't that what he was trying to achieve with this covert operation at the mill? To heal his battered soul, to forgive by doing something to benefit someone other than himself?

The news about the grave was worse than he had imagined. Carter was not fabricating a tall tale— misery and regret were clear on the boy's face.

"Wollstonecraft, I heard Muggeridge has returned to Earl Shilton. He is staying at the inn. Perhaps you can approach him with this news," Paris said.

The queen's representative. Perfect. He turned to Cristyn, took her hand, and kissed it. "I must take my leave and seek out Muggeridge immediately. I'll return early in the morning. Carter, you will show me then where this grave is located?"

The boy nodded.

About to turn on his heel to depart, Aidan stopped and held out his hand to Middlemiss. "Thank you for all you have done for Lottie." The doctor took his hand and shook it.

Aidan turned to Cristyn. "And to you, Nurse Bevan. As always, my deepest thanks."

She gifted him with a warm smile in reply.

Aidan exited the small clinic and walked briskly toward the inn. Once he asked Atwood for Muggeridge's room number, Aidan located it and knocked. A middle-aged man with graying hair opened the door.

"I am Aidan Wollstonecraft. Could you spare me a few moments of your time? A grave situation has arisen and I will need your assistance." *Grave, indeed.*

The man arched an eyebrow at him, giving him a dubious look.

"I am the heir to the Earl of Carnstone."

"Come in, by all means, Lord Wollstonecraft." Aidan crossed the threshold. His grandfather's name opened more doors than not. "Your father is Viscount Tensbridge. We've been corresponding about the situation here."

There was only one chair in the room, so Aidan remained standing, and wasted no time relaying all that had happened since he'd arrived in the village.

"Good God," Muggeridge murmured. "Bodies of children in a mass grave is serious indeed. We could be talking of gross negligence, manslaughter, or at least criminal neglect. I am a barrister, so I know of what I speak."

"What would happen to the mill if McRae were arrested?" Aidan asked.

Muggeridge rubbed his chin. "I would imagine, if he were found guilty, the crown would seize the property until a suitable buyer could be found."

"If that should come about, I wish to purchase it. Please contact me before anyone else. Can you do that?" Him? The owner of a cotton mill? Why the hell not? "I would not mistreat, neglect, or harm the workers. Every rule and regulation would be followed to the letter." Aidan would find capable local men who could run the day-to-day operations—Miller came to mind.

"I will. But we are getting ahead of ourselves. What is your plan?"

"When dawn breaks, I'll be taken to the grave by the lad I told you about, and we will commence digging."

"I want to be there. But before that, I will send for a number of soldiers from Leicester. They will keep order, and also keep people away from the dig site. You are sure of this boy's tale? If we're wrong, it could bring about a whole collection of tribulations."

"I believe him. Besides, you're the queen's representative. No feeble threats from McRae will ever transpire."

With a shake of hands and an agreement to fetch Muggeridge at dawn, Aidan hurried to Samuel's room. Once inside, he relayed all that had happened that evening. "We will need at least one other man to assist us with…" He paused. *Delaney.* Was he still in the vicinity? Why even consider him when Aidan wanted to keep the man firmly in his past? His brawn would certainly come in handy, not only for the digging, but in keeping others away. "Remember the large man who forced his way into the clinic this past February?"

Samuel nodded.

"He's here, in the village. Not staying at the inn; he prefers to rent rooms. I need you to locate him. We have spoken and cleared the air." *More or less.* "Find him, and bring him to the inn later tonight. You remember what he looks like?"

"Aye, sir. Are you sure you wish to include this man?"

"Yes. Ask around; he's not hard to miss. We will also need shovels." Aidan thought of the gardening shed in the rear yard. "I will collect some. Go, Samuel."

Once Samuel departed, Aidan headed to the shed. It wasn't easy stumbling about the yard in the dark. Damn it, a padlock!

By the time he found Atwood, asked permission to borrow the shovels, gathered them, and brought them to his room, Samuel had arrived with a hulking Delaney.

"Never thought you'd ask to see me again," he grumbled.

"Neither did I. But I have a job for you. It pays fifty pounds."

"Oh, aye, and I'm to leave right after?" he snapped. "Sounds like another bribe."

"It's not. Have you started working for the stocking masters?"

Delaney curled his lip in disgust. "Aye. It involved me bullying poor folk to part with their meager coins to pay rent on the frames. Doesn't sit well with me."

"Then the fifty pounds will eliminate your need for the job. If you wish to stay in this area, there may be more respectable employment for you in the future. Or you can move on. The decision is yours."

Delaney gave him a dubious look. "And what do I have to do for this money?"

"Grave digging. At dawn. Do you accept?"

"I can't figure you out," Delaney said, shaking his head.

"I've been told that on many occasions," Aidan replied. "Taking the work, then?"

"I'll not ask what it's about, but I'll take it."

"Be here as soon as the sun rises."

As Delaney nodded and turned to leave, Aidan exhaled. Never had he imagined he would be working alongside him, considering their past association. But though the man physically resembled a brute—and often acted like one—Aidan had come to believe that Delaney had his own code of honor. Tomorrow would bring revelations of all sorts.

* * * *

They set out at dawn, a group of the unlikeliest men you could imagine: Aidan, Samuel, Delaney, and Muggeridge, along with Carter Rokesmith. The queen's man informed them he'd sent a message to Leicester last night, and a contingent of soldiers was arriving at the mill presently.

Carter led them to the edge of the property, a flat piece of ground nestled between clusters of oak trees. It afforded them a modicum of privacy. Samuel and Delaney began to dig. Aidan removed his coat, rolled up his sleeves, grabbed a shovel, and assisted.

They hadn't excavated far before Delaney said, "I've hit something." He cleared away loose dirt and discovered a canvas sack. Delaney opened it. Inside was the desiccated corpse of a child. "Bloody hell," he murmured. Aidan was sickened. "We had best keep digging."

\* \* \* \*

Cristyn arrived at the clinic shortly after dawn. Carter had departed to lead Aidan and the others to the grave he'd spoken of the night before. For two hours she kept busy attending patients; she set a young boy's broken humerus, treated a woman's cut from slicing meat, and attended to Lottie, who thankfully had made it through the night. With a few moments to herself, she sipped a cup a tea, and her thoughts turned to her sensual encounter with Aidan. Heavens, she was truly playing with fire. But she was not ashamed. Not of her actions, and not of her feelings. She was in love, and no matter how this concluded, she would never, ever regret saying and showing how she truly felt.

A commotion in the front of the clinic caught her attention. She set the mug upon the table and hurried toward the noise. A man who was waiting to be treated stood and headed for the door. Outside, a number of people scurried past. "What is going on?" she asked.

The man turned to face her. "My brother came in and said there's a to-do at the mill. Soldiers. Men digging in the ground. Master's yelling at the overlooker, who be in the thick of it. Going to be a fight, I'll be bound." He exited the clinic and followed the crowd.

*Oh, no.* Her expression must have reflected her worry, for Paris said, "Go to him. I will stay with Lottie."

Lifting her skirt, she stepped outside, then followed the rush toward the mill. Her heart was in her throat. Surely the soldiers would not allow the situation to deteriorate to such a state that two men would exchange blows.

Arriving on the scene minutes later, she observed three soldiers holding back the gathering crowd. Cristyn pushed her way forward. A number of men stood on the corner of the mill property, with McRae and Aidan inches apart, shouting. Another man with gray hair and spectacles was trying without much success to place distance between them.

With a few quick dodges, Cristyn slipped through the throng and eluded one of the soldiers. Nearing the scene, she stopped in her tracks, her hand flying to her mouth in shock—for on the ground she counted eight burlap sacks. One was open, showing a corpse. Considering the size, it was as Carter described: a child. Neglected, buried, and forgotten. Tears formed in her eyes.

"You miserable bastard!" Aidan roared. He grabbed McRae's neckcloth. "You cold-blooded, murdering whoreson!"

"They died of injuries and sickness," McRae sneered, spittle flying across Aidan's cheek.

"Fire!" someone screamed. Other voices joined in.

*Dear God, what next?*

More people joined in raising the alarm, pointing frantically toward the mill. Aidan released McRae and they glanced in that direction. The residence portion of the mill was on fire. Smoke poured out of the closed windows, as they were obviously not well-sealed. One of the windows shattered and flames whooshed forward, causing the crowd to gasp and shout.

"My son!" McRae yelled.

"Your wife is in there too?" Aidan questioned.

"Yes. Oh, God!"

The gray-haired man called to the soldiers, "Make sure those inside the mill make it to safety!"

The soldiers nodded and ran with all haste toward the main entrance.

Unlike the mill's brick exterior, the residence was wood-framed. The structure was quickly being consumed by the roaring blaze, which grew in intensity with each passing minute.

It occurred to Cristyn what Aidan was about to do. *No.* He would be hurt, or killed. "Aidan, no!" she cried out.

He stopped, met her gaze, gave her a regretful smile, then ran toward the inferno.

She was about to head after him, but a strong hand held her arm, halting her. "No, miss. I'll go. I'll watch out for him."

She gazed up into the rough face of Delaney. His eyes reflected sadness, and her heart ached. Words would not form; all she could do was nod.

Delaney fell in behind Aidan. They disappeared around the rear of the building, and Cristyn's blood froze in her veins. The crowd attempted to move forward, but a few soldiers—along with the gray-haired man and a younger one, who must have been Aidan's Samuel—kept them at bay.

Carter ran to her, his expression reflecting the worry she felt. Cristyn slipped her arm about his shoulder.

*Aidan, my love, be careful.*

If she lost him, her heart would never recover.

# Chapter 22

With a swift kick, Aidan tore the door to the residence off its hinges. He stepped aside, waiting for the roar of flames to greet him, but nothing came—it hadn't spread to the stairwell yet. *No time to waste.* Delaney caught up to him. "I'll grab the boy, you find the wife," Aidan said.

"Aye. Lead the way," Delaney replied.

There was nothing else for it but to dash in, locate them, and escape before the roof caved in or the passageway caught fire. Aidan ascended the stairs until he reached the French double doors. Through the glass, he could see small pockets of flame consuming draperies and furniture and climbing ever higher to the ceiling. Through the smoke, he saw Mrs. McRae slumped on the sofa. Where was the boy?

Upon opening the doors, the fire was met with a blast of oxygen, but the rush of flames was not as serious as it could have been due to the fact the window had already been smashed, allowing air into the room. Or so Aidan surmised. Before he'd arrived, he read up on how serious a fire could be at a cotton mill. If the fire spread to the mill proper—it didn't bear thinking about. Hopefully the workers made it to safety. Aidan pulled the draperies down to try to slow the spread of the fire, but it insidiously consumed everything it came in contact with: cushions, rugs, wooden cabinets filled with expensive treasures.

Delaney lifted the unconscious woman over his shoulder. "Never mind the fire, find the boy!" he yelled at Aidan. "I'll wait."

*Right.* Aidan sprinted into the narrow hallway, coughing as the black smoke grew thicker.

"Come out, lad!"

He had checked two rooms and was about to exit the third when he heard a whimper. Crouching down, he found McRae's son curled into a ball under a bed. "Take my hand!"

The boy didn't move or respond. Aidan grabbed his leg and pulled him from his hiding place. Copying Delaney, he slung the boy over his shoulder and ran to the parlor. Aidan's eyes were watering; the heat was overwhelming, making breathing difficult. "Ready—"

"Look out!" Delaney shoved him out of the way, causing him and the boy to sprawl across the sofa. A large section of the ceiling fell on Delaney, scattering him and Mrs. McRae in sparks and flame. That Delaney managed to stay upright and still have a firm hold of the woman was impressive. But the sleeve of his coat had caught fire, the flame spreading upward, catching part of Mrs. McRae's skirt, then in turn spreading to Delaney's face and hair.

McRae's son was screaming at the top of his lungs as Aidan jumped from the sofa. He grabbed a cushion and tried to beat the flames into submission. He'd managed to snuff out most of it when Delaney yelled, "Go, before the rest of the ceiling comes down on us!"

Aidan threw the cushion aside, grabbed the hysterical child, and rushed through the wall of flames that was spreading into the stairwell. When they reached the outside, Delaney collapsed, part of his sleeve still burning. Muggeridge shrugged out of his coat and smothered the remaining flames.

Aidan lowered the screaming boy, and when he located his father he stumbled toward him. Cristyn ran into Aidan's arms and he held her close, grateful to be alive, thankful he could hold her once more. Hell, he could not imagine never holding her again. Life would not be worth living. His eyes burned from the smoke, as did his lungs. He coughed, trying to catch a decent breath of air.

"I must check on the others." She kissed his cheek and moved to Delaney's side. Mrs. McRae lay next to him, unconscious.

Samuel pulled up in one of the mill's wagons. "Sir, we had best leave. The fire is spreading to the roof of the mill."

"Is everyone out?" Aidan asked between coughs.

"Yes, sir. The village doesn't have a fire brigade; we could use the water from the river."

"Perhaps it is better that it burns." *Evil place.* He cast a glance at McRae. *Evil man.*

Muggeridge motioned to a couple of soldiers. "Take Mr. McRae into custody. There is a jail in Hinckley. Take him there, and I will follow directly. We will have to locate Hanson, this former overseer."

"My family knows where he is. I will send word." Aidan rubbed his stinging eyes. "And the bodies?"

"We will have to find a suitable place. Do you believe Dr. Middlemiss is up for the task of examining the remains?" Muggeridge questioned.

"Yes. More than competent."

"Good. We will make arrangements when we take the injured to his clinic."

"And the fire?" Aidan's voice had grown hoarse. God knew how much smoke he had swallowed.

"The remaining soldiers and men from the village have already set up a bucket relay to try to keep the fire from destroying all in its path. I would hazard to guess the residence is a complete loss. Perhaps also the roof of the mill."

"If the flames come in contact with the cotton fibers in the air, or the bales of cotton, the place will become a raging inferno. It is best everyone stay away and let it burn itself out. Try to prevent it spreading to the surrounding woods by all means. But the mill? Do not risk any lives to save it."

"I will heed your advice. Now, Lord Wollstonecraft, climb on the wagon and go with the others. You must be examined by the doctor. You have done enough heroic deeds for one day."

Heroic? Him? He didn't feel it. Rubbing his stinging eyes, Aidan cast a glance at the crowd watching from a distance. All the workers of the mill were now out of work. The children as well. How, exactly, had he helped these poor people? The poverty in this area would increase tenfold. And what would happen to the children? Would they be taken to another workhouse, where they would be sold by poor law guardians to another master to work as slaves?

Dejected, he hoisted himself onto the rear of the wagon. Delaney was grunting and writhing with pain. The man had saved him when he pushed him out of the way of the falling, fiery debris. It was not something he would soon forget.

\* \* \* \*

Bedlam broke out at Middlemiss's clinic once the wagon arrived. The doctor examined Delaney first, with Cristyn's assistance, treating the burns on his arm and part of his face. Next was Mrs. McRae. Middlemiss had stated he could smell laudanum on her breath. Using smelling salts, she awoke at last, but would not speak to anyone except to say she had no knowledge of how the fire had started.

But the boy, who said his name was Jonathan, spun a different—and interesting—tale. His mother had observed them digging on the property. Downing numerous glasses of water no doubt laced with laudanum, she became agitated. Storming about the room, she knocked over a lit kerosene lamp. Jonathan, scared at her violent ramblings, ran for the safety of his room. Apparently his mother behaved this way often. Once the fire started, he hid under the bed. When pressed, Jonathan recalled his mother screeching that his father's secrets were going to destroy them all.

Which indicated that his wife was complicit. When Muggeridge arrived at the clinic two hours later, he stated he would be taking Mrs. McRae to Hinckley jail for questioning.

"And the boy, Jonathan?" Aidan asked.

"We will find a relative to take him in, I am certain."

"The mill?"

"We managed to keep the fire from spreading to the surrounding wooded area, but as you predicted, once it reached the cotton, it burned dangerously fast. Not much remains of the structure, except the brick walls. The good news is no one was injured; the horses and wagons were rescued, as well as some of the cotton bales. Is it worth rebuilding? That is the question."

"What will happen to the workers in the interim? The children? They are blameless in this sordid episode, yet will suffer the worst," Aidan snapped. He shook his head. "Forgive my temper. It's all so blasted unfair."

Muggeridge nodded. "It is. But I will approach the queen on this. Perhaps there can be a sort of temporary financial assistance until this village and the surrounding district is put to rights. The hold that masters have on their workers, whether at the mill or in the making of stockings, is coming to an end. You have my word, and I speak for the crown."

Well, that was good news. "The nineteen children…"

Muggeridge flipped through his papers. "I thought there were twenty-one?"

"Two are staying under my direct care. I do not wish for the remainder to be sent to the workhouse. Surely we can locate a decent orphanage for them. They must be given a chance to find a family willing to take them in. I'll pay for their upkeep until it can be achieved."

"I may know of a couple of places. Allow me to contact them. In the meantime, however, where will they go?"

Aidan rubbed his forehead. He had an almighty pain throbbing across his temple. "Where are they now?"

"Some of the villagers have taken them in."

"Then perhaps the villagers will continue to see to their care until they can be relocated. Again, I will take up the expense. I will ask Samuel to go door-to-door and make arrangements."

Muggeridge held out his hand. "Then I had best be off to Hinckley. I can assure you, justice will move swiftly. As for the bodies of those poor, unfortunate children, I have taken possession of a barn near the mill. They are under guard. Your man, Samuel Jenkins, knows where it is. I will speak to Middlemiss before I depart, for I wish for him to examine them as soon as he is done here."

Aidan took the man's hand and shook it. "Until we meet again."

"May it be under better circumstances."

Muggeridge departed to find Middlemiss. Cristyn moved to Aidan's side and slipped her arm about his waist. "You must sit. You're as white as a sheet."

Aidan allowed her to lead him to a chair. "How can you tell under all the soot?"

Reaching for a damp cloth, she gently washed his face. "I am a nurse; I can tell."

"A highly competent nurse." He grimaced. "My damned head is aching."

"I will get you something to relieve it." She continued to stroke his cheeks. "You're a true hero, Aidan. *My* hero. You never gave it a thought; you ran into the burning building to rescue the woman and the boy. I was frightened. If anything had happened to you..."

He took her hand and kissed the palm. "But nothing has. And Lottie?"

"She's awake and sitting upright. First, allow me to fetch your headache powder. I will place it in a cup of tea." Cristyn kissed his forehead and left him alone.

The clinic was quiet for the first time in the past two hours—except for Mrs. McRae crying quietly as she and her son were taken to the wagon outside. He should feel sympathy for their predicament, for the lad at least. He would wind up with a relative, and hopefully would be protected from the worst of what his parents had done. But the woman? If she was complicit, she deserved justice. Hell, he had not imagined this operation coming to such a dramatic conclusion.

He couldn't wait; he had to see Lottie. Upon entering the back room, Aidan nodded at Middlemiss and Delaney and continued on to Lottie's bed. Carter was showing her a picture book.

Her face lit up when Aidan sat next her. "Hello, sir," she whispered. The child looked fragile, bundled in blankets with a large bandage about her head. It made his heart ache to see how she'd suffered, but he was also relieved she was recuperating. She smiled broadly. "My prince. You saved me."

"I'd do it again." He took the girl's small hand. "How would you like to come live with me? You and Carter. You will not have to work anymore. I will care for you. Nothing or no one will ever harm you again. Either of you. Would you like that, Lottie?"

She looked to Carter, as she often did, and the boy smiled and nodded. Lottie squeezed his hand and gave him a sweet smile. "Yes, sir. Would you be my father?"

Aidan's heart swelled. "I will be whatever you want me to be. Your father, your friend, your prince—or perhaps all of them rolled up together. You do everything the doctor says and get well, my dear."

He felt a hand lay gently on his shoulder. It was Cristyn—he knew it instinctively without turning around, for sizzling heat traveled through him. How much had she heard? "There's a good girl." He kissed Lottie's hand and released it.

After he'd followed Cristyn out of the room, he took the cup of tea she offered and sipped it, savoring the warmth. They stood in the doorway, and he inclined his head toward Delaney. "How serious are his burns?" he murmured.

"All burns are serious, but Paris states it hasn't reached the inner layers of skin. He will be in some pain and discomfort, but he will recover."

Middlemiss and Delaney were out of sight, but within earshot.

"Am I going to die?" Delaney rasped.

"Not if I can help it. There will be some scarring," Paris replied, his voice gentle.

Delaney scoffed. "Then I will be uglier than before." He paused. "I've got nowhere to go, Doctor. No way to pay for my keep and care. I don't want to wind up at one of those miserable workhouse infirmaries." His voice shook on the last sentence. There was real fear in his whispered tone.

Once Aidan paid Delaney, he would not be destitute, but he remained silent, not wanting to disturb the intimate conversation.

"Here, take my hand. You will stay with me as long as you like. I will care for you. See you well. On that, I promise. You will not have to go through this alone." The doctor's voice was soft with compassion.

A gruff but wretched sob escaped Delaney's throat.

Aidan took Cristyn's arm and led them away from the private moment. "Middlemiss, he prefers—"

"Men?" Cristyn replied in a quiet tone. "Yes. It's why I said he hadn't any romantic interest in me."

Aidan arched an eyebrow. Delaney and Middlemiss? It would be an odd pairing, if anything came of the emotionally charged atmosphere. It was also none of his business.

"I am weary beyond all reasoning," he murmured.

"Then perhaps we should head to your room. You must be hungry. It is past three in the afternoon."

"We?"

"Yes. Carter is looking after Lottie. Paris is looking after Delaney. Allow me to care for you. Anything relating to today's events can wait until tomorrow. I am your nurse, and you must heed me."

Aidan nuzzled her neck. "I do enjoy it when you order me about," he murmured. "And when you care for me." He was laying hot, insistent kisses along her neck, moving toward her chin and, ultimately, her mouth when Samuel burst in through the front entrance.

"Begging your pardon, sir. Jacob arrived with a message from Wollstonecraft Hall. Says it's urgent." He handed the sealed note to him. Aidan tore it open.

*Aidan,*

*Please come at once. Sabrina has gone into labor. It is too early, and she is in distress. Dr. Faraday has been sent for. It may be all over by the time you reach here, but I need you. Pray it is not the curse.*

*Riordan*

Fuck it all, what else had to happen? The words "Pray it is not the curse" had chilled him. Jesus, what if it was?

Cristyn squeezed his arm. "What is it?"

Exhausted beyond words, he handed her the note. She scanned it, her brows furrowing.

"I will have to leave at once. Fetch my horse, Nebula, from the stables, Samuel, and—"

Cristyn shook her head. "No, Aidan."

A flash of annoyance tore through him. "I teasingly mentioned enjoying you order me around, but I'm drawing a line. My brother needs me; nothing else matters." Aidan was annoyed—he would be damned if he were pushed about. "You stated you abhor men making your decisions. Grant me the same courtesy."

"You're right," she murmured. "I am sorry. I didn't mean that you should *not* go, just not today. This note is dated three days past. Your brother's wife has already had the baby—as a nurse, I can guarantee that. Rushing there while you are exhausted is not wise. Wollstonecraft Hall is—what? Well over a hundred miles away? Even riding full-bore you'll need sleep, meals, a change in horses. Samuel, how long did it take for Jacob to arrive here?"

"Two and a half days, miss. He is in my room, sleeping. He's done in."

Aidan cast Samuel a furious look, but the man didn't wither under his gaze. "Miss Bevan is right, sir. Forgive me for speaking out of turn, but why not use the carriage and leave in the morn? Jacob will be recovered from his fatigue by then, and so will you. I will remain here, act on your behalf until you're able to return."

There was merit in what Samuel and Cristyn said. He doubted he could even keep upright in the saddle. It would be reckless, and he was bloody well done with irresponsible behavior. "Does Jacob know anything of my sister-in-law's condition?"

"I thought you might ask, so I quizzed him before he took to bed. All he was told was that she was in labor. Sorry there's not more to tell, sir."

"I will leave in the morning, then. Ensure all is prepared. Nebula will return with me. The horse Jacob came on? It will stay here for your use. And yes, Samuel, you will be acting in my stead. After I rest, I will come to you with instructions. For now, I need you to accompany Dr. Middlemiss to where the bodies are being kept. He must examine them with all haste." He turned to Cristyn, softening his expression. "Will you stay here until Middlemiss returns?"

"Of course, if you will go at once to your room. I'll join you there later." She gave him a shy, but seductive smile. He kissed her forehead.

After speaking to Middlemiss, and to Delaney, stating their account would be settled soon, he stepped toward Lottie's bed and kissed her cheek, remembering her words: "My prince, you saved me."

He was Lottie's prince, Cristyn and Carter's hero.

Perhaps his life was not a total waste after all.

# Chapter 23

It was close to seven in the evening before Cristyn was able to make her way to the inn. Hopefully, Aidan had been sleeping the past few hours. How she wished Cyn was nearby to discuss all that had happened—especially the intimacy with Aidan. She had confessed in her last letter that she was in love with him, and had told him. Cyn had been nothing but supportive in her reply, revealing that she, too, had boldly spoken her true feelings for Davidson. It had all led to a happy ending.

But Aidan was not a vicar, a man who lived a moral life. No, he was much more complicated, which in turn made this entire situation a thorny and difficult journey. But as she had concluded previously, to her, Aidan was worth it.

Especially since she'd witnessed his tender and heartfelt conversation with Lottie. Her heart had swelled when Lottie called him her prince. How apt. Offering to take the children in had more than proved his innate goodness and honor.

When she stopped at the front desk of the inn, a woman looked up from her ledger and gave her a polite smile. "May I help you, miss?"

"I'm Nurse Bevan, assistant to Dr. Middlemiss, here to see Mr. Black. What room is he in?" Such duplicity, but one must at least try to keep up appearances.

The innkeeper's wife gave her a surprised look. Yes, she was a young woman about to go into a man's room alone. But this was a professional call—at least on the surface.

"Room fifteen, Miss Bevan, top floor. Is he well?" The woman leaned in closer. "Is the tattle accurate? Mr. Black dashed into a burning building to save the master's wife and child?"

"Yes, that's correct. It is why I'm here, to ensure there are no complications. Would it be too much trouble to have a pot of tea and sandwiches delivered to his room? Unless he has already eaten?"

"No, he hasn't. I'll see to it personally, miss. I must say, I'll be sorry to see him leave. Polite to a fault. A true gentleman. And generous."

"Yes, he is that."

Climbing the stairs, she thought about the note from his brother and the word "curse." She had decided against bringing up the subject in front of Samuel, but it was one of the many subjects they must tackle.

She knocked, and the door opened to reveal Aidan looking tousled and darkly appealing, as if he had woken from a nap. Giving him a brief smile, she entered.

Removing her shawl, she glanced at the quilt hanging off the edge of the bed. "You've slept?"

"I ordered a bath first. Hopefully the odor of smoke no longer lingers." In two strides, he gathered her into his arms. "How do I smell?" He smiled teasingly.

She gazed up at him. "Clean, with a faint whiff of bergamot." As hard as it was to leave his warm embrace, she placed her hands against Aidan's chest and stepped back. "I ordered sandwiches and tea. They should be here directly. How do you feel? Does the headache persist?"

"I must bow to your medical wisdom. You were correct; I would not have been able to travel by horseback today. Yes, my head still hurts. I also feel slightly nauseous. Not sure I will be able to eat."

"From what I've read in my father's medical books, you're suffering from inhaling too much smoke. Does your chest hurt?"

"A little."

"Your voice isn't as hoarse. A good sign. Traveling by carriage is entirely more prudent." They sat in the chairs. "I have news. Paris examined the bodies of the children. Two of the more decomposed ones showed evidence of fractured skulls." Cristyn shook her head. "What kind of men would treat children as if they mattered not at all?" she whispered miserably.

Aidan thumped his fist on the arm of the chair. "It churns my guts to see how children are used and abused, all in the name of industry. I could tell you horror stories of children laboring in coal mines, far worse than what we have witnessed here. Anyway, can it be proven McRae or Hanson committed murder?"

"Paris sent word on to Mr. Muggeridge in Hinckley, but from what he knows of the law, murder will be hard to prove—unless the men turn on each other. Manslaughter might be a more practical avenue."

Aidan snorted derisively. "So Muggeridge said."

A knock sounded at the door. Cristyn rose. "Must be Mrs. Atwood." She walked to the door and opened it, and the innkeeper's wife bustled in, laying the tray on the small table by the window.

"Beefsteak sandwiches as you like, Mr. Black."

"Thank you, Mrs. Atwood. You are a treasure," he crooned.

The older woman blushed and giggled. Aidan could charm anyone. Once a rake, always a rake? It was hard to know. Mrs. Atwood departed, closing the door behind her.

Cristyn poured the tea and passed Aidan a cup. "What did your brother mean about a curse?"

Aidan didn't answer right away. Instead, he ate a wedge of sandwich, working out a response. "Speaking of it to anyone outside of the family is not something I like to do, though I spoke of it to your father. I was first told of it at age thirteen. My grandfather escorted my brother and me to the family cemetery. He explained that most of the graves were of women who had married into the family—or, on rare occasion, were born into it. The Wollstonecraft men are cursed, never to keep love."

He ate more of his sandwich before continuing. "My grandfather had three wives. My mother died when I was three. My aunt died shortly after birth. Not all the unfortunate women died in childbirth, but many did. Hence my brother's worry. This curse goes back hundreds of years."

He took a sip of tea and frowned. "There was no way to break it, no magical spell, no great expedition to find a sacred object. Merely the directive: 'do not love.' That's it. It is why we have all remained unattached—until recently. Garrett believed in it more than any of us. He turned from love at age eighteen because of it. All it did was make him and Abbie miserable for years. And there was a child."

"Oh, my."

"Garrett only recently found out he had a fourteen-year-old daughter. Well, he couldn't deny the love any longer. They were married in Scotland."

"I remember you mentioning the nuptials, but I had no idea of all the complications and the history behind it." Cristyn sipped her tea, staring at him over the rim. Heavens, the family was cursed? How preposterous, but she wasn't about to mock it, as Aidan obviously took it seriously. Or did he? "Do you believe in this curse?"

"That trip to the cemetery had more of an impact on me than I led my family to believe. I decided I would never marry. Never involve myself in any affair of the heart. Once I became old enough to appreciate women and indulge in casual dalliances, I held true to my belief."

Cristyn felt sick to her soul. They had no future. He'd made it more than clear. If she had any sense, she would say goodbye and leave immediately. Try and forget him. But how? Aidan had a hold on her heart. She would never be able to give it to anyone else. In placing her cup and saucer on the tray, her hand shook.

"But," Aidan said quietly, "that is firmly in my past. Yes, I hit the lowest point any man could. But that wasn't why I was a physical and emotional wreck." He looked down into the depths of his teacup. "The reason I came on this excursion was to cleanse my soul, mold myself into the man I always wanted to be. An honorable man. A man worthy of the name Wollstonecraft."

"You are, Aidan," she said, her voice soft. "More than worthy."

"I hope that is the case. My father told me once to never allow anyone to tell me a man cannot show emotion, that it makes him weak. A man secure in his own skin will allow his feelings to show. Compassion, a stout heart, and a genuine concern for one's fellow man are collected in tears. I didn't heed him. Instead, I hid my emotions. I never cared for anyone but myself. It appears I was *not* secure in my own skin. But no longer." He wiped his eyes, and the sight of his tears caused some to form in her eyes.

"My past is behind me, and it is because of you. My angel of mercy. My comfort." He looked up at her, and his eyes shimmered with emotion. "My heart. From the moment you touched me, speaking to me in your soothing tone, I was completely smitten. I remember all our conversations—once I became lucid enough to participate in them. You adore hot mince tarts with fresh cream, and reading medical journals. You have strong opinions, especially on how the poor do not receive the medical care they deserve. I believe it is another worthy cause for the Wollstonecrafts to embrace." He gave her a warm smile.

"And to find that you saw away on corpses makes you infinitely more interesting than most women. You are forthright, honest, yet with a quick temper. I adore the fire that burns within you. You are passionate. Beautiful. And if I haven't made it plain: I love you, Cris. With you I am whole. Complete. Secure in my skin at last. You must stay with me. Forever. So that I may avoid ruination, for without you, I am Lord Nothing."

The tears spilled down her cheeks at his passionately spoken words. She vaulted out of her chair, right into his lap. Aidan laughed. Oh, he needed to do more of that. Cristyn would make it her life's work to ensure he loved and laughed with total abandon. Cupping his freshly shaven cheeks, she said, "I love you, Aidan. I will never run from you. I will fight for you, support you, and love you, regardless of your past, or a family curse. On this, I swear. It is only the future that matters. Our future."

He kissed her, and it contained all the love and passion he was feeling. She could taste it, for it matched hers. "Let's go to bed," he murmured, hungrily nibbling on her bottom lip.

"Don't we have more to discuss?"

"After."

"What about the headache? Nausea?"

"Completely gone."

Cristyn laughed, and once they stood they frantically removed their clothes. Aidan assisted her in removing the pins from her hair. As she reached for the waistband of his trousers, he halted her. "I had better lock the door. We're going to be at this all night. You will stay with me?"

\* \* \* \*

Aidan waited for her answer. My God, he'd told a woman he loved her, a declaration he had sworn he would never make. But the events of the past couple of days made his muddled emotions shift into clearer and sharper focus. Speaking with Delaney helped to truly place the past behind him, and speaking of it to Cristyn, telling her of truths long kept secret, also gave him the courage to own his feelings.

He needed time to show her how much he loved her, to taste every inch of her skin, lick and nibble every sensitive part of her body. To allow her to explore him the same way. She stood before him in a thin chemise, her nipples hard, begging for him to suckle them. Her glorious raven hair hung past her shoulders in thick, glossy waves.

"Yes. All night," she replied.

Aidan ran his fingers under the straps, pushing the chemise down until it pooled at her feet. Seeing her naked caused his heart to hitch in his chest. "You are stunning," he murmured reverently. He strode to the door and locked it. Then he unbuttoned the fall of his trousers, pushed them and his smalls to the floor, and kicked them aside.

"You're stunning as well," she whispered.

They were in each other's arms, skin to skin, kissing as Aidan walked them to the bed. He laid her flat, her legs dangling over the side. Then he hit his knees before her. Cristyn leaned up on her elbows, looking at him quizzically.

"I'm going to taste you." Draping her shapely legs over his shoulders, he gave her a wicked grin. Running his fingers along her slit, he moaned at the wetness that coated them. He ran his tongue along her folds and Cristyn shuddered, a soft whimper escaping her lips. "Do you like it? Do you wish me to continue?" he asked, his voice laced with desire.

She tunneled a hand through his hair. "Yes. Taste me."

Aidan didn't need to be told twice. Over the years, he had become quite skilled in giving women oral pleasure. He put all he'd learned to good use and had Cristyn writhing and moaning. Flicking his tongue across her clitoris caused her to cry out, then tremble with her swift and sudden release. "Oh, my."

"Indeed."

With a sigh, she sat up and cupped his cheek. "How wicked. May I do the same to you?"

Aidan rubbed his cheek against her palm. "Do what, exactly?"

"Put my mouth on your cock?"

He groaned, for he loved that she was not the least bit shy at speaking in succinct erotic terms. "Absolutely." He lay flat on the bed. "Explore whatever part you like."

Cristyn sat by his side, trailing the tips of her fingers along his arms and down his chest, leaving a trail of heat in their wake. "You are recovering well," she murmured. "More delineated muscle, and the extra few pounds show that your health is returning in full vigor."

"Thank you, nurse."

She grasped his painfully hard prick, giving him a couple of quick strokes. A ragged groan tore from his throat. Cristyn lay on top of him and began kissing and stroking his chest, moving slowly downward, his anticipation sparking. When she encased the head of his cock with her sweet, hot mouth, he nearly came off the bed. Gripping the blankets, he surrendered, allowing the sensations of her unpracticed motions to send him soaring. He couldn't recall any of his past sexual encounters—this beautiful woman had erased them. And he was glad.

He gently caressed a lock of her hair. "Enough, my love."

Cristyn no sooner sat back when his climax tore through him. "Jesus. Hell," he moaned.

"Will there be more?"

Never, ever would he tire of this glorious woman. "Insatiable minx. Later. Over by the basin, bring me a cloth, if you please."

Completely unconcerned that she was naked, Cristyn strode to the basin, wet the cloth, and returned. As he reached for it, she gently swatted his hand aside. "I will clean you."

Once she had, they lay on their sides, and he held her close. They rested for close to thirty minutes. Having her in his arms caused him to harden. He lifted her leg and rested it on his hip. Then he entered her, and, with slow deliberation, made love to her. They reached their peaks at near the same moment, and he took care not to spill inside her. Pulling her once again into his arms, they fell asleep.

Aidan awoke and lit the oil lamp by the bed. Hours must have passed, for they had awakened, made love once again, and slept some more. Rubbing his tired eyes, he glanced at the clock on the wall. Cristyn stirred and cuddled closer to him.

"What's the time?" she murmured.

"After midnight. Today is my birthday. Correction: mine and Riordan's birthday. Happy birthday, Brother."

She caressed his chest. "Happy birthday, my love."

"It's one of the best, with you here in my arms." He kissed her forehead.

"Charmer. When will you depart? Dawn? Later?"

"You mean when will *we* depart."

Cristyn sat upright, holding the sheet against her. "We?"

"I never asked, did I? I merely assumed. I wish for you to travel with me to Wollstonecraft Hall. Obviously, we will not depart until we have seen to every detail. I need to see Samuel, for there is much to address. There are certain people at the mill I want looked after. Miller, Tessie and her family, the children. Then there are Carter and Lottie."

"I cannot go anywhere without speaking to my father. Besides, regardless of what we've shared privately in this room, I cannot travel with you to your home. What will it say publicly? There is a societal difference in our stations."

Damn, he was making these plans and had not even explained how Cristyn would factor into them. "When I said I want you at my side forever, I meant us, married. Partners in life—and love. I would not dream of making any decisions without you. Ever. As for different stations, neither I nor my family holds with such strictures."

"Others will," she whispered.

"Hang them all." He took her hand. "Will you marry this newly molded man? Riordan told me what he said to Garrett, that love means taking a chance. Will you take a chance on me?"

She nodded, and gave him a brilliant smile. "I will marry you."

"Then we can make a slight detour to Standon. As you said, the baby is already born. Rushing there is not going to change the outcome. We will speak to your father, and if you both wish for me to travel on alone, I will. Whatever you wish."

"I agree."

"Now, regarding Lottie and Carter."

She laced her fingers through his. "I heard what you said to them. You were wonderful. A true prince, as Lottie said. I agree wholeheartedly with the plan."

"A ready-made family, my love. It will be a challenge."

"We will meet it—and any other challenges—together."

Aidan pulled her into his arms and kissed her fiercely.

Happy birthday, indeed.

* * * *

It took several hours to prepare for their departure. Cristyn packed her small trunk and spoke with Mrs. Trubshaw, who said she would gladly look after the children until their return. They spoke with Carter and Lottie, to say their goodbyes and explain how the four of them would soon be a family. Lottie threw her arms around Aidan's neck.

Carter, however, stood stiff, not saying a word. Aidan seemed to understand, and said, "It's all right, lad, to show how you feel. A man secure in his own skin will allow his feelings to show." Aidan looked up at her and smiled. His father's words. Carter sniffled and leaned against Aidan, as if needing the support.

Next they spoke to Paris. "I will admit I had concerns, but I am glad you are traveling to Standon to speak with Gethin," Paris said to Aidan. "Now that I know the particulars, may I say I admire how you have handled this situation at the mill? I wish you both a lifetime of happiness." He held out his hand and Aidan shook it.

Aidan moved to Delaney's bedside and slipped money into his hand. He was sitting upright; his arm and part of his face were heavily bandaged. "For services rendered, as agreed. And thank you, for pushing me out of harm's way."

Delaney snorted. "We couldn't muss that pretty face, could we?"

Aidan chuckled. "I will return in a few weeks. I may be reopening the cotton mill—there could be a job in it for you, like an overseer. If you're staying in the area, that is."

Delaney and Paris exchanged knowing looks. "Aye, I'll be staying."
It was close to two in the afternoon before they were underway. Together
in the carriage, they talked, kissed, cuddled, spoke of the future. Aidan
told her of the progressive school his brother wished to build. "Perhaps
we could propose a live-in portion for the school, for a small number of
orphans we wish to sponsor."

"What a lovely idea! You are thinking of the children from the
mill, aren't you?"

"I am. I'm aware I cannot rescue every child in dire circumstances,
but I will be rescuing them. I also thought perhaps we could include a
free medical clinic on the property of the school, one you could oversee.
It would be a shocking waste for you not to ply your medicinal skills. Of
course, we will have to discuss this with the family—"

Cristyn kissed him. How she loved him. While she was more than
ready to become a wife and mother, she had wondered if she would be
able to keep a hand in medicine. After all, one day she would be wife to a
viscount. Then an earl. Heavens, she would be *countess!* How wonderful
she would be marrying into a family with her same views.

But first, they must see her father.

When they arrived the next day, the look of surprise on his face turned
to one of concern. They adjourned to his office, and Cristyn began a
breathless narrative of all that had happened since she and Aidan had
reunited in Earl Shilton—leaving out the more intimate details.

"Marry?" Her father's eyebrows furrowed.

"As soon as I can arrange it," Aidan said. "By special license, if need
be. We both wish for you to be there. But more than anything, we wish for
your blessing. Dr. Bevan, you are well aware of my past, my struggles,"
Aidan said. "And now, so is Cristyn. I've told her the entirety of the tale. I
love your daughter with all my heart, and want nothing more than to make
her happy. She will always remain independent. I will never smother her or
deny her anything. She is my world. The moon and stars. She is everything."

Her father nodded as Aidan spoke. "I can see that you love each other,"
he said in a soft voice. "But there will be obstacles, aside from the class
difference. Taking on orphan children? And what of your addiction?"

To Aidan's credit, he kept his temper under wraps, though Cristyn
observed him clenching his fist. "There will be ruts in the road—there are
in any marriage. But as Cristyn said, we will meet any and all challenges
together. My family will approve of the match wholeheartedly. All we
wish is for you to do the same."

Her father sighed as he looked at her. "My dear, I will miss you terribly. What will I do without you, not only in the clinic, but in my heart? Your absence will leave a gaping hole."

Tears gathered on her lashes. "I won't be all that far. It's time for you to hire another doctor, one who can cover for you when you come to visit us. Several times during the course of a year, I pray. We have your blessing?"

"With the whole of my heart."

Cristyn rushed to her father's arms and hugged him tight. Now there was only Aidan's family to see.

They arrived at Wollstonecraft Hall two days later, and when it came into view, Cristyn gasped at the size and scope. Once the carriage pulled into the circular drive, she was swept up into a buzz of activity. The front hall, which looked ancient and medieval, was filled with handsome, formidable men—it wasn't hard to see where Aidan got his stunning good looks. She was introduced to each of them, and became reacquainted with Garrett's wife, Abbie, and his daughter, Megan. With hugs and delighted laughter, Aidan's father, the viscount, introduced his betrothed, Alberta Eaton. The wedding would take place the first of next week. Good heavens, her head was spinning from all the enthusiastic chatter.

"Enough suspense. Has Sabrina safely delivered?" Aidan asked worriedly.

"The difficult delivery was touch and go, but I am the proud father of a little girl. We named her Fiona, after Mother." The two brothers embraced warmly.

Abbie slipped her arm through Cristyn's. "Sabrina will never forgive me if I do not bring Cristyn up to meet her immediately—the perfect opportunity, with Bastian taking a much deserved nap. We must coo over the baby. Gentlemen, tea in one hour in the Georgian parlor."

Abbie led her toward the staircase, the other women following behind. "I know it can be overwhelming, but you could not have chosen a more loving and caring family to marry into. I am pleased for you and Aidan. I thought I sensed a spark all those months ago. I admit to a feeling of satisfaction in knowing I was correct."

Cristyn laughed. Yes, a loving and caring family. But to her, Aidan was the most loving and caring of them all. Her notorious rake. Her hero. Her true love.

\* \* \* \*

The men headed to the earl's study, and once Martin served the drinks he left them alone. Aidan gave them a condensed version of what had occurred the past several weeks. "But enough about my adventures; I want to know what happened with Sabrina. That note chilled my blood."

The men exchanged glances. "It chilled ours as well. Sabrina was not due for at least another three weeks." Riordan took a large swig of scotch. "We sent for Bastian—Dr. Faraday—but it took several hours for him to arrive, so we had to settle for Phillips in the interim. He did what he could. God, Sabrina was in labor for close to two days. Hearing her scream was agonizing. I stayed with her during the delivery. The baby arrived, but both mother and daughter were in distress. There was a chance they would not make it." Riordan's hand shook as he lifted the glass to take another draw. "Then when it appeared all was lost, they began to recover. Now, five days later, Sabrina and Fiona are hale and hearty. I cannot explain it."

"I can." Garrett turned to look at Aidan. "When did you tell Cristyn that you loved her? Said the actual words?"

"Monday night. Why?"

"The curse is broken," Garrett murmured. "Broken at long last, for Monday night was when Sabrina and the baby began to improve."

Aidan gave his uncle a quizzical look. "What are you on about?"

"Son, we made a discovery while you were at the sanatorium," his father stated. "A journal entry from the Earl of Carnstone from the early eighteenth century. He wrote that a Scottish sorceress said the curse can only be broken if all the men living form a love bond within a lunar year. And we all have. You were the last."

Aidan couldn't believe this. "You didn't think to tell me when I arrived home at the first of June?"

"We decided you had enough to deal with," his grandfather replied. "Besides, you were on a difficult undertaking and needed no distractions. But it appears you had one at any rate."

The men all chuckled, but soon sobered. All were lost in their thoughts. The curse was broken.

Damn it all, he believed it, for he felt it deep in his soul. It was as if a weight had been lifted, his soul was no longer blackened and diminished. But Cristyn had more to do with that than any ancient curse. How gratifying it worked out for Riordan, Sabrina, and baby Fiona.

There was a birthday to celebrate, a wedding, an engagement. He had yet to mention the children he wished to take in.

Time to put the past behind him and forgive himself, and with Cristyn at his side, the future looked bright indeed. Aidan held up his glass. "To the Wollstonecrafts."

And to living life to the fullest. He would. Always.

# Epilogue

A beautiful summer afternoon was the perfect background for the wedding of Megan Hughes and Jonas Eaton. With the ceremony completed, the family gathered outside in the garden, where a large table had been set up for the wedding brunch, served Wollstonecraft style, with assorted dishes laid out for the guests to serve themselves. Liveried footmen moved about, filling beverages, while Martin, the butler, watched over the proceedings.

Much had happened in the ensuing five years—the most astonishing was that the family had grown by leaps and bounds. Health, happiness, and love filled the hall, the curse forever banished.

Sitting at the table was Julian, Aidan's father, who had married Alberta Eaton and was now the proud father of four-year-old Hannah. Sitting next to them was Aidan's grandfather, the Earl of Carnstone, and his countess, Mary. Next were close family friend and physician Bastian Faraday and his new bride, Lydia Monckton, daughter of Baron Monckton.

Riordan sat with Sabrina and their five-year-old daughter, Fiona. Garrett and Abbie, proud parents to the bride, sat on the opposite side, with their four-year-old son, Alec, named for Garrett's Scottish grandfather. Abbie was with child again, and would deliver later in the autumn months.

Next to them sat his ward, twenty-year-old Carter Rokesmith, home on holiday from Oxford, where he was studying to follow his late father into law. With Aidan's assistance, he'd been able to recover a portion of his inheritance, but he wanted nothing to do with his uncle again. As he'd told Aidan on more than one occasion, the Wollstonecrafts were his family. Never too far from Carter's side was Lottie, now eleven and, when adopted, given the name Elizabeth Wollstonecraft. Lizzie had few memories of what had happened at the cotton mill. The faint scar on her forehead was the only reminder.

As for the mill, it reopened under Aidan's ownership. The changes regarding factory rules in Earl Shilton and the surrounding region had lessened the poverty a great deal. The mill made a small profit, and Aidan ensured it was run according to the latest standards. Miller was the new master, and by all accounts, liked and respected by all. McRae and Hanson were serving time at Newgate for criminal neglect and manslaughter.

As for Paris Middlemiss, he had sent along his best wishes. He was living in an isolated northern region of Scotland, continuing his quest to bring medical care to those less fortunate. Delaney accompanied him, acting as assistant, but in private was much more. Aidan was happy for them.

His gaze slid to Lizzie, who gave him a brilliant smile, then to Gethin Bevan, sitting next to her. Cristyn's father still had his clinic and was finally gaining recognition for his good work. He had married Deena Williams, his widowed housekeeper, last year. She nodded at Aidan and smiled as his gaze traveled along the table.

There sat the love of his life, his beating heart, his beloved angel. Cristyn. She was busy with their fraternal twin boys, rambunctious and noisy at two years of age. Julian was the oldest—they called him Jules—and the heir. The future of the Wollstonecrafts was assured. Both had their parents' midnight-black hair, though Jules had light blue eyes and his younger brother, Bennett, had his mother's violet-blue shade.

At the head of the table was the young bride, Megan, and Jonas Eaton, head groom of Wollstonecraft Hall. They would be moving into the Eatons' small manor house, now vacant since Julian and his family had moved to a nearby estate.

Riordan built his progressive school, and, as Aidan had hoped, it included an orphanage and a free clinic. Many of the children from the cotton mill had been adopted—some in Earl Shilton, more in the Kent area, and others went on to apprentice in good trades. Riordan and his wife and daughter lived in a three-story house they had built not far from the school.

Megan's home for those with special needs opened in Sussex, not far from Eastbourne. The Duke of Gransford and his heir, the Marquess of Tennington, also interested in progressive causes, donated the land and a large portion of the proceeds. It was called the Hornsby and Wollstonecraft Residential Home.

Garrett and Aidan and their families lived at Wollstonecraft Hall, along with the earl and his countess. Aidan and Cristyn had talked more than once of moving elsewhere, but she confessed she loved it at the hall, as did the children. Cristyn often volunteered at the free clinic and had found great satisfaction in using all she had learned.

As for Aidan, never had he been so happy. The clay had set, and he became the man he had always hoped he would be. He kept busy assisting his father and grandfather behind the scenes in parliament, preparing for the eventual day he would sit in the House of Lords. He assisted Garrett with running the estate and Riordan at the school and orphanage. There was more than enough to fill his time and give his life purpose. But nothing brought him more joy and contentment than Cristyn and the children. They were his anchor, his lighthouse beacon.

He was notorious no longer, there was only unwavering love.

# Meet the Author

Karyn Gerrard, born and raised in the Maritime Provinces of Eastern Canada, now makes her home in a small town in Northwestern Ontario. When she's not cheering on the Red Sox or traveling in the summer with her teacher husband, she writes, reads romance, and drinks copious amounts of Earl Grey tea.

Even at a young age, Karyn's storytelling skills were apparent, thrilling her fellow Girl Guides with off-the-cuff horror stories around the campfire. A multi-published author, she loves to write sensual historicals and contemporaries. Tortured heroes are an absolute must.

As long as she can avoid being hit by a runaway moose in her wilderness paradise, she assumes everything is golden. Karyn's been happily married for a long time to her own hero. His encouragement and loving support keeps her moving forward.

To learn more about Karyn and her books, visit www.karyngerrard.com.

# Author's Note

Earl Shilton suffered from grinding poverty in the 1840s, and Queen Victoria did send a representative to investigate the situation in 1843. I changed the year to 1845 to match my narrative. While the village was a busy industrial area, making stockings and boots, the cotton mill was completely my invention.

Concerning addiction, it was the generally accepted opinion during the Victorian era that it was merely a bad habit or a moral flaw, not a disease. Treatment was nonexistent, and since drugs like opium were legal, they were not considered a crime. The treatment Aidan received did not come into use until the early twentieth century, after World War I. The word "addict" in relation to drugs was not used until 1909.

As for the Factory Act, a revision in 1847 limited the number of hours women and children could work to ten. It took close to fifteen years to bring about this "Ten Hours Act." It wasn't until the Factory Act of 1878 that improvements were made for child workers, like compulsory education, and those between the ages of ten and fourteen could only work half days. It wasn't until 1901 when the minimum working age was raised to twelve.

In the 1840s, there was no formal training for nurses. It did not become a respected vocation until 1860, when Florence Nightingale laid the foundation of professional nursing by establishing a school at St. Thomas Hospital in London.

Printed in the United States
by Baker & Taylor Publisher Services